A MIDWINTER DAN[...]
A CAST PARTY AMONG THE STARS.
AN ODE TO A FALLEN RAP LEGEND.

*Contemporary audiences have always craved reimaginings of
William Shakespeare's classic works. Now, today's best writers for teens
take on the Bard in these fifteen whip-smart and original retellings . . .*

PRAISE FOR

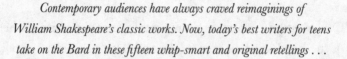

"From comedy to tragedy to sonnet, from texts to storms to
prom, this collection is a knockout."

—BuzzFeed (Best Book of the Year)

"This sumptuous anthology reframes Shakespeare's work,
linking themes to contemporary concerns while bringing a
critical eye to the originals' cultural assumptions. With its
range of narrative styles and diverse protagonists, this collection offers much to savor." *—Publishers Weekly*

"*That Way Madness Lies* is a must-read for theater kids ready to
consider their favorite comedies and tragedies in a new way,
as well as Shakespeare skeptics." *—Booklist*

"The stories stand capably on their own merits but will be enriched by familiarity with—or, better yet, reading alongside—Shakespeare's original plays and sonnets. Budding writers may even be inspired to put their own spins on the Bard of Avon's timeless tales." —*BookPage*

"Queer and diverse, this Shakespeare anthology takes fifteen of the Bard's most iconic works and builds an eclectic collection that successfully subverts the original white heteronormative canon. Built-in curriculum potential and excellent representation mean school libraries in particular will find this anthology a worthy purchase." —*School Library Journal*

"Ranging from grim and gritty to starry-eyed and futuristic, these fifteen stories retell the Bard's works as they've rarely been presented before. A radical reimagining and avant-garde interpretation of Shakespeare." —*Kirkus Reviews*

"*That Way Madness Lies* is a stunning collection of laughs, heartbreak, and beauty. The authors and the source material shine in this book." —*Paperback Paris*

"*That Way Madness Lies* is a spectacular, spellbinding Shakespearean collection that you will fall deeply in love with. Each tale is a gem in the glittering crown of this anthology, which is one of the best I've ever read."

—*The Nerd Daily*

That Way MADNESS LIES

*Fifteen of Shakespeare's Most
Notable Works Reimagined*

EDITED BY
DAHLIA ADLER

FLATIRON
BOOKS
NEW YORK

THAT WAY MADNESS LIES. Copyright © 2021 by Dahlia Adler. All rights reserved. Printed in the United States of America. For information, address Flatiron Books, 120 Broadway, New York, NY 10271.

"Severe Weather Warning" © 2021 by Emily Wibberley and Austin Siegemund-Broka. "Shipwrecked" © 2021 by Mark Oshiro. "Taming of the Soul Mate" © 2021 by Kayla Ancrum. "King of the Fairies" © 2021 by Anna-Marie McLemore. "We Have Seen Better Days" © 2021 by Lily Anderson. "Some Other Metal" © 2021 by Amy Rose Capetta and Cory McCarthy. "I Bleed" © 2021 by Dahlia Adler. "His Invention" © 2021 by Brittany Cavallaro. "Partying Is Such Sweet Sorrow" © 2021 by Kiersten Brazier. "Dreaming of the Dark" © 2021 by Lindsay Smith. "The Tragedy of Cory Lanez: An Oral History" © 2021 by Tochi Onyebuchi. "Out of the Storm" © 2021 by Joy McCullough. "Elsinore" © 2021 by Patrice Caldwell. "We Fail" © 2021 by Samantha Mabry. "Lost Girl" © 2021 by Melissa Bashardoust.

www.flatironbooks.com

Designed by Devan Norman

The Library of Congress has cataloged the hardcover edition as follows:

Names: Adler, Dahlia, editor. | Shakespeare, William, 1564–1616.
Title: That way madness lies : fifteen of William Shakespeare's most notable works reimagined / edited by Dahlia Adler.
Description: First edition. | New York : Flatiron Books, 2021.
Identifiers: LCCN 2020047442 | ISBN 9781250753861 (hardcover) | ISBN 9781250753854 (ebook)
Subjects: LCSH: Short stories, American. | Shakespeare, William, 1564–1616—Adaptations. | CYAC: Short stories. | Shakespeare, William, 1564–1616—Adaptations.
Classification: LCC PZ5 .T31347 2021 | DDC [Fic]—dc23
LC record available at https://lccn.loc.gov/2020047442

ISBN 978-1-250-75387-8 (trade paperback)

Our books may be purchased in bulk for promotional, educational, or business use. Please contact your local bookseller or the Macmillan Corporate and Premium Sales Department at 1-800-221-7945, extension 5442, or by email at MacmillanSpecialMarkets@macmillan.com.

First Flatiron Books Paperback Edition: 2022

10 9 8 7 6 5 4 3 2 1

.⋅≈⊰⊱≈⋅.

FOR MICAH,
WHOSE STORIES ARE ONLY JUST BEGINNING

.⋅≈⊰⊱≈⋅.

INTRODUCTION

THE WORKS

COMEDIES

A SONNET

TRAGEDIES

LATE ROMANCE

Introduction

illiam Shakespeare may well be the most widely read author of the Western world, which comes with incredible influence. His works have sparked countless adaptations, from films like Baz Luhrmann's *Romeo + Juliet* and the *Taming of the Shrew*–based '90s rom-com *10 Things I Hate About You* to musicals like *West Side Story* and *Kiss Me, Kate*. He's also the wordsmith behind a stunning number of phrases that remain in common parlance; for instance, if you ever say something is a "foregone conclusion," you are pulling from *Othello*.

Four hundred years after Shakespeare shuffled off this mortal coil (we owe that one to *Hamlet*), the stories and themes of his brilliant and evocative comedies, tragedies, histories, and late romances still resonate deeply, but as we've seen time and time again, so much is gained by giving them new settings, genres, and especially points of view.

Shakespeare's unique ability to craft characters with humor, pathos, and ambition combined with his ubiquity has given his stories a kind of power that has allowed for his work to define people for centuries. This includes both those whom he chose to portray and those he did not. Although most writers of his time were no different, to say Shakespeare did not do marginalized people any favors is an understatement; many of us still live with the effects of his caricatures and common story lines today.

As in my prior anthology, *His Hideous Heart: 13 of Edgar Allan Poe's Most Unsettling Tales Reimagined*, the authors here have deconstructed and reconstructed an inarguably brilliant but very white and very straight canon. I wanted to give authors the power to revisit and give new spirit to these narratives, much in the same way that I, as a Jewish author, eagerly anticipated remaking *The Merchant of Venice* to give the Shylock analogue considerably more agency.

The result is a collection that explores different cultures, celebrates a variety of genders and forms of love, and addresses different kinds of emotional pain head-on.

I hope you love the result as much as I do.

—DAHLIA ADLER

COMEDIES

SEVERE WEATHER WARNING

Inspired by The Tempest

Emily Wibberley and Austin Siegemund-Broka

Though with their high wrongs I am struck to th' quick,
Yet with my nobler reason 'gainst my fury

Do I take part. The rarer action is
In virtue than in vengeance.

—ACT 5, SCENE 1

O brave new world,
That has such people in 't!

—ACT 5, SCENE 1

I haul my sister's luggage down the stairs, letting the suitcase strike every step. The noise reverberates into the house and joins with the echoes of thunder in a foreboding rhythm. Nevertheless, I feel a sliver of pleasure whenever I drop the wheels onto the undeserving hardwood.

I'm angry, as angry as the storm outside. When I reach the entryway, I hear the screen door rattling, the hinges and mesh shaking while the wind whips past the porch. On the front table is the folder of documents Mom prepared this morning before hugging Patience goodbye and heading to work—my sister's boarding pass, emergency contact information, the credit card Patience got special for this summerlong internship in New York. I'm seventeen—one year older than

Patience—and even I don't have a credit card. And I'm certainly not getting on a plane anytime soon. I'm stuck in Nowhere, Oklahoma, for the foreseeable future.

"Patience," I shout up the stairs. "We have to go."

There's no reply except the storm, howling up the driveway and shaking the windowpanes. I check my phone. We should have been on the road twenty minutes ago. The reason we're not is Patience's boyfriend, who just *had* to drop in and say goodbye in person. For thirty minutes. In Patience's bedroom. With the door closed.

Patience has done everything before me. Credit card, job, trip out of Oklahoma—and boyfriend. The only thing I have on her is my driver's license. Which right now just makes me my sister's chauffeur.

It's the irony of our names. Patience has never had to practice patience in her entire life, what with how quickly everything comes to her. Whatever she wants, whenever she wants it. Whereas I, named Prosper—the whim of a mother who loves poetry—haven't seen a whole lot of what passes for prosperity in high school. Not when it comes to internships or summer opportunities or homecoming dates who aren't Netflix.

I start back up the stairs, the wood groaning under me like it's protesting its earlier mistreatment. Everything creaks in this house. Every cupboard, every door. Whenever there's humidity or wind, everything makes noise, like the house carries on wordless conversations with itself.

Presently, I'm hoping the wood speaks loud enough for Patience to hear. I doubt it will. I'm fully prepared to walk in on my younger sister having sex with Benjamin Campos.

I knock once on the door. There's no response.

"You're going to miss your flight," I call out. Despite how jealous I am of her leaving, I want her to make her plane. It's the one upside of her flying to New York today. I won't have to see her this summer—won't have to be reminded of what was stolen from me.

When I knock for the second time, the door flies open.

Patience doesn't look short of breath, or flushed, or sweaty. She looks pale. Her skin's practically porcelain white, her hair—auburn like mine—tucked behind her ears like she's pushed it there compulsively.

Behind her, Benjamin's standing in the middle of the room, *crying*.

"I'm ready now," Patience says. Benjamin sniffles.

I'm not sure if Patience cringes. Her hazel eyes remain unreadable. I'm stunned, watching this scene, uncomprehending. Is Benjamin this distraught my sister's leaving? It's not like Patience isn't coming home, not like she's being shipped off to some deserted island or exiled from Oklahoma permanently. Her internship is only six weeks. I feel bad for him, even if I can't empathize with sadness at my sister's absence.

"Are you sure?" I ask.

Patience doesn't glance over her shoulder, doesn't hesitate. "So sure. Let's go." She sounds like she's leaving a boring party, not her bawling boyfriend.

I peer past her. Benjamin doesn't look like he's noticed I'm even here. His eyes balefully roam my sister's room, as if searching for solace in her furnishings or the random collection of items Patience has picked up throughout her effortlessly successful childhood. Trophies from kids' soccer, photos of her playing with school orchestras, spelling bee ribbons. From their haphazard placement, I don't even feel like she's proud of them. She just needs places to put her accomplishments.

I nod slightly in Benjamin's direction. "Is he . . . ?"

"He's fine," Patience replies quickly. She grabs her backpack and walks past me out of the room.

Benjamin, however, stays right where he is. He has the gangly frame of a fifteen-year-old boy, and his slightly greasy hair hangs down his forehead like he has no idea how long hair should be. The crying helps none of it, wet streaks running down his light-brown cheeks. "Do you, um, need a ride?" I ask him.

He looks up. Then he bursts into sobs. "My brother's outside," he chokes out.

I stand in the doorway, hoping he'll take the hint and leave Patience's bedroom. Before he can, my phone starts emitting a siren. Benjamin's starts up the next moment, followed by the echo of Patience's downstairs.

While the noise continues, I pull out my phone.

It's the worst possible time for what I know I'll find. I read the words of the notification with frustrated dread. *Tornado watch.* I've lived in Oklahoma my entire life. I know to expect the occasional tornado. This one's just spectacularly inconvenient.

Over the asynchronous sounds of our phones, I hear Benjamin's voice.

"I told her I loved her," he says, like he's speaking mostly to himself, "and she broke up with me."

❧

Now dealing with three problems—a weeping boy, a sister who's extremely late for her flight, and a *tornado*—I gently close the door of Patience's bedroom and go interrogate my sister. When I reach the foot of the stairs, I find her packing the folder Mom prepared for her into her backpack. "You *broke up* with him?"

Patience shrugs her backpack onto one shoulder. "Yeah, with the internship and everything, it was time." She sounds like she's commenting on the weather. Well, the weather on a normal day. Not this weather.

"Wait," I say when she reaches for the door. "What're you doing?"

"We should have been on the road by now," she says seriously, like I'm the one who needs reminding. "We'll have to hurry if I'm going to make my flight."

Her presumptuousness would piss me off if I weren't worried about her walking into gale-force winds. "You're joking," I say.

Patience looks at me quizzically. "It's just a tornado *watch*. Look, it's fine outside."

She walks to the front window and opens the curtains. It does not look fine outside. I knew it wouldn't. While a tornado watch doesn't mean a tornado's happening, it means there are the right conditions for one. Out the window, black clouds blanket the day. It looks like night, and it's two in the afternoon. The official recommendation for a tornado watch is to "have a plan." I'm pretty certain a good plan doesn't include driving to the airport.

Before I can explain this to Patience, the front door opens. I jump, thinking the wind's blown it open.

It's not the wind. It's Sam Campos, who is dripping wet. His hair—darker and wavier than his brother's—is plastered to his forehead, and rainwater runs down his long, straight nose. "Hey, Prosper. Can I, uh, wait in here?" he asks. "The storm is looking kind of intense."

"Of course," I reply. I'm friendly enough with Sam. We kissed once in seventh grade. It was very awkward. We didn't speak for three years, despite only having fifty people in our grade. Now, we're going into senior year, and we still don't really hang out. We mostly know each other from situations like this—shepherding our younger siblings on dates and to each other's houses. We're high school in-laws.

Or we were.

Sam steps farther into the room and pulls off his soaking raincoat, flinging a few drops onto Ariel—our cat, who was lounging on the heating vent, like he does. When the water hits his fur, he flees the room. Sam's shirt sticks to his skin, revealing, one might say, other differences from his brother. The elder Campos sibling is not gangly. He's a swimmer, and, well, he has the receipts.

While I want desperately to look away, I can't, and he notices. "Sorry," he says, humor and no cockiness in his voice. "I had to walk up the drive, and the rain was practically horizontal."

"Oh, yeah. Totally—fine." I congratulate myself on coming off cool and collected. "Do you, um, need a towel?"

I dart into the bathroom where I pull one of the hand towels off the rack. When I return, Sam's draped his dripping raincoat on the hooks next to the door. "You excited for your internship?" he asks Patience, mussing his hair with the towel I gave him. "Benjamin told me how competitive it was to get."

I ignore what the praise does to me. Not because it's Sam but because I really don't need to hear yet again how impressive my younger sister is.

"Well, I'm going to *miss it* if we don't leave." Patience fires her words in my direction.

Fed up, I take out my phone and search Patience's flight number. "Look." I wave the screen in her face. "Your flight's delayed. Because of, you know, the tornado?"

Patience's eyes narrow, her gaze withering. "Eventually the storm will lift? And I'll need to be at the airport?"

I grimace. We're at the passive-aggressive point where every statement is spoken as a question.

"I want you to be on that flight more than anyone, but I'm not driving in this," I say, folding my arms over my chest.

Like the weather is listening, the pounding on the roof intensifies. "Hail," Sam says. Out the front window, small chunks of ice patter the ground. Patience looks miserable and like she has nothing to say, which Sam notices. "Hey, at least this gives you and Ben some extra time together. Where is he, anyway?"

He's obviously trying to cheer her up, but Patience forces an uncomfortable smile. "I'm going to call the program coordinator from Mom's room and explain the delay," she says to me.

She disappears down the hallway. I'm left with Sam, and I realize it's my job to explain what my sister didn't want to. He faces me, looking understandably confused. "Where *is* my brother?"

"Upstairs. In Patience's room," I reply. Sam starts for the stairs. "Um. He might need some privacy."

"Oh god." Sam pales. "Did you walk in on them? Is that what's behind the weird vibe in here? One time I went into his room not knowing Patience was over . . . I'm really sorry if you had to see my brother's butt. I know how traumatizing it is. He's young, but hairier than one would expect—"

"No!" I cut him off. "No. I didn't walk in on them. They broke up."

His eyes widen. "No. No way. They're, like, sickeningly in love."

I understand his disbelief, and in my head, I commend his perfect word choice. "Sickening" is exactly how I'd describe the one movie night where they didn't know *I* knew what was going on under their blanket. *Moulin Rouge* will never be the same for me. "Benjamin is crying upstairs," I inform his brother.

His expression flattens. "Your sister *dumped* him?"

"In fairness, I don't know the full story. The decision could have been mutual," I protest weakly. Sam gives me an unconvinced look. "Fine. She dumped him."

"He must be really upset. I have to check on him." He starts up the stairs, his expression endearingly nervous.

While his footsteps join with the sounds of the hail on the roof, I go to the window. The weather worsens with every minute. In the neighbors' yard, the wind knocks over the plastic play structure, pushing it into the fence. The rain is incessant, and new clouds have gathered on the horizon.

I know one thing for certain. We're all trapped here—together—for a while.

🌹

"I'm so glad you're not out on the roads," Mom says over the phone. She speaks frankly and fast, and I've never known whether it's just who she is or a product of her hectic job, keeping everything moving and everyone calm in the hospital where she's a nurse.

I'm in my room, idly counting the lights strung over my desk. "I know," I say. "How's the weather where you are?"

Mom couldn't get out of her shift to drive Patience to the airport. Her hospital is thirty minutes from our house on the edge of what could generously be called a small town. It feels more like an island, with miles and miles of straight, dusty roads separating us from the rest of everything.

"I already have a couple storm-chaser injuries. I don't think I'll be able to get out of here before tonight," Mom says. "Will you guys be okay on your own?"

"Don't worry about us," I reply. I'm used to Mom's long hours, and I honestly don't dislike the freedom it leaves me. "Benjamin and Sam are also here."

"Oh, fun. Tell them to stay until the tornado watch is over. No one should be on the road right now."

I don't bother to dispel her idea of how "fun" it'll be having Benjamin and Patience's drama one room over. I glance out my open doorway to the other end of the hall, where my sister's door is closed. Neither Ben nor Sam has emerged.

"Of course," I reply.

"I've got to go, kiddo. Be gentle with your sister. I'm sure she's upset about her flight," Mom says, and I feel my mood darken like the clouds outside.

"Right. Talk later." I hang up, frustrated. Everything is about Patience's feelings, her internship, and never what she did to me. At least I can thank this storm for making Patience's life fractionally more difficult. Meteorological payback.

Her door opens. Sam wanders into the hall, looking lost for a moment. His eyes find mine, and he smiles slightly. In just two steps of his swimmer's legs, he's sauntered up to my doorframe.

"How is he?" I nod in the direction of Benjamin in Patience's room.

Sam walks into my room and closes the door. He surveys my walls for a few silent seconds. He's never been in my room, and I find myself wondering what he thinks. I've put effort into my decorations—the lights over my desk, the cross-stitched sayings in frames on one wall, the shelves packed with used paperbacks from garage sales. I'm proud of my room. I figure if I'm stuck here, I want it to look nice.

"He's not great," Sam says, not mincing words. "He wants to talk to her, but I convinced him it's not a good idea while he's so emotional. I hope I did, anyway. How's Patience?"

I shrug. "Fine, I'm sure."

Sam watches me uncertainly. "They had a pretty intense relationship. Even if she did the dumping, I bet she's upset."

The suggestion makes me laugh. "If I know Patience, she's started planning her life in New York. Benjamin just doesn't fit in."

"That sounds a little mercenary." Sam's voice is delicate.

I huff. "You're joking, right? Do you know my sister?"

He sits down on the bed. It's kind of forward, but I kind of don't mind. He looks comfortable there. Not necessarily because he's in the habit of sitting on girls' beds. I get the impression it's because his thoughts haven't left his brother. "Patience has dinner with my family every Sunday night. I've gone to every one of her orchestra concerts with Benjamin. I've given her more rides to places than I have most of my friends. So, yeah," he finishes. "I know her some."

I should just let it slide. Dragging Sam into drama with

my sister isn't necessary. But I feel suddenly claustrophobic in my own head, like everything I'm unable to say—to Mom, to Patience—needs out right now. "Did she tell you how she got the internship?"

Sam frowns, uncomprehending. "No. I'm guessing she applied?"

"Yeah," I start. "She applied, after never saying she was interested in the internship *I'd* wanted and *I'd* found. I was the one who knew about the Duchy Law Group from my friend's dad. She watched me spend months working on my application. When the results went out, I learned that not only did she secretly apply, but she got it over me." Even saying the words heats me with embarrassment I resent. It's not that I particularly care about the job itself. I'm not dying to be a lawyer. I just wanted the summer in New York City, a summer outside the isolated emptiness of where we live. More, I wanted something I could call mine.

"Ah." Sam shifts the collar of his now-drying shirt. "No, she didn't mention that."

"Of course not." I face away from him, not wanting him to see the hurt flush spreading in my cheeks. "Don't worry about Patience. She's getting what she wants."

"It must suck. Watching her head off to the internship you wanted," Sam says measuredly.

I'm conscious I just dumped a whole lot of very personal resentment on him, and I don't care. It felt good. "What sucks is knowing your younger sister is smarter than you."

He reclines onto one elbow. The bottom of his shirt pulls up, revealing the skin of his stomach and the sharp line of his hip bone, which I distract myself from by remembering he's sprawled on the white, crochet blanket Grandma knitted the year before she passed away. *Focus on your dead grandma's blanket, Prosper.*

"I don't know," Sam says, his lips curving playfully. "She did just dump my really awesome brother."

I laugh, improbably. "At least we don't have to drive them to dates anymore."

"Or see them making out at school."

"Or hear them playing the 'you say goodnight' game on FaceTime at one in the morning." Sam laughs now, and it's nice, feeling my frustration with Patience ebb just a little. "Sometimes I wonder if Patience only pursued Benjamin because she knew you were my first kiss," I say softer. "Like she has to do everything I do, but better."

Sam draws back, faux indignant. "Oh, so you're saying my brother is a better first kiss than me?"

Heat of a very different kind returns to my face. It's the first time we've ever openly acknowledged our disastrous attempt at kissing in seventh grade. "Obviously, *I* don't want to kiss your brother," I clarified.

"You sure? Because I hear he's recently single." He raises his eyebrow.

"I'm just saying," I start, my lips wobbling into a smile, "our first kiss was objectively the worst. You know it was. You couldn't even look at me for weeks."

While he looks chagrined, there's humor in his eyes, like he's enjoying this. "To be fair, you did drool on my shirt."

I drop my head into my hands, and my hair falls over my elbows. "I know," I groan. Looking up, I point a jokingly accusatory finger in his direction. "*You* stuck your tongue directly down my throat."

"Okay, yes, it was the worst." He rubs his neck, uncomfortable. It's kind of sweet, this objectively hot guy feeling abashed remembering his middle-school kissing incompetence.

"So I told Patience what happened with us, and what does she do? She makes sure your younger brother is *her* first kiss. First everything, just to one-up me," I say, not minding how petty I sound. I remember when Patience told Mom and me nonchalantly over dinner that she'd kissed Benjamin. Benjamin Campos, she confirmed, looking right at me.

Sam doesn't look indignant on my behalf. He pauses thoughtfully, running the edge of Grandma's blanket in his fingers. "Maybe Patience just wants to be like you," he suggests.

It's an idea I'd never considered, one I can't fathom. The rain picks up on my windowpane, newly insistent. I say nothing, weighing how to reply. If you want to be like someone, wouldn't you be nicer to them?

I don't have the chance to ask the question out loud. Sam's voice is hesitant when he speaks. "You know, after we kissed, when I avoided you, it wasn't because of anything you did." I frown, and he continues, "Okay, I didn't love the drool. But really, I was embarrassed. I'd had this huge crush on you, and finally I got to kiss you, and it was an absolute disaster. I didn't know how to come back from that."

"You had a huge crush on me?" The question leaps out of me. I'm surprised and struck by how confidently he confessed it. I'd always assumed he just wanted his first kiss. Everyone wanted their first kiss on record in seventh grade, myself included. I never figured he wanted *me*, with my face full of freckles, frizzy red hair, and overly large soccer sweatshirts.

"Why did you think I kissed you?" He sounds puzzled.

"Just because?"

"Wait." Sam looks uncomfortable, like he was hit with a sudden stomachache. He sits up straighter on the bed. "Did you kiss me *just because?*"

I remember seventh-grade Sam, his shaggy hair like every other guy's in his grade, his scuffed skate shoes. "I thought you were really cute," I say, his honesty encouraging mine. I really did. When Sam walked up to me during Chloe Michaels's birthday party, I wondered if the fluttering in my stomach was the result of the cups of orange soda I'd had, then I decided it wasn't.

Reassured, Sam flops back on the bed. "Well, that's something." His eyes find mine, livelier, a flicker of impulsiveness in his dark irises. "I'm guessing the kiss erased that though, huh?"

I still, startled by the implications of his question and the new direction of this conversation. Even the rain and wind outside seem to subside for the slightest moment, like they're waiting.

Neither of us ends up splitting the silence. Shouting erupts from downstairs. Sam's and my wordless gazes fly to the door. In seconds, we rush into the hall and down the stairs, the whole house creaking and straining. I reach the living room, Sam on my heels, and find Patience in front of a hiccupping Benjamin.

"Just tell me what I did wrong," Benjamin pleads, his voice raised plaintively.

Patience replies with uncharacteristic—well, patience. "You didn't do anything wrong."

"Hey, Ben, what did we talk about?" Sam steps forward. "Maybe we should go back upstairs?"

Benjamin ignores him. He's fixated on Patience, while my sister's eyes remain determinedly on the corner of the room where the wall meets the graying carpet. "There has to be a reason," he demands.

I know my sister well enough to recognize the exact moment she's pushed past her limit. Her face flushes, her eyes flinty. "I just don't love you!" It's like the wind's finally ripped the door open and stolen the oxygen from the room.

Nobody moves, everyone horrified and feeling incredibly uncomfortable. I want desperately to know how to fix this situation. Unfortunately, I have nothing. When a wailing echoes into the room, I wonder for a second if Benjamin has started some sort of weird keening.

In the same moment, each of us realizes it's not Benjamin. It's none of us. It's the severe weather warning siren, whining distantly over the rooftops outside. Our phones sound off next, one by one. I read the screen of mine. *Tornado warning. Take cover.*

Relief rushes into me. Even the upgrade of *tornado watch* into *tornado warning* isn't uncommon in Oklahoma. It's sometimes slightly scary but statistically unlikely to hit our house. Right now, it's sparing us from the horrible tension in the room.

I lead Benjamin and Sam to the safest room, the first-floor bathroom. While it's tight for four people, it has no exterior walls. Patience follows the boys in, and they cluster around the toilet and the tub. I don't join them, instead heading to find Ariel, whom I know will have hidden himself under my mom's bed.

Like usual, he protests. When I return to the bathroom, it's with fresh scratches and a yowling cat. As I close the door, he wriggles from my arms, and when I look up, I realize the pissed-off cat is the least of my worries. Benjamin's perched morosely on the lid of the toilet. Patience is on the floor near the tub, her back to one wall, the seashell-decorated hand towels nearly touching her shoulder while she stares at her phone. Sam, in the corner, looks painfully relieved he's no longer the only other person in the room.

I realize with dawning discomfort that it's silent in here. The sounds of the storm and the sirens don't reach this inner part of the house. Which is the point, I know—it's safest in the small interior space. Safe and stiflingly awkward.

"Anyone know any jokes?" I offer into the silence.

Sam laughs. Patience doesn't acknowledge I've spoken.

"Our love was a joke," Benjamin says. He sniffles exaggeratedly.

Sam's smile fades, and now Patience glances up, glaring. "Can you just *try* not to cry anymore?"

Her ex-boyfriend's face reddens. "Oh, I'm sorry my *feelings* are an *inconvenience*." He puts dramatic emphasis on his words, and it's different from his desperation earlier. He's veered into anger. Behind the toilet, our furious cat hisses in what feels unnervingly like agreement.

Patience drops her eyes to her phone, and I notice her expression's no longer indifferent. She says nothing, her cheeks pinker. Compulsively, she pushes her hair behind her ear.

Benjamin sniffles again then wipes his eyes.

I catch panic flit over Patience's face. She's not enjoying this. She didn't break up with Benjamin because she's cruel. She just doesn't love him, and now she's trapped in this tiny bathroom watching him cry. It's a nightmare. For the first time in a long time, I feel compelled to help my sister.

"Sam, um." I grope for a conversation starter. "What are your plans for the summer?"

Sam glances at his brother, obviously picking up on the need for distraction. "I'm volunteering at the museum. How about you?"

I'd intended to make idle conversation and didn't expect I would find his reply interesting. The only museum nearby is an art museum forty minutes from here, where we went for a field trip in freshman year. I didn't know Sam was into art. "I'll be working," I say, resenting the reminder of my usual checkout job at the grocery store. "But I'm thinking of taking a community college class."

Patience looks up. "You are? In what?"

Her interest surprises me. "I don't know," I say honestly. "Poetry maybe?" I shrug. I used to scribble poems in my middle-school planner, the product of reading Shakespeare's sonnets in class and listening to a whole lot of Panic! At the Disco. Getting back into it could be fun.

"I think that would be really cool," Patience says. It's sincere, and while it's far from an apology for the internship, the gesture is nice.

I return a smile. "Thanks." Patience nods. I look to Sam. "Are you an artist?"

"I draw a little," he says. His voice is soft in a way that tells me it's a lot more than a little.

We pass the next half hour in conversation about art and poetry and our plans for senior year. While it feels like an eternity, I notice Benjamin's crying grow intermittent, and the conversation with Sam flows easily. Finally, Patience relaxes, her shoulders loosening as she scrolls on her phone.

When she tells us the tornado warning has lifted, I leave the bathroom feeling like I've survived something.

🌹

"Thank you for that." Sam's followed me into my room, while Benjamin has returned to Patience's room, and Patience to Mom's. Sam doesn't drop onto the bed this time.

"What? Talking to you?" I shove my hands into my back pockets.

"Distracting them from each other," Sam says.

"Well, it's not like talking to you was a *huge* imposition for me," I reply.

He grins, and only now, not during the half-hour tornado warning, do I feel the currents of air in the room changing. It's a nice grin, fuller on one half of his face in an inviting, genuine kind of way. "Glad to hear it," he says.

I'm about to face away from him, letting the pleasant moment pass, when I catch myself. I've allowed Patience to take from me and done nothing except enjoy how the weather inconvenienced her. Instead, I might be happier if I pursue what *I* want without worrying about what my sister does. It's not just right to let this grudge go—I deserve to let it go, to dwell on new hopes instead of old wounds.

I step closer to Sam. "I still think you're cute. By the way." His face furrows in confusion, which, I can confirm, is indeed cute. "Our first kiss didn't erase it," I clarify.

He looks surprised, but not in a bad way.

"Redo?" I propose.

His smile relaxes, and his eyes sparkle, like he wasn't expecting this but is completely into it. Delighted, even. I'm enjoying how my heart is pounding, the heady rush of him stepping closer to me.

"I feel compelled to point out I don't do that tongue thing anymore," he murmurs, putting a hand on my hip.

I laugh, hardly noticing when my hands find his waist in return. "Unfortunately," I say, lifting my chin, "I do still drool." I feel his grin widen, his lips a breath from mine.

"I'll take my chances." He does, closing the distance and kissing me. I do too, and I *love* taking this chance. It's delicious enough for me to forget everything else—flight times and work shifts and weather warnings.

I realize instantly we've each learned a few things since our first kiss. He's gentle yet not hesitant, his tongue brushing mine deliberately, like he's proving what he can do. I deepen the kiss, directing instead of just enjoying. He wraps his arms around me, and I feel his fingertips against my shoulder blades. It's not a long kiss, just long enough to know, *yeah, there's something here.*

We part.

"Well," Sam says.

"Not bad," I reply.

"Far from terrible, really."

"Promising, at the very least."

Promising feels nice. It's been a while since I've felt promising. I'm leaning in for a second go when I'm interrupted— *we're* interrupted—by Benjamin's voice from the doorway.

"Seriously? *Already?* Were you just waiting for me to get dumped?"

Sam releases me and faces his brother. He's opening his mouth to reply when the sirens start up once more from our phones.

With the way this day's going, I find I'm not even frustrated or stressed by the outstandingly poor timing. I'm stifling a laugh.

※

This time, the tornado warning lasts for twenty minutes. I wind up covered in new cat scratches, and Sam tries for ten minutes to talk his brother down. It doesn't work, and Benjamin climbs into the bathtub, drawing the shower curtain to hide himself from view. Patience returns to her phone. There's no conversation, only me and Sam catching each other's eyes, holding in our grins.

When the sirens finally die down and our phones confirm the storm has passed, we file to the front door. Benjamin wordlessly stalks to his brother's car. I survey the driveway and the sky. The damage doesn't look heavy, and only the neighbors' upended play structure and a few garbage cans look out of place. Leaves litter the waterlogged ground. It's no longer raining, and sunlight filters past the clouds.

Sam lingers in the doorway. "Should I call you, or did you only kiss me 'just because'?" He studies my expression.

I roll my eyes. "Call me," I say, "and we'll find out."

He kisses me, earning a labored moan from Benjamin in the front seat of Sam's car.

"Okay, then." He flashes me a smile. I watch him walk the whole way down the drive, permitting myself to enjoy the view of his swimmer's stride in skinny jeans. He circles his car, opens the driver's door, and climbs inside.

I close the door, finding Patience watching me uneasily from the other end of the room. "I found a red-eye," she says stiffly, "so Mom can drive me when she gets home."

"Okay," I reply.

Patience sighs. My sister looks stressed, and I would guess it's not just from the flight rescheduling. "I guess this storm was payback for what I did to you with the internship." Her expression is fragile, like it's finally hitting her she really hurt me.

The thing is, over the past hours, I've let my resentment die down and drift off like the winds of the storm. Still, it's nice of her to say. I shrug. "No, it wasn't. Not even you deserved to be trapped in a bathroom with your ex."

Patience laughs, her face brightening like the lining of the clouds outside. "Looks like you had fun, though," she says leadingly.

I smile. "Yeah," I say. I feel lighter somehow, and I realize it's part of what's nice about moving on. You're freer to look forward. To imagine museum dates, poetry classes, and kisses.

Maybe spending the summer stuck in Oklahoma won't be the worst.

Shipwrecked

Inspired by Twelfth Night

Mark Oshiro

Oh, time, thou must untangle this, not I.
It is too hard a knot for me to untie!

—Viola, Act 2, scene 2

Vi entered the gymnasium through the eastern door.
They smoothed down the lapels of their red velvet suit. Over and over and over. A nervous reaction born of the cliff that seemed to open at their feet.

Be you.

Tell everyone.

Suffer the consequences.

The suit fit well. At least they had that. It had been Seb's idea—their twin, the only person Vi trusted with their truth. He had asked Duke Pennington for help, and Vi was *so* grateful for Duke, since it was not like Vi had ever done anything like this. Duke was the one with style; he was the one with the knowledge of how to best use clothing to boost one's confidence; he was also the boy who was attracted to literally anyone and proud of it.

Seb, Seb . . . he was supposed to be here already. Vi was terribly nervous, too jittery to look for him.

They had a plan to enact. But what if everyone confused the two of them for each other? They were twins, after all.

Seb had assured Vi that they should do what they wanted. "Do you want to wear a suit?"

"Well, yeah," they had said. "But what if we look *too* similar?"

Seb's eyes went wide. "Then you need to see Duke," he said. "If you want to make a statement, then he's the one to see. And I only want the *best* for you, sib."

So Seb had arranged it.

(How did he always know the right things to say?)

But was it still a good idea? Were they jumping out of a plane without a parachute?

They almost turned around, almost gave in to the certainty of giving up.

No, Vi, they told themself. *You will regret it if you leave.*

They took one more step forward.

Shit, was this like walking the plank?

Who the *hell* came up with having a midwinter dance styled after a *shipwreck,* anyway?

Olivia. She'd allowed it in student council. So it was Olivia.

For Vi, though, it was *always* Olivia.

Most of the reason Vi was here was because of Olivia. Not *directly,* but it was Seb's love life that got Vi interested in this ridiculous dance in the first place. Seb liked Olivia and, at least according to Antonio, wanted to impress her. Most of this year had been so hard on Seb, so Vi jumped at the chance to make their twin brother happy.

And apparently, that was by impressing Olivia.

Vi was never going to tell anyone the truth: Olivia made Vi feel alive. Being around Olivia was like having a personal sun.

Like finding a hundred dollars in the front pocket of a pair of jeans on laundry day.

Like an impossibility.

An impossibility because Olivia rarely seemed aware that Vi was in the same room with her, even though they saw each other once a week. Vi wanted Olivia, but they also wanted Olivia to reciprocate their feelings. It didn't mean anything if this interest wasn't mutual. Still, Vi couldn't stop thinking about her and the desire that ripped through their body. They sometimes craved being romantic and cute with Olivia. All the other stuff didn't matter; that wasn't Vi's thing.

But Olivia didn't ever seem to notice the secretary in those student council meetings. Besides, Olivia was for Seb, and the sacrifice would be worth it, if only to make Seb smile again.

So maybe this was a miscalculation. Maybe now was not the time to do this, to make their first public declaration, their first attempt to be wholly themself.

But . . .

Maybe.

Maybe it *was*.

Maybe Vi had to do *something* for themself in all of this.

Maybe this *was* like walking the plank, except that the plunge wasn't into a cold, dark, and unforgiving sea.

Maybe it was a leap into the future.

To new beginnings, they thought.

They ran their hands down the lapels of their red velvet suit.

It was time for Vi to *become* Vi. And in order to do so, in order to shed who everyone saw them as, they were going to impress the hell out of Olivia.

For Seb, of course.

Seb entered the gymnasium through the southern door.

Oh, this is a terrible, terrible idea, he thought. *A shipwreck? How is that romantic* or *entertaining?*

The lights pulsed around him, and the DJ was playing an awful Katy Perry remix. Actually, he wasn't sure there were *any* good Katy Perry remixes. Or songs. At all. Yeah, he could do without all of them. Someone should make them . . . walk the plank? Oh god, was he going to start *thinking* in terrible ship-related puns?

He did not like this.

But Antonio said that attending this cheesy dance was the only way to impress Olivia, and Seb had no reason to distrust Antonio. Antonio, who had pulled him out of the burning remains of the car, who made sure that Seb stayed still on the side of the road, who sat beside him in the ambulance. Antonio, who had stuck by his side through all the physical therapy, who had sacrificed so much of his time to be with Seb when Seb most needed a friend. A *best* friend.

And sometimes, best friends set you up on dates with pretty women.

There was just a tiny problem, one that Seb was still keeping to himself. He had almost confessed it to Vi, moments after Vi had told him all about the whole nonbinary thing. He knew they would be trustworthy, that they would understand, but Seb worried that he would be stealing their spotlight. They had a new name! One that was spelled so damn cool, that was just a single syllable so they could match Seb; one that allowed them to step fully into who they were.

Seb couldn't take that moment away from them.

Thus, this whole absurdity began.

Antonio stepped up beside him, slightly out of breath, and his best friend looped his arm in his. "Are you doing that thing again?"

"No!" Seb exclaimed. "I'm enjoying the dance. Bruh. Why are you breathing like that?"

Antonio ignored his comment. "You've been here for a whole sixty seconds, and I bet you've already made a bad Katy Perry joke in your head."

Seb was going to act scandalized, but Antonio knew him so well. Seb leaned into the cane in his left hand. "It wasn't *that* bad," he said.

"Was it a pun about ships?"

Seb scowled. "We truly spend way too much time together."

"I don't know," said Antonio. "We're around one another a lot, but it's not so bad, is it?"

Oh, Antonio.

Antonio, who bonded with Seb's parents by first speaking Spanish then complimenting his abuelo's cooking.

Antonio, who researched online for hours to find the right kind of cane to reduce the pain in Seb's joints.

Antonio, who once spent the night and slept on the wildly uncomfortable couch for just an hour so he could drive Seb to an early physical therapy session before school.

And now, Seb's best friend thought that setting him up with Olivia—who was perfectly fine and perfectly pretty and perfectly not at all his type—would make him happy. Why had he talked about wanting to be Olivia's friend so much? He truly meant it! But just as a *friend*. So it was a sweet gesture really, but come on. Wasn't it obvious? Didn't Antonio just *know*?

He looked to the right. Saw Vi coming in through the doors on that side of the building. They looked so damn *sharp*, and Seb's heart was in his throat. Oh, he should have said something to his twin. Vi would have been exactly the right person to tell.

But this was their moment, and Seb was so proud of that suit.

"You want to actually go *in* the dance, Seb?"

Antonio tugged his arm.

And his heart.

And yeah, it was cheesy to think that, but Seb didn't care. He wanted to be cheesy with Antonio Vasquez.

Olivia entered the gymnasium through the western door.

She was immediately and utterly over it all.

First off, the music was *terrible*. Olivia believed that Katy Perry had lost the right to produce music after trying to cover Whitney Houston, but apparently the DJ had not gotten the memo. Second: the *gymnasium*? No one could come up with a better venue? This place smelled. She'd just gotten new box braids in, and she was certain that by the time she got home, they'd stink of unwashed boys' underwear. The stench was *everywhere*.

Great.

To her left was Mal. Olivia wasn't sure why Mal came, but could she judge? Here Olivia was, without any interest in dances or her gross classmates hitting on her, still in the school gymnasium. THE. GYM. Mal had gone all out, had rented a tux that was *way* too expensive for literally *any* school's midwinter dance, let alone this travesty. Was someone on the school council a huge fan of *Titanic* or something? Who in all honesty thought giving a school dance a shipwreck theme was a good thing?

Yes, Olivia was on the student council, and yes, she had technically approved the idea (mostly to end a meeting that had gone forty-five minutes past the scheduled time), but did they have to go and make something so *tacky*? Maybe she should have paid more attention during all those meetings.

Mal bumped into her arm. "I'll go get us some sparkling apple cider," he said. He fussed with the big swoop of blond hair he had coiffed up, and every time he did, he messed it up more.

He darted off, and as soon as he was gone, Olivia's best friend and council vice president, Maria, leaned in closer. "Olivia, I *swear,* he is deadweight. He's like one of those logs you find washed up on the shore. Or something."

"I don't understand your metaphor, but I respect it," said Olivia, but then she dismissed the comment with a wave. "And I've been friends with Mal since elementary school. He's fine."

Maria squinted at her. "Is he, though? He's basically a . . . what's a less genital-specific word for cockblocker?"

"Maria!" Olivia shouted. "Why you gotta be so nasty?"

"Am I wrong?" Maria held her hands up. "Has he ever let *anyone* get close to you since—"

"Don't say it." Olivia already had a finger in Maria's face. "Don't say his name."

"Okay, okay, I won't." Maria shook her head. "It's been two years, Liv. Surely that's long enough."

"Nope. Seven years."

"Seven? Where did you even get that number?"

"It's how long I need," said Olivia. "Seven years, and then I'll be ready to fall in love again."

But even as Olivia said it, she knew that wasn't true. After *he* had broken her heart, Olivia had sworn off all potential relationships. Yes, she was still in high school, and yes, she was going to wait. Besides, she wasn't into the same things her peers were. She was confident sex was not going to be her thing; she just wanted everything else. The romance. The attention. Even kissing!

So here was a convenient out: seven years of devotion to herself. Then she didn't have to explain what was *actually* going on with her.

Besides, there was not one human being at this "dance" (and she certainly made air quotes in her mind when she thought that word) who could excite her.

Well. She had to make her appearance as a student council member. Mal would inevitably find his way back to her and spend the rest of the night shooing off anyone who tried to talk to her. A part of her appreciated that, but another . . . she knew Mal liked her. Like *that*. But how could she tell him the truth? He would stop being her friend, wouldn't he?

Maybe he wasn't actually a friend if his idea of friendship required sex.

She thought about that as Maria guided her into the fray. The truth was that she wanted something that felt so cliché, so *normal*, and yet it was her truth.

Olivia just wanted to be swept off her feet.

❧

Antonio had entered the gymnasium through the north door.

He'd scoped out the room immediately. Swept his eyes across to the left.

Seb, Seb, Seb, where are you?

Nowhere to be found, apparently.

Oh, this was not going to go the way Antonio wanted it. It wasn't that he *didn't* want to help Seb! That was second nature to him. But what happened when the nice thing you did for someone else contradicted the nice thing you *wanted*?

He watched Olivia come in, surprised that she was here before everyone else he knew. Even though she was student body president, she notoriously hated coming to school functions. It was part of the reason she got elected, after all. And yet there she was with her friends, drifting through the crowd.

There was Vi, and Antonio waved. No response.

Where are you, Seb?

And then the Katy Perry song started playing.

Antonio had to laugh. If Seb was in the room, Antonio knew exactly what was going through his head. Disgust and annoyance first, and then . . . boy, Seb really liked coming up with bad puns. Really, really, *really* bad puns. He'd lay one out then look to you to see if it made sense or was even a little bit funny, and the corners of his eyes would wrinkle up because he was so worried and—

There. To the south.

His body betrayed his desires, and Antonio initially rushed his way through the crowd, his nerves racing. But then he froze before Seb could see him, and Antonio was a static thing in the shifting rhythm of the other dancers.

Damn it, he was doing it again. It was so easy for Antonio to let his fantasy run wild, to ignore that he was so deeply in love with someone who definitely did not reciprocate it. They were just "friends." It was a boundary that Seb enforced by . . . well, by mentioning it every chance he got.

Here's my friend Antonio, Mom!

My best friend is taking me to therapy, Papi.

My best friend is—

Few things were more crushing: wanting more but being unable to have it. Yet Antonio could not resist. It was like every part of him wanted to help Seb, to do things that made him smile, to show him how much Antonio adored him.

Because maybe, just maybe, Seb would do the same things for him.

So here he was, about to set Seb up with one of the most popular people in school. To be seen with Olivia was like being witnessed with royalty. Seb had often mentioned how much he enjoyed Olivia's style. Her chaotic humor. Her confidence. So, Antonio roped Vi, who at least knew Olivia, into making sure she and Seb met. Sparks would fly, because who *didn't* like Sebastián Rojas?

Antonio cut around the table with apple cider so he could seem to have effortlessly joined Seb, as if he had always been beside him. It was such an inconsequential thing, but the little details mattered so much to Antonio.

Seb's suit was dark, a navy blue, while Antonio's own was a deep green. Both of them chose colors that would pop against their brown skin, and when Antonio curled his arm around Seb's, he tried to hide the fact that he'd run over here.

But Seb picked up on it. He was so much more observant than he gave himself credit for.

Except about the one thing that mattered.

Antonio had been waiting for Seb to put it all together. The nights spent at his house; the dedication; the loyalty; the way Antonio looked in Seb's eyes as if eternity could be found there.

But Seb just smiled, and the two moved out on the dance floor, and Antonio burned with shame.

It was never going to happen.

To be in love with someone who did not love you back was the loneliest thing in the whole damn world.

✿

The actors were in place.

The play began.

✿

It was a complicated dance.

The looks started immediately. Quick, furtive glances from Vi's fellow students, then double takes, and then they caught Beau Johnson full-on staring at them, his mouth slightly open, like a door left ajar.

Vi had to ignore him. They puffed their chest out a little more, smoothed down their lapels, pointed their chin a bit higher.

They walked like royalty.

Through the crowd, past couples moving their hips against one another.

Through the crowd, ignoring the comments.

Through the crowd, one destination in mind.

Olivia.

Olivia was standing near the chaperone check-in area, and Maria was by her side, wrapped up in something on her phone. So Vi took the opportunity and strolled right up to Olivia.

Bowed in front of her.

Extended their hand so she could take it.

Watched as Olivia gave them a quick glance then a second one that was much longer.

Then.

"Seb? Are you . . . are you asking me to *dance*?"

Wait.

No.

What?

Maria's attention flicked up from her phone. "Sebastián Rojas? Asking Olivia Bellweather to dance?"

No, no, no.

This wasn't supposed to happen.

And yet . . .

There was a thrill. It rose from deep within their belly, sent waves of energy through their body. Vi and Seb had not been mixed up all that often by their peers, yet Vi *had* been worried this would happen.

But . . . no reason to get excited, right? Olivia didn't like them; she liked Seb.

(Even if, for the briefest span of time, Vi could imagine that the excitement *was* for them.)

"Follow me," Vi said, taking Olivia's now outstretched hand. "I have a surprise for you."

Olivia's mouth dropped open. "Oh my *god*. A surprise? Seb, you are doing *way* too much."

But then she extended *her* hand.

Took Vi's.

Her friend Maria seemed so pleased. "I don't know where Mal went, but I'm getting *you* a drink," she said and then disappeared.

And Vi vowed to make this perfect for their brother.

I'm going to sweep her off her feet.

And together, they walked toward the other side of the room.

✤

Antonio was on the lookout again, but he found it challenging. Challenging because he just couldn't stop casting glances at Seb. (Who allowed such a jawline to exist? And those *cheekbones*? *Rude,* he thought. *Absolutely rude.*)

His eyes fell upon Vi, who was escorting Olivia across the dance floor as planned, toward Seb, toward a destiny that was inevitable. Antonio's heart raced, pattering violently in his chest. Did he really want to witness this?

Vi and Olivia paused.

The two of them spun around.

And then Olivia's hand was on Vi's back, her other hand in theirs.

And they spun again.

Again.

Again.

Okay, perhaps Antonio was imagining—

No, nope, that was definitely—

Oh, wow, they were *really* close now, and Olivia was whispering something in Vi's ear and—

Vi's eyes went wide then locked with Antonio's.

Oh, no.

Something had gone horribly wrong, hadn't it?

"Come this way," Antonio said—a sudden, thoughtless change. This was pure reaction, nothing else, as he guided Seb away from the dance floor and toward the table of all the nonalcoholic drinks provided with the cost of the ticket. "Let's get something to drink first."

"But I'm not thirsty," said Seb, looking over his own shoulder back into the crowd. "And I kinda have to pee, and is that—"

"Perfect, then let's go to the bathroom!"

Seb's features twisted as he was guided to the bathroom. "How is it perfect that I have to pee?"

Nice going, Antonio, he thought. But he had to move past this moment and get Seb to safety. Seb would be *crushed* to see Olivia with literally anyone else, but with his own sibling? That would be a tragedy of epic—

"Is Vi dancing with Olivia?"

Antonio stopped and put his face in his free hand. No, no, *no!* This was not going how it was supposed to go. Antonio was supposed to make Seb happy by introducing him to the future love of his life, and now it seemed like Vi had perhaps stolen Olivia away from their own brother.

"It might be," said Antonio. "I can't see too well in the dark, so maybe it's someone else."

Seb tilted his head to the side and scrunched his face. "It's not *that* dark here, Antonio."

"Maybe we should have petitioned to have better lighting installed in the gym," suggested Antonio.

"Dude, the lights are fine. Most of them are just *off.*"

It was clear from the look on Seb's face that Antonio had now *completely* lost him. "Never mind," Antonio said. "Let's get some air. You want some air?"

"Bruh, *no.*" Seb frowned. "I want you to stop being so *weird.*" Well.

That wasn't what Antonio wanted to hear.

And when Vi and Olivia spun into view behind Seb, Antonio could not push down the frustration building within him.

He was going to make this right, no matter what it cost him.

Olivia figured it out within a minute.

And she was more than fine with it.

She had never seen Vi like this. *Vi,* rhymes with "ski." Vi Rojas. She rolled the name around in her mouth. Vi had whispered it in her ear toward the beginning of the dance, once Olivia admitted to mixing up the twins.

And maybe she was attracted in some platonic way to Seb—she had not really considered it before—but *this* feeling? The energy that Vi gave off? The way Vi held their chin high? Whoa. Where did this come from? Why hadn't Olivia paid more attention during those student council meetings?

Maybe this felt so exciting because Vi was finally being themself.

The pair spun around together, even though the song wasn't meant for slow dancing, wasn't intended for two people like them, but who cared about intent? Who cared about plans and dreams and futures when someone came into your life like this?

Vi had always been so quiet during those meetings.

Or . . . wait.

Had they?

Or was Olivia mistaken in how she remembered the past? Could her perception of Vi be flawed? If so, how could Olivia possibly know what kind of person they were?

Vi smiled at her.

"This is very strange," they said.

"I like strange," she said back. "And chaotic. And *different.* This school can feel so . . . so . . ."

"Typical?" Vi offered.

"Yes," said Olivia. "That word."

Olivia's disinterest in much of life at school stemmed from *that*: everything here felt so typical. So cliché. So exactly like you expected it. But . . . not Vi. Not this moment. Olivia knew this wasn't love at first sight. That wasn't how things worked with her; never had, never would.

But right here, right now . . . something else was happening. Vi was a *fantastic* dancer, knew how to take the lead, knew how to look into Olivia's eyes and make her feel like there wasn't another person on the whole planet, and . . .

Well, the rest of it, Olivia would have to find out. And what an exciting idea that was.

Not love at first sight. That implied that otherworldly forces were at work, that some magical energy was pushing them together.

Nah. This was a *choice*.

"What are you *doing*?"

The moment was shattered. Olivia's back was to whoever had yelled, but she quickly realized it wasn't meant for her.

There was Seb, right there, and next to him, that boy with the dark hair and thick brows who was always at Seb's side. Like right now, his face twisted in anger. "Vi, I thought you were supposed to help me!" the boy said.

Vi let go of Olivia, and seconds later, Maria was back, two drinks in her hands. She looked from Olivia to Vi, then to Seb, then *back* to Vi.

"Um . . . did I miss something?"

Help him?

Help him *what*?

"I'm so confused," said Seb. "Antonio, why are you yelling at Vi?"

"This isn't how this is supposed to happen!"

Antonio was *way* upset. More than Seb had ever seen him. (Had Seb ever seen him angry?)

(Damn it, he was kinda hot while mad!)

(Focus, Seb, focus!)

"What exactly is supposed to happen?" Seb asked. "I don't see what's wrong with Vi dancing with—"

"It was supposed to be *you*!"

Antonio's face twisted in agony, and Seb took a step back. Oh. This was *serious*.

"Antonio . . ." he began then sighed. "I just . . . oh, *no*." He gently placed his head in his hands. "You think I wanted to like . . . *date* Olivia?"

"You're always talking about how cool you think she is!" Antonio shot back.

"Wait, really?" Olivia said, her hand over her heart.

He grimaced, certain he was about to disappoint another person, then faced Olivia. "Like . . . as friends. But yeah. I do think that."

Ugh, that sounded so terrible, he thought. But there was nothing wrong with wanting to be friends with someone! It wasn't any less of a relationship than a romantic one. How, though? How could he explain that to her?

"But you—" Antonio grasped for the right words, and Seb discovered that he *also* looked cute when flustered. "You always said you wanted to be around her, and I asked Vi to help, since they're on the student council, so this was supposed to be your grand introduction, and . . . oh, *fuck*." His hands flew to his face. "Did I mess this up? How badly did I mess this up?"

Olivia laughed.

She *laughed*.

"Wait," she said, swinging her braids back. "Did . . . did you try to set me up with Seb? Instead of getting with him yourself?"

The wind was knocked out of Antonio. As he took a step back, Seb tried to save the moment.

"He's my best friend," Seb shot back. "What are you doing with Vi, anyway?"

"Whatever I want," Olivia said. "And am I wrong about you two?"

"But that wasn't the plan!" Antonio said, moving closer to Olivia.

"Am I not allowed to make my own decisions in all this?" Vi said softly. "Olivia didn't want to be set up with my brother. And *I* wanted to dance with *her*."

"I truly wish I had a bowl of popcorn," said the girl standing next to Olivia, her face awash with glee. "This is so entertaining!"

"And who are *you*?" Antonio asked.

"That's *my* best friend!" Olivia cried.

Right as Olivia said this, Seb looked down.

To see Olivia gripping a hand tightly.

Vi's hand.

Oh.

Just that.

Then:

She made a choice.

The realization awoke within him burning desire and the terror of rejection—simultaneous monsters that he needed to conquer. They had kept him too silent for too long.

So now these feelings made him *bold.*

Seb stretched his own hand down. Ran his fingertips over Antonio's skin, toward the fingers he then interlocked with his own, and Seb squeezed tight.

Once. Twice.

Then looked at Antonio.

Because if Vi could make their own decision, then damn it, so could Seb.

"I *told* you," said Olivia. "Now can we get back to dancing?"

Vi and Olivia spun off. Antonio hesitated, and Seb saw the glassy eyes, the quivering lip, the dawning realization.

"Really?" said Antonio. "You mean it?"

He pulled Antonio in for a kiss. It was short, but it was enough for now.

"Yes," said Seb. "I mean it."

Right then, Sebastián Rojas got to see a new expression on Antonio's face.

The one where he was both surprised *and* delighted.

🌹

Maria sipped at her apple cider and tried not to choke as she watched this scene unfold.

So, if she understood it: Vi was in on the attempt to get Seb and Olivia together. This new boy—Antonio, maybe?—was clearly doing all this to get Seb's attention because he was absolutely head over heels in love with Seb and perhaps thought this bit of self-sacrifice would be seen as noble? *Maybe?* And while Maria had been gone for the whole of five minutes, Olivia finally found someone that interested her, and it was the mega-hot (seriously, that suit!) sibling of Seb, so that made this a love . . . square? Except it wasn't all perfectly mutual?

Oh, god, this was the most delicious thing Maria had ever seen in her sixteen years on this beautiful earth.

Except there was one piece of this messy disaster of attraction and romance that was heretofore unresolved, and Maria had to make sure things went smoothly.

Which is why, as she spotted Mal making a determined beeline for Olivia, she deftly maneuvered out of this love fest to pull Mal to the side.

"Hey, Mal, we should talk," she said.

But he was already staring over Maria's shoulder. "Who is talking with Olivia? She probably needs me."

Maria put a hand out to stop Mal from going after her friend. "No, Mal, you can't."

"I can't *what?*"

"You can't keep trying to control Olivia's life," she said, and even as the words left her mouth, she thought that perhaps this was too cruel.

But it felt true. In the years since Olivia's heartbreak, Mal had only gotten more protective of her. And Maria was, too, to some extent, but . . . not letting her make her own decisions? How was that fair?

"I'm not *controlling* her," he said, his mouth dropping open in shock. "How could you *say* that?"

"Look at her!" Maria gestured to her bestie, who was dipped low by Vi then spun up and around. "She's having a good time. And maybe she'll get her heart broken again, but she should be the one to decide to take that risk."

Mal pursed his lips. "But . . . I don't like seeing her hurt."

"Who does?!" Maria shot back. "That doesn't mean you get to swoop in and stop her from feeling happiness, too."

She thought she knew what he was going to say next: that

he loved her, that he had *always* loved her, that this wasn't just about protecting Olivia but protecting *himself.*

She thought she had it all figured out.

And then he turned around, his eyes searching the crowd, and then . . .

A boy came toward Mal.

They kissed.

Was that . . . was that Duke Pennington?

Maria coughed. "I'm sorry . . . are you two . . . ?"

Mal pointed at himself then at Duke. "You mean . . . are we . . . ?"

Duke shrugged. "I always thought he was cute."

"Don't you think *everyone* is cute, Duke?" Maria asked.

Duke smiled ear to ear. "Doesn't make Mal any *less* cute."

"But . . . you and Olivia," Maria began, pointing toward Mal.

Mal burst into laughter, a loud, earsplitting sound. "What, did you think I *wanted* Olivia? This whole time?" The next round came from his gut. "Oh, honey, no. Not in a million years! I just want the best for her, you know?"

And now Maria was left feeling . . . well, a little foolish.

The actors were all in place.

And then—in possession of the truth, standing in their own selves, breathing the air of possibility—they danced.

They did as they would.

And the night went on.

TAMING OF THE SOUL MATE

Inspired by The Taming of the Shrew

K. Ancrum

No shame but mine. I must, forsooth, be forced
To give my hand, opposed against my heart,
Unto a mad-brain rudesby, full of spleen;
Who wooed in haste and means to wed at leisure.
I told you, I, he was a frantic fool,
Hiding his bitter jests in blunt behavior,
And to be noted for a merry man,
He'll woo a thousand, 'point the day of marriage,
Make friends invite, and proclaim the banns;
Yet never means to wed where he hath wooed.
Now must the world point at poor Katherine . . .

—KATHERINE, ACT 3, SCENE 2

Right there in the supermarket?"

"Yeah, apparently she was grabbing some chips off a high shelf and heard him gasp loudly behind her, and when she turned around and saw him . . . *boom!* Full color and everything," Katherine said.

"Gross—*Lucentio*? Good god." Sabrina gagged dramatically before continuing to swipe on her mascara. "I would die if he was my soul mate. He has muttonchop sideburns."

Katherine leaned against the doorframe and checked her phone. They were already a solid hour late to Lucentio and Bianca's elopement party. "I bet if he was your soul mate, you wouldn't care about the sideburns," she said. "It literally turns you into a fool who would fall in love with anyone. I would blind myself to avoid it, if only I didn't like seeing so much. I don't even know if getting to see colors for the first time is worth that kind of embarrassment."

"Yeah, okay. But what if your soul mate was really hot or a celebrity?" Sabrina replied, dusting her under eyes with setting powder. "You'd change your tune then."

"I think you should be able to choose who you wind up with—"

"I know," Sabrina interrupted. "That's why you're dragging me, your only friend, to an engagement party with less than three hours' notice. An engagement party thrown by high school seniors, no less. There better be at least a few college freshmen like us or this will be a waste of makeup."

Katherine sat down on the floor so she could pull on her light-gray boots. "It's an elopement party, not an engagement party," she clarified, zipping up the sides. "Our dad's being weird about the family trust, and there are a bunch of archaic rules in it about the eldest getting married first. Neither I nor Bianca cared about that until now, because we were both really focused on getting an education. But I'm pretty sure he's going to hunt her down when he finds out that she's beating me to the altar," she finished darkly.

Sabrina whirled around, her gray curls flying. "So, you don't like the soul mate thing because it's supposedly forcing you to choose someone you might otherwise not have liked. But your dad having a rule about your and your sister's relationships is somehow worse than that? To the point where you're fully supporting your younger sister running away with muttonchop man?"

Katherine paused with one arm in her coat. "His mutton-chops are bad. He's also seventeen and not even in honors classes. This?" She waved her free arm around wildly. "This whole thing isn't a best-case scenario. But I love Bianca, and it's not fair for her to have to stand there and not get to be with her soul mate, just because I'm focused on my first college finals in three weeks instead of getting hitched to the first guy I see. Also, hurry up, you look fine."

Sabrina tossed her sparkly gray lip gloss into her makeup bag and cackled. "Wow. Way to bury the lede, Katherine. You should have just told me that first. Bianca would be seeing in color for years before you let a guy get close to you like that. You should've let me set you up with Janet."

"I'm not dignifying that with a response. You get five minutes before I'm driving away." Katherine zipped up her coat and marched toward the car.

***

Sabrina scuttled in, seconds before Katherine was preparing to rev the engine threateningly. "Jeez, you could have waited for me to get my shoes on."

"You don't have to look good for Bianca's friends," Katherine said. "They're all bros, and by the time the weekend is over, you'll be back to hanging out with bio majors anyway. Don't waste your energy."

"I know, Katherine, but you never know who *you'll* meet," Sabrina said, checking her face one last time in her compact.

"They're all terrible, and my best friend deserves better than that. They're super-immature, and we're going to be pre-med. Bianca has been telling me stories about them, and they're all horrible. Lucentio's best friend even ate a goldfish on a bet. He's probably going to be the best man."

"Really? Gross. Did he chew it?"

"Does it matter? That's the quality we're going for here? And it's going to be a small group, so don't get any ideas. We can go to a restaurant afterward if you're so desperate."

"Are you *sure* it's going to be a small group?" Sabrina asked.

"Bianca doesn't lie to me. Just keep it together."

"I wasn't speculating. I can hear the music from here, Katherine."

The door was already open when they pulled up to Lucentio's house, and people spilled out onto the lawn. Katherine scowled. Clearly the "intimate get-together" had gotten out of hand.

Sabrina looked down at her tasteful, knee-length, gray wool cocktail dress then over at Katherine's modest light-gray turtleneck and gave her a dry look.

"If you're uncomfortable, I'm sure we can make an appearance for support, give them some cash, and head back home," Katherine snapped.

"It's not that I want to leave," Sabrina said. "I just didn't know this would be a cool party, and I look like a teacher's assistant."

"I'm sure Bianca has something you can wear if you want to change." Katherine parked the car an extra block away to be safe. "I, on the other hand, will be keeping these clothes on. I prefer to look intimidating. We are not their peers."

They pushed through the crowd to get inside. Already, Katherine could smell weed and the salty tang of too many people in a small space. The living room was packed, but Bianca's white-gray hair shone brightly from the back of the room. She was sitting in the middle of the couch, pressed snugly against Lucentio.

"Oh, wow, Lucentio shaved them off . . . ," Sabrina pointed out brightly, bumping up behind Katherine as a tall boy shoved past them.

Katherine's eyes flicked over to Lucentio, and his mutton-chops were indeed gone. It was a drastic improvement. His dark-gray hair was also brushed, and he was wearing a well-fitting button-up shirt and nicer jeans. Katherine would never have considered Lucentio to be good-looking, but he looked good happy. She elbowed her way past the people in front of her and called out Bianca's name.

"Katherine!" Bianca shrieked, tearing her eyes away from her fiancé to throw her arms open for a hug.

Katherine held her sister close and rocked back and forth, the way they always did after not seeing each other for a while.

"Oh, god," someone to her left said, before leaping off the couch with such urgency that they knocked into Lucentio hard enough to send him careening into the side of Katherine's shoulder.

"Asshole!" Katherine shouted after him and gently touched Lucentio on the side of his head. "You okay?"

"Yeah!" Lucentio said, rueful. "Sorry, that was just my man Petrucio. Maybe he drank too much. Anyway, thanks so much for coming. I know the situation isn't what you might have wanted . . ." He trailed off, looking kind of sheepish.

"Don't worry about it. I'm not the one you should be trying to impress," Katherine said. "Welcome to the family. Bianca is a peach, but you'll definitely regret the rest of us. Here, I have a gift for you both." She pulled an envelope out of her purse and handed it to Lucentio. "Don't spend it all in one place . . . or if you do, try spending it on housing."

Sabrina hugged the couple as well then plopped down into the newly vacated space on Lucentio's other side.

"These heels are for sitting, not standing," she said, glaring up at Katherine. "Where is the food? Please tell me there's food here."

Bianca and Lucentio were staring at each other again.

"Bianca," Katherine called.

"Yeah," Bianca said distractedly.

"Sabrina's hungry. Which way is the kitchen?"

Bianca didn't respond, she just sighed and leaned her head against the side of the couch, snuggling up closer to her soul mate. Lucentio's face was still lit up like Christmas.

Katherine threw her hands up. "I'll find it myself." She turned and began trying to elbow her way through the crowd.

"If there's chips, bring me chips!" Sabrina called after her.

"Yeah, yeah, chips." Katherine pushed past a kissing couple and into the hallway. It was darker past the living room, and there was a snaking line for the bathroom, packing everyone much tighter. Katherine slid against the wall, inching her way past the bathroom and around a corner. Kitchens tended to be brighter than most rooms in a house, so if the light at the end of this hallway was any indication, she was getting closer.

Katherine ducked under a swinging arm and slapped away a hand that touched her hip, forging determinedly toward her goal. She rose up on her tiptoes to try to see over a guy in front of her who seemed to be pushing in the same direction when a hand came out of nowhere, grabbed her arm, and dragged her through a dark doorway. Her assailant slammed the door hard behind her and covered her mouth with his hand.

"Ow! What the fuck!" She pushed with all of her strength,

hoping whoever had grabbed her would fall backwards, but she'd overestimated the size of the room, and they both slammed against the wall with a gasp. This was a closet, not a bedroom. Katherine grabbed at the door and only felt a hole where a doorknob should have been.

"I'm sorry, I'm sorry." It was a soft, deep voice.

So, it was probably a guy.

"Let me the fuck out of here!" she shouted into what she hoped was his face.

"Stop yelling, just listen to me," he said, reaching toward her.

She slapped at his hands wildly and shoved him hard again, then she turned and began beating on the door.

The guy wrapped his arm around her shoulders and pulled her away from the door, switching their positions so his back was against it and she was stifled between winter coats. "STOP!" he yelled. "Just stop!"

Normally Katherine wouldn't have stopped screaming, but he sounded scared. Or at least more scared than a rapist probably would have sounded. She stopped screaming and opted instead to yank one of the metal hangers out of a coat, bend it sharply, and stab it in his general direction.

He grunted then hissed in pain. "Fucking hell, is that a hanger?"

"If you don't let me out of here," Katherine said, "you'll leave bleeding. Now tell me what the fuck is going on."

"Okay, OKAY, that's what I've been trying to—"

She poked the hanger harder.

"Ow. God, I'm sorry! Just, let me . . . okay." He calmed his wild breathing and backed away as much as he could. "Katherine. I need you to lower the hanger so I can reach up and turn on the light."

"You can turn on the light from here just fine," she said coldly. "And how do you know my name?"

He huffed in frustration. "Please. The hanger's on my neck, and I don't want it to go in by accident. Here, move it to my chest or something."

Katherine felt a tug on the hanger and stubbornly didn't move for a second before letting him lower it just a bit.

"God. Is this how—" He sighed angrily. "Whatever."

After a bit of fiddling, the light turned on.

The first thing she thought was, *I've never met this guy before.*

The second thing was less of a thought and more of a feeling as gray and black and white became painful to look at and the colors began to tear through. His hair was . . . like the way bread looked when it was cooking, dark and shiny. His eyes were the same hue . . . but lighter, like the way weak tea tasted. His face was bright, the way she thought the sky looked on a cloudy day.

She didn't have words for the colors. She knew how to list them: red, blue, pink, green, yellow, brown. She knew that she was seeing them, but she didn't know which was which. His cheeks looked like the feeling of heat, and his mouth looked the same but hotter. He matched some of the hats hanging on the inside of the door. Beyond the colors, he was tense. His jaw was set, and his gaze crackled with intensity. As the realization of what was happening—who he was to her—began to sink in, Katherine closed her eyes. Just to make sure.

When she opened them again, he was still there and so were the colors. There was no turning back—she was color-born. Even though the hanger in her hands had cut the side of his face and a thin line of dark also dripped from his neck, he was silent. Just staring back at her, his eyes flicking away every so often in obvious humiliation.

Katherine lowered the hanger and finally tore her eyes away from him to take in the vibrancy of the rest of the closet. There was a coat in a color so bright, it hurt her tender vision again, just like the first time. There were also coats in shades she was already familiar with: dark gray and light gray. There was a scarf on a shelf that reminded her of the smell of grass and another that made her think of the texture of strawberries.

She looked down at herself. She realized she didn't like the colors she was wearing and felt a pang of embarrassment. Her skirt was a warm color and her shirt was a bright color and her shoes were something in between that didn't quite look right. It took a second before she remembered that most of the people at the party wouldn't be able to tell. Just Bianca and Lucentio, probably. And, of course, *this* guy.

When she finally managed to look back up into this stranger's eyes, she frowned.

"My name is Petrucio," he said firmly. "And I'm your fucking soul mate."

"No, you're not," she said reflexively.

He just looked at her with a pity that she loathed on his face. She also noticed his clothes seemed to match, even though color was clearly new to him, too.

"You're not my soul mate, because the likelihood of me finding the only soul mate I'll ever have in the *same town* within the *same week* of my sister is astronomically low," Katherine tried. "Maybe it's someone out there in the hallway. Maybe it took a second for the colors to kick in and my soul mate is waiting for me outside."

Petrucio didn't say anything.

"Maybe someone is playing a joke on me, and when I come out, they'll all yell surprise. Maybe I angered a fucking demon or something. Just to check, you aren't Lucentio's friend who ate a goldfish for money, are you?"

Petrucio reared back. "It wasn't for money, it was a bet that I lost!" he cried, offended.

Katherine laughed mirthlessly over his explanation. *Cool. Very cool, my new soul mate is a childish dork who eats live animals.* "Are there any other horrible surprises for me?" she cried to the heavens. "Anyone else going to ruin my day today?"

"Ruin your day?" Petrucio repeated in disgust.

"This isn't exactly part of my four-year plan, Petrucio!"

"You're acting like you're the only one impacted by this!"

"Oh, you think I'm *acting* like I'm the only one impacted by this?" Katherine spat. "It's not like I'm not dealing with enough nonsense, it's not like I'm about to conceal my sister's elopement a few weeks from finals. You have no idea the amount of stress I'm under right now. I can't do this."

"At least *you* aren't supposed to be perfect for the bitchiest girl in the entire history of our high school. At least *you* don't know you'll spend the rest of your life with someone who loves making people miserable. You don't know me at all, Katherine, but I know *you.* Everyone knows about you, and how happy everyone was when you finally graduated. People were dreading you even showing up to this thing. The only thing I'm bringing to this situation is some story you heard about me doing something ridiculous." He paused. "Lucentio got to swoon into a flower store display. I got stabbed in the throat. What does this say about you? And more importantly, what does that say about me? That we supposedly fit?"

Katherine's throat began to sting, and her face felt hot. "Move. I want to get out of here."

"Stop." Petrucio put his hands against the door. "Think about what you're doing. This is Bianca and Lucentio's party."

"I don't care," she said, trying to push past him.

"They're still in the honeymoon period of being colorborn!" he argued. "Why are you going to ruin this for them? Don't make them associate this day with us and with your fucking bullshit. I didn't pull you into this closet for a game; I did it to avoid ruining this party. We need some time outside of here to sort this situation out, and if you don't understand that—"

Katherine pushed against his chest and tried to breathe out of her mouth so she wouldn't remember what he smelled like. It would be easier to never see him again that way. She'd heard that smell was involved in the soul mate process, and she wasn't risking getting attached to his. "Good point!" she huffed, pushing even harder. "That's how I know you're not my soul mate. Because if you were, we'd be in the honeymoon period, too."

"We *would* be if you weren't so self-centered," Petrucio said. "Even if you don't care about your sister's feelings, I definitely care about Lucentio's, and you're not going to wreck this for him."

"I *do* care about my sister's feelings!" Katherine shouted. "How dare you even say that?" He didn't know her, and he didn't understand anything about their family.

"What do you think is going to happen?!" he yelled back. "Do you think I just casually hang out in closets? Do you think I pull people where they don't want to go, regularly? God, Katherine, you're so . . . ." He closed his eyes and rubbed his forehead.

"Look. What would you have done if you'd walked in, hugged your sister, turned to hug Lucentio, and saw me? Huh? What would you have done, if you were looking at me in front of everyone and the colors started coming and you knew it was me, Lucentio's meathead friend? Would you have laughed it off? Kept it to yourself and come to talk to me about it later?" He paused. "Of course not. You would have gotten angry and everyone would have come to see what was the matter and the entire night would have been about you. Calming you down and mocking the idea of how laughable it is that we would be suited for each other and god knows what else. So. When I saw you, instead of getting to spend time looking into my soul mate's eyes and discovering color together, I had to run and hide before you could see me and make things worse. Why? Because I'm a good fucking friend, Katherine."

Katherine covered her face and sank down to the floor. She could sense Petrucio standing, looking down at her. "What are we going to do?" she asked quietly.

After a moment, Petrucio kneeled across from her. He pushed his curly hair back with one hand and scowled up at the light. "What happens about this on your end? Bianca mentioned . . . something about your dad?"

"My dad's brother will get the lion's share of our grand-parents' inheritance if Bianca gets married before I do. If I had met my soul mate before she did, then Bianca would have been free to have a big wedding like she always wanted instead of settling for this slapdash party and running to City Hall afterwards. I was supporting her by helping pay for the license because I knew she'd have to get it in secret. Our father can't find out before it's done."

Petrucio paused to let that sink in. "And you're still going to let her have that slapdash City Hall wedding anyway, even though the circumstances have changed? Wow."

"I need you to stop pointing out my flaws, okay? It is taking everything inside me to not kill you right now. Let's work together to stop that from happening." Katherine's hands were still firmly over her face.

Petrucio scoffed. Katherine looked up just in time to see him roll his eyes.

They sat in relative silence for a while, the party still raging outside. The music was so loud, they could feel the vibrations through the floor. No one had tried to open the closet door yet, which was more comforting than Katherine would have thought.

"Can you turn off the light? This is a bit overwhelming for me. My eyes still hurt from . . . you know," Katherine admitted.

She listened to Petrucio climb to his feet, pull the string that plunged the room back into darkness, then settle back across from her, his knees bunched up under his chin and the toes of his gym shoes pressed against the wall on her left side.

"Why do you hate men, anyway? Bianca said you don't date girls either, so what gives? Are you asexual? I have a cousin who's asexual . . ."

Katherine sighed angrily. She didn't want to share this with a stranger. She barely shared her feelings with Sabrina. But Petrucio was waiting patiently. She could feel his body heat from across the small space, and even though she couldn't see him, she could tell, somehow, that his face was warmer than the rest of him.

"It's not that," she said finally. "It's not that I don't . . . like . . . men. It's more that I don't have time for them right now. I wanted to focus on school then focus on my career.

Most people don't meet their soul mates until they're in their late twenties or early thirties. I should have had more time. And I wanted to be the one to choose my partner. I wanted to be able to meet someone and work together to build a relationship. Not have instant love tell me what I was going to do and who I should trust. It doesn't seem fair."

The closet was still for a while as Petrucio thought. "How we react to our circumstances is a choice. We don't have to do anything we don't want to do, you know. We could choose to react one way to this, or we could make the best of it." She heard him take a deep breath. "For example, I know that you're . . . ambitious—which is a good thing," he interjected quickly. "And that you have strong principles and you stick to them. I know that family is important to you, but your values are *more* important to you and that you're willing to work hard to defend them. I know . . . that you have high expectations and that your high expectations make people around you try harder. I know you're a fighter and that you can defend yourself if need be," he said with a wry grin that she could hear. "We might not have ever locked eyes before this, but your reputation precedes you. I called you names earlier, but I really meant that you're tough. Strong, I guess."

Katherine lowered her hands from her face and scrunched up her knees so she could rest her cheek on them and listen to his voice.

"I know that you're responsible," he continued. "I know that Bianca looks up to you, which means you're worth looking up to. It's . . . it's not the worst that I could find, you know?"

Katherine snorted and rubbed at her eyes. "What are you planning to major in when you graduate?" she asked, trying for another topic.

Petrucio sighed in irritation. "Of course that's what would be important to you. I'm majoring in business with a minor in theatre."

"That's a weird combination."

"Fuck you," Petrucio volleyed back mildly. "It's expensive to go to college. I'm going to do what I want, no matter what anyone says. Also, it's good to have a hobby, even if I'm trying to get a good job." He sniffled.

"Are you crying?"

"I'm not crying," he said firmly. "My eyes just hurt. No one told me that your eyes hurt when you first see color."

"My nose kind of hurts, too," Katherine admitted. "Kind of like when you drink something fizzy and inhale it the wrong way."

"Yeah," Petrucio agreed. "I was reading somewhere that you can smell your soul mate from really far away after a while. Which is kind of gross."

"The entire concept of soul mates is gross, so I'm unsurprised." Katherine snorted.

Petrucio was quiet after that, and Katherine could feel a frisson of pain coming from him. She couldn't tell yet whether it was from his multiple hanger wounds, or if their new connection was forcing her to perceive his feelings. It hadn't occurred to her that he would have felt differently about this. Boys didn't seem to care about romantic stuff, so she had assumed he would be on her side about feeling disdain for the whole thing. But now that they were sitting in silence, her words felt like more of a misstep than she'd intended them to be.

"You . . . have some good qualities, too," Katherine started, tentatively. "You seem to be smart, and you can think on your feet. You're considerate of others' feelings. You're a good friend, and you're protective of the people you care about. You . . . uh . . ."

Petrucio sniffed again.

"You don't care what people think of your hobbies. I like that."

Petrucio sighed, and Katherine could hear him wiping at his face.

But when he began to speak again, his voice didn't have any tears in it. "You know, we can do this however we want. We can pretend we're not soul mates until we can announce this at a better time. We're basically strangers, Katherine. The only thing we owe each other, really, is consideration. I know you've got a lot of stuff going on and that this wasn't a part of your plan, and I respect that."

"You would let me go? Just . . . let me do what I want?" Katherine asked, leaning closer. It was an unusual offer. Not unheard of, but certainly not traditional.

"Yes!" Petrucio cried. "I don't want someone who doesn't want me. We don't have to . . . you know. Be a couple. We can just be partners or companions. Or not even that, if you don't want. But whatever we pick, it's ours to choose. Just because we . . . just because . . ."

Petrucio scrunched his legs up so he was farther away from her. "It doesn't have to be anything we don't want it to be," he continued, quieter. "You can finish school and go start your career. I'll stay here and finish up my degree. Maybe we can live in the same city and get coffee every so often, see each other once a week so that neither of us gets heartsick and fades away like soul mates do when one of them dies. Maybe spend a couple days together every year. You don't have to meet my family or anything."

"Maybe you can get a sweet girlfriend who will actually be nice to you, instead of 'the biggest bitch in the entire school.'"

Petrucio chuckled. "I'm not taking that back. But to be honest, even though that's how I feel now, I don't know if that will matter much when I'm older and there's no school for you to be the biggest bitch of."

"How do you think you'll feel then?" Katherine asked.

To her surprise, Petrucio answered immediately, "Lonely. But I would never make that your problem."

Someone slammed against the door loudly, and both of them flinched. Laughter leaked in from the hallway, and the body pressed against the door moved away.

"What do *you* want?" Petrucio asked, when both of their hearts had stopped wildly pounding.

Katherine thought for a while. "I want . . . to be respected. To be loved by someone who won't tie me down and force me to do things I don't want to do. I want to be independent but know that I have someone to come home to. I want to be myself and to not be mocked."

"You say that like those are incredible things to ask, but they're not. That's basic. Everyone wants to feel like that, it's not special. And if someone cares about you, they'll give you that stuff without you having to ask for it," Petrucio said.

"And what about you?" Katherine asked. "What do you want?"

"I want to turn on the light and look at you," he replied thickly. "I just want to *look*. It doesn't have to be anything more than that."

The knot in Katherine's throat grew bigger, and her chest began to ache. "What would you do if I never let you?" she whispered.

She could hear Petrucio move, scrabbling on the floor for something, then he lightly felt up her side until he found her arm. He took her hand and gently placed something round and heavy in her palm and closed her hand over it. She turned the object over in her hand until she understood what he had given her: the doorknob.

Her heart thundered behind her ribs. Katherine slowly got to her feet and placed the doorknob into the door. Petrucio made a small wounded sound, a noise so quiet that if they'd been in the hallway instead of the closet, she would have missed it.

Instead of opening the door, she reached her arm up and pulled the chain to turn on the light.

The colors were still there, still bright and achy as he looked up at her from the floor with his weak-tea eyes and warm-bread curls and the heat of his cheeks like the sun on her skin. This boy, who was hers. Who she didn't know, who she knew better than anyone, who didn't know her but was willing to learn her anyway. Who ran from her when she first walked into the room but wasn't running now.

Her stranger, companion, not yet a friend, who thought she was a bitch, who gave her a doorknob like he was giving her his heart. Who was still growing up, who was so far behind. Who offered her freedom after keeping her inside a closet until she was able to see the freedom he offered her.

Who was just a boy looking up at a girl by the flickering light of a dying lightbulb. On the first floor of his best friend's house, at an elopement party loud enough to get shut down by the cops.

With his pupils blown wide, in full colorbirth, in honeymoon, alone.

Katherine let go of the doorknob and slowly, to not startle him, kneeled until they were the same height. Petrucio looked at the door and at the feet casting shadows from the outside into this little room, then he turned back to her. She reached out to touch his cheek, but he flinched, ready for her to hurt him again.

Katherine hushed softly until he unwound, face less pinched, eyes less frantic, then she placed her hand on his cheek. Petrucio closed his eyes and let out a breath. She hadn't noticed that he'd been shaking until he stopped.

"Are you ready to leave the closet?" she asked. "I'm ready now, if you are, too."

Petrucio covered her hand with his and leaned his face into her palm.

"Not yet, Katherine. Not yet."

Well, come, my Kate. We will unto your father's
Even in these honest mean habiliments.
Our purses shall be proud, our garments poor
For 'tis the mind that makes the body rich;
And as the sun breaks through the darkest clouds,
So honor peereth in the meanest habit.
What, is the jay more precious than the lark
Because his feathers are more beautiful?
Or is the adder better than the eel
Because his painted skin contents the eye?
O no, good Kate; neither art thou the worse
For this poor furniture and mean array.
If thou account'st it shame, lay it on me.

—PETRUCHIO, ACT 4, SCENE 3

KING OF THE FAIRIES

Anna-Marie McLemore

That very time I saw (but thou couldst not)
Flying between the cold moon and the Earth,
Cupid all armed. A certain aim he took
At a fair vestal thronèd by the west,
And loosed his love shaft smartly from his bow,
As it should pierce a hundred thousand hearts.
But I might see young Cupid's fiery shaft
Quenched in the chaste beams of the watery moon,
And the imperial votaress passèd on,
In maiden meditation, fancy-free.
Yet marked I where the bolt of Cupid fell:
It fell upon a little western flower,
Before milk-white, now purple with love's wound.
And maidens call it "love-in-idleness."
Fetch me that flower. The herb I showed thee once.
The juice of it on sleeping eyelids laid
Will make or man or woman madly dote
Upon the next live creature that it sees.

—OBERON, ACT 2, SCENE 1

They are white, all of them. Endlessly and unrelentingly white.

The fairies have long been hailed as fairer than high Taurus snow. It is part of their name and nature. Each morning, the pale wind crowns them as princes and princesses of pure white.

And each evening, I stand among them, a brown-armed girl, lonely as a jasper set in alabaster.

Here, in these bewitched woods, they dance.

They dance between ponds so clear, they make crystal seem clouded.

They dance beneath the moon, beholding her silver form in the water.

They dance beneath arches of perfect primroses and on grass the moon has decked with liquid pearl.

They dance, and I remain still.

While they flit over petal-strewn ground, the gold of my skirt remains still.

I have lived and grown in this place, among these pale bodies.

The fairy court, which declared itself my home without ever asking if I cared to belong to it.

Peaseblossom and Cobweb turn their filmy skirts to the lutes' song. Titania laughs from her cowslip-adorned throne.

Oberon rises from his, gesturing to the musicians.

"King of the Fairies," he orders, and the court raises its cheer, hailing the king and his choice of song.

Titania gives him a fond smile.

But I remember when they glared at each other so keenly, I thought their eyes would leave wounds.

"Floria," Titania calls to me, a laugh tinkling through her voice.

The relative youth of the king and queen still unnerves me. Titania and Oberon have lived a thousand seasons yet hardly look old enough to have a child my age, nearly grown. They call me their changeling daughter and boast of how the fairy court has enchanted me with the same steadfast youth. But the court whispers that I will age no more quickly or slowly than a being who is half fairy and half mortal, that I will likely die before the king and queen's hair has even turned more gray than gold.

Titania extends a hand toward the fairies, and the moon finds her crown, as pale as her hair. "Dance," she says.

I bristle, as I have for years. She wants to show off this changeling daughter, pretty and brown and ever willing to do as she says.

I suppose anyone reasonable would blame me for my inaction all these years, as I've grown from child to young woman. Anyone might ask why I did not protest, did not demand I be taken back to my family.

But to any such question, I would say that I was small when Titania plucked me from my father's arms. I was small enough that now I remember my family only by their warmth and their specific shades of brown. I had thought the fairy queen was merely taking me on some living dream, to then return me to my bed by day's gentle approach.

By the time I realized this was not some fairy dream, that Titania and Oberon would never return me to my father, I did not know how to leave.

I did not know how to be anything but that changeling who exists to delight them.

What I did know, what I know still, is that fairies are long used to having what they like.

I did not want to learn what would become of me if I denied them.

Puck leaps across the bower, amusing the king. Puck, ever the happy uncle to me, has been Oberon's faithful attendant longer than I have lived.

Moth and Mustardseed spin, skirts fine as if they were woven from water.

With the parting of their bodies, a sliver of color startles me. Brown.

Brown, among all the white arms and blossom-pale gowns.

At first, I wonder if a pond has left its bed, if it holds itself up to me as a mirror.

But the brown does not belong to me.

This brown belongs to a boy.

He does not wear the jewel purples and greens of the fairy men.

He wears a green as soft and dull as olive leaves, white softened into cream-beige, brown as deep as the earth.

And he dances more precisely than any of the mead-drunk courtiers. Light-heeled, each step is as crisp as the horned edge of a crescent moon. He skips forward as easily as water over stones, and the air smells a little more sweetly of wood-bine and honeysuckle.

The set to his mouth shows both his concentration and his disregard for the way the fairies pause to watch him.

"Stop." Oberon signals the musicians.

But the musicians, too, are watching the boy and continue their playing as though entranced.

The fairy court grows so still that the trees seem to shift, breathing, stretching out their arms to intertwine branches.

"Stop, I say!"

Oberon's bellow silences the musicians.

Even the boy stops dancing.

"You." Oberon rises, regarding the boy who seems now to be the still center of the rustling woods. "Approach."

The boy does.

And he stays upright.

The court seems to hold its breath, all of them together, waiting for the boy to realize his mistake.

He remains standing at his full height.

An angry flush rises from Oberon's neck up to his fine hair and silver crown.

"You dare show your king no reverence?" Oberon asks. "Bow, you intruder."

The boy lowers himself to his knees, the usual first deference for a court visitor. So he knows enough of fairies to know their way. But he lowers himself slowly, so slowly, I can hear Oberon's sigh of impatience.

This, together with the curve of the boy's mouth, the bow of his lips, makes the gesture seem mocking.

"What is your name?" Oberon asks.

Even in raising his glance to Oberon, even in the small flick of the boy's eyes, there is defiance.

"You know my name," he says.

The court gasps.

I pray for the woods to tie up this boy's tongue before Oberon orders him drowned in a pond.

But Oberon chuckles.

It is a sound so unexpected, I startle.

"Ah." Oberon finishes his laugh as though savoring a fig. "The bastard changeling. What was the name you called yourself?"

The boy glares up at the king.

The king seems more pleased at this than offended. "Yes." He pretends to have a sudden recollection. "Narciso. I do hope you're pleased with it, for unlike those of us named by our fathers, the only quarrel left to you is with yourself."

"I did not name myself," the boy says, "the first or second time, and you know it."

Titania sees my confusion and offers an obliging smile. "As the ivy enrings the barky fingers of the elm," she says, inclining a delicate hand, the way she always does when explaining something to me, "so the boy before you must enring his own form in cloth beneath his clothing."

The court murmurs its incomprehension.

But understanding flashes through me, fast as lightning in the coiled night. That Titania would declare this before the entire court sickens me, even if half does not understand.

As the ivy enrings the elm.

She is talking of Narciso binding his chest.

She is talking of how, to be taken properly as the boy he is, he must wrap cloth around himself beneath his shirt.

I have learned that, for as flighty and lovely as fairies are, the fairy court has little patience for anyone who wishes to step out of the dresses or trousers they were handed at their birth. I've heard that fairies raised in the depths of the wood live as they wish, but the queen has always said that what may be fine custom for the far meadows is unseemly at court. Once, I asked to clothe myself in the deep colors reserved for fairy men, the night blue and dewed-grass green, and Oberon asked why I should want to mar my girlhood. I once asked Titania if I might wear pants to a midnight dance, and she gave no reply but the bell song of her laugh.

My soul and my stomach fell each time.

I cannot imagine the grief of this boy who was likely given a girl's name at his birth.

But I find in his face no shame or fear. Only that defiance. He holds Oberon's gaze.

And still, with that pitying laugh, Oberon speaks. "Rise," he says.

Narciso obeys.

"I banished you as a child," Oberon says. "Do you imagine greater forbearance now that you're grown?" He flicks a hand. "Skip hence."

Narciso gives a small bow, a gracious nod.

Not to Oberon.

To me.

I did not realize he had noticed me.

But as he exits, it is only me he acknowledges, a brown-armed girl among these pale sylphs, as though it is I who commands him, not the king of the fairies.

Once the gleams of the moon have faded and the fairies have taken to sleep in their bowers, there is little time before the king and queen argue.

From behind the heavy elm where I hide, where I have hidden during their quarrels for years, their words are crisp as new grass.

"It is blasphemy," Oberon says.

"He is nothing." Titania tries to flatten the king's bluster.

"For him to dance our dance—I cannot even think on it."

"He is a bead, an acorn," she says. "Nothing next to the king of the fairies."

Her voice is more that of a reasoning sister than a soothing wife. Their marriage is woven more in power and esteem than in love. Titania forswore his bed long ago, and he minded little. She has her elves who sing her asleep, and their beds. He has Puck, whom I hope he loves in at least half the measure Puck loves him.

"I will not see that bastard darken our court again," Oberon says.

Two words in the single declaration sting me.

Bastard. Oberon said the same word when he first saw Narciso, but I didn't think he meant it as more than insult. Now, hearing it again, hearing Oberon's anger seething beneath it, I understand. So this is why Narciso performed the dance so well, how he knows the particular bow of fairy courts. He is some fairy, some mortal.

Darken. To Oberon, to make something darker is to make it worse.

How little he would have wanted me if Titania had not wanted me first.

"Are you quite finished?" Titania asks. "He's no threat to you."

Her patience is wearing. The weaving together of their rising voices draws me back to when I was that small child, their stolen changeling.

Titania gained my mother's devotion, and more of her, I imagine, though I do not know if Titania loved her, too. She claims my mother cared for my father but did not want the life and land they had grown on. That she wanted to leave the milpas and farming seasons of her youth. That she grew bored with the three sisters of squash, corn, and beans growing in earth as rich black as the night sky.

But in the same breath, Titania spins the loveliest tales of my mother's homeland, the land where I was born. She waxes about the ash-rich earth beneath volcanos, the emerald and garnet of quetzals' flight, the millions of orange-and-black butterflies that cover the land every autumn.

Titania tells me how she bid the sails of her ship to grow big-bellied with wind, that she sat with my mother on Neptune's yellow sands, that my mother would delight her with the bright fruit of the hillsides.

Titania tells me that my mother would have wanted her to have me.

It should have been no surprise to Titania that if she claimed something pretty and rare, the king would want it for himself.

They laugh of it now, the row over me. How Puck, Oberon's good robin, fetched a bewitched flower, struck by Cupid's arrow. How its potion made Titania fall in love with Bottom, a man who, just for that night, had the head of an ass. How she declared her unending love to the gentle mortal, offered him jewels and a bed of pressed flowers. They marvel at a love enchantment strong enough to make Titania's heart turn toward any man at all, and Bottom's toward any woman's, even the queen of the fairies. (Bottom, true to his name, happily follows every order of his gentleman Quince.)

Their happy concord was to share me, their changeling child.

Except that now, their changeling child slips away into the dark.

With each step, my heart pulls on me, trying to tug me back toward the fairy court. But I keep on.

I lost my mother. I was stolen from my father. I was taken from the land that grew my blood.

I will not lose the chance to know the first brown-skinned boy I have ever seen at the fairies' court.

＊

When I find Narciso, I watch him in his lonely vale. Only wild thyme and nodding violets attend him.

I hide, as I am well used to doing, appearing only when it will please.

Narciso flits through the steps of that same dance, the exact clicking of heels and turn of the calf. His lips move, as though he is counting out music that is not playing.

The silver boughs seem to acknowledge him. Even the hardwood of birches bends and sways, their rustling a kind of music for him. The eglantine and musk roses incline their blooms toward him. The land itself seems to breathe with him, as though he might turn the far-off mountains to clouds.

He finishes a step, swift as a shadow.

Then he looks at me.

Not *for* me.

At me.

With a small, exact glance, he places me precisely where I stand.

He smiles.

I withdraw into the dark. The satin bag I've brought with me swings against my legs. I stole a good portion of apricots and dewberries, purple grapes and green figs, and a heavy glass full of honey. It seemed only fitting considering our court's lack of hospitality.

Now the offering seems paltry, almost comical.

I turn, and Narciso appears before me.

He has moved through the bush and briar as quickly

as the piping of the wind. The shifting woods seem to produce him.

I draw back.

"Set your heart at rest," he says. "I will not hurt you."

This close, he smells of the cold brooks silvering the mountains.

"Not that you would take my oath, given what your mother and father say of me," he adds.

This boy's brown skin and soft smile loosen my tongue.

"They're not my mother and father," I say.

"They seem to have assumed otherwise," he says. "I know well how they love to declare reign over things they want."

"Did they want you, too?" I ask. "To keep you."

"Hardly." Narciso laughs. "I am the bastard son of a mortal father and a fairy from another wood. My mother feared the wrath of her own fairy king, little better than the one you know, and so I was raised by that mortal father and the mortal woman he later married. She loved me as her own when the mother who bore me could not."

What must that be like? my heart asks before my thoughts can quiet it. *For a woman to care for you as a child and not as an ornament?*

I remember the weight in my hands and give him the bag.

He seems neither suspicious nor delighted. "Well, you've taken the trouble to find me, and it seems not to have been on Oberon's word." Narciso sits on a fallen tree. "I suppose you deserve the story."

He offers me some of the fruit I've just given him. I demur. For as much as I usually enjoy eating, my stomach flutters too much for it now. And I fear if I move too much, he might reconsider. Not only telling me what happened between him and Oberon but also speaking to me at all, letting me near him.

He opens an apricot. "So you're the child they rowed over."

Now I wish I could vanish so I would not have to meet his gaze.

"I was a child that summer, too," Narciso says. "Older than you but by little. You were likely too young to remember Oberon's love potion."

"I have heard enough of it," I say. "I marvel that you remember. You were small yourself."

"So you know of the flower."

"The one he bade Puck fetch him," I say, pained to think of it. If Oberon wants something, Puck will put a girdle around the earth in forty minutes to see it done. "Yes. I've heard much of it."

"But do you know the tale?" Narciso asks. "The mermaids, and the arrow."

"The who and the what?" I ask.

"The story Oberon tells is of a mermaid on a dolphin's back, her song so dulcet and harmonious that the rude sea grew civil," Narciso says. "The sky loved her music so well that certain stars shot madly from their spheres. And among them, Cupid flew between the cold moon and earth, if you believe such things. And if you can hear Oberon speak of Cupid's 'love shaft' without laughing."

I cannot. Plainly. I laugh loud enough that the trees prick up their leaves, wondering at me.

Narciso smiles, seeming pleased, though he still has not eaten the apricot. I wonder if he is wary of its provenance or simply distracted. Its amber sugar mixes with the scent of wild thyme on his shoulders.

"According to Oberon and his fairies," he says, "the arrow's fire was quenched in the chaste beams of a watery moon. And so it missed its mark, and in doing so, struck a flower."

"Milk-white," I say, for I know this part of the story, the flower itself.

"And then purple with love's wound," Narciso and I say together.

"And maidens call it *love-in-idleness*," I say. I have heard this story a hundred times over, the bawdy tale of how Oberon made Titania fall in love with an ass. How Oberon set the juice of that flower on her eyelids, cursing her to lose her head and heart over the next being she saw.

"But what had that to do with you?" I ask.

"A few years from that summer, Oberon learned my family had a gift for finding certain plants," Narciso says. "And so he commanded me to find a thousand more flowers like it. He dreamed of what mischief he and Puck might undertake, what power he would command with a glade of love potions."

"But you were still a child," I say. "How could he expect you to find a thousand more?"

"Because I could," Narciso says. "There was a meadow of such turned flowers, and within my heart, I kept its secret. And Oberon knew it. So when I would not lead him there as he asked, when I would not give him and his sweet queen what they ever consider their due, there could be no concord. Titania and Puck would not let him harm a child, so all that was left to him, and for me, was banishment."

"He tried to make you lead him to it?" I ask, softly, not in surprise but in recognition.

Narciso gives a sad breath of a laugh. "As though I were a pig bred to find truffles."

I watch him turn the apricot in his hands.

"I am sorry," I say.

He shakes his head. "It's not your task to explain for the king."

It is not the first time I have wanted to apologize for the fairies who have claimed me. Oberon could ask Puck to sprout the wings of a griffin, and the poor man would give his life to trying.

I wince to think of Titania's words during the dance. The elm and the ivy.

"And I am sorry for what the queen said of you," I tell Narciso. "How she said it. And where."

"I say again, such things are not yours to excuse." Narciso bites into the apricot.

"May I ask you something?"

Narciso dips his head once, a slow nod.

"You were"—I begin the question without knowing how I will end it—"given the name of a girl at your birth?"

He laughs. "A fine and kind way of asking. I am well impressed."

I am learning his laugh, the low music of it.

"Yes," he says. "Given a girl's name, and it fit me no better than a wrongly cut blouse. But renamed by my good stepmother upon realizing the mistake. And since that day, I have been Narciso."

"Narciso," I say, letting my amusement show. "The name of the hunter who died for love of looking at himself in a pond?"

This boy holds little in common with that hunter. Yes, he is beautiful, and he seems to know it, but he also seems far too interested in everything around him to be caught by his own watery reflection. His eyes flit as easily as robins' wings, missing nothing. Not a cloud passing over the moon, nor the turning of leaves.

"A name," Narciso says. "And my stepmother's reminder to be neither too taken with myself, nor to leave myself unexamined." He hands me the second half of the apricot, the corner of an eyebrow quirked, as though daring me to try my own fruit.

I accept it. I bite into it, my eyes not leaving him, to show him both fruit and its bearer are safe to him.

I swallow the earth-laced sugar of the apricot. "Why did you return?"

Now he flushes, the brown of his cheeks warming to match the bloom on the apricots.

For the first time since we began talking, he will not meet my eyes and will not let me have his.

"I heard there was someone like me in Oberon's court," he says. "It seemed worth the peril."

The quiet of his voice does nothing to dampen the weight of his words. This, the twin lodestars of our loneliness, pulls on us as surely as a moon.

I thought I had come here looking for him.

But he came here first, looking for me.

"So now you have the story," he says. "Oberon wanted something, and I wouldn't give it to him. Not for his favor. Not to avert his wrath. Not for anything. I was an obstinate child, so he decided I would come to nothing but a defiant youth, dangerous when full grown."

"Was he wrong?" I ask.

The corner of Narciso's mouth matches the quirk of that eyebrow.

"In this instance," he says, "I think it falls to the questioner to decide."

I try to let sleep take me. I try to let my body sink into the green give of the bower. But I think only of the smell of wild thyme on the wind and a brown-skinned boy who would not do as these pale beings bid him.

All I have tried to shut away, he has brought back, quick as any dream.

When I was small, when Titania and Oberon argued over me as though I were some disputed necklace, they called me *Indian,* a word I have learned that pale men—fairy and mortal—use for anyone with a color near mine, no matter what blood made them. To them, we are enough alike that we should share one word. To them, the differences between us are mere trifling detail. They think nothing of the cost to those who should rightfully decide the word's meaning and those of us who would call ourselves by others.

That midsummer, the one in which Titania and Oberon declared me theirs, has become etched in court legend—a season in which the trees themselves breathed love. A season in which the love tangled between two men and two women became sorted in these woods, and in which the love of a changeling child, along with a few fairy spells, settled a dispute between fairy king and fairy queen.

Of course, none of that is exactly true. Simply ask Helena or Hermia.

Oberon credits himself with mending the unions of Hermia and Lysander, Helena and Demetrius, when the truth, says Puck, is that the four of them staged the entire affair. They played the parts of lovesickness for each other. They did not want their parents to suspect the truth—that two and two would wed but that man and man would share a bed as well as wife and wife.

That summer found a happy conclusion for the king and queen, but not for me. For ever since then, I have lived here, in this flowering court where pale fairies eat swans not for the taste but because they are beautiful, and because they want to remind themselves that beautiful things are theirs to consume.

This flowering court, where a fairy king and queen each wanted a brown-skinned child only because the other wanted her.

Even now, almost grown, I am more pet than child. And they remain, to me, more king and queen than the mother and father they proclaimed themselves when I was too small to realize I was not just being brought to see the fairy court.

I was being folded away into it.

The warning Narciso's stepmother gave him, the one laced into his name, finds me now. How much have I left unexamined? How many times have I heard Titania's wistful claim that my mother would have wanted her to have me? How often have I heard assurances that nothing good waits for me outside the fairy court, that I should want nothing to do with anyone beyond it, not even the fairies who live deeper in the woods? How long have I thought this place of fear and bitter loyalty is the only one that would have me?

I could carry on chanting hymns to the cold, fruitless moon.

Or I could follow the dream that burns in me, bright as Venus in her sky. I could pull against the draw of this court on my very being, heavy as a stone in my chest.

The trees part as though to show my way back to the vale. The bowing of their branches guides me through the dark-dyed night.

At first, I think Narciso is asleep, the night butterflies fanning the moonbeams from his eyes.

But at my approach, he sits up, unhurried, as though he were only watching the wandering moon.

As though he has been expecting me back.

For the moment it takes him to stand, the words are caught in my throat. It seems an easier task to move storms than to loosen my tongue.

But I do.

"I don't want to live unexamined either," I say.

Without letting a moment fall between us, he asks, "And what do you propose to do for it?"

In the little time I have spoken with Narciso, I have learned his voice and manner enough to know this:

These words he has spoken are not challenge.

They are not dismissal.

They are an invitation.

🌹

The moon is a horned lantern the night of the midsummer masque.

Half-covering masks painted as wings and fanned with feathers hide portions of their faces, a gesture of modesty to the sky and all her stars. I wear my own, autumn blue embroidered with gilt, the same as my dress.

Because Oberon and Titania think I will obey, because I have always obeyed, they do not notice me bringing a handsome stranger into their midst. A mask of gilt-edged autumn leaves covers half his face, obscuring him. They do not note the brown of his exposed jawline, or his dark hands against the evergreen cuffs of his shirt—a shirt I stole for him. Alongside the rich cloth, the brown of his wrists looks as a branch within leaves.

Oberon calls, as he always does, for the musicians to play "King of the Fairies." And when they do, I draw Narciso onto the grass, cool beneath our feet.

We dance, our hands drawing apart and then intertwining. Narciso's fingers are warm as sun-touched bark.

We dance, our brown arms grazing each other's waists and shoulders. We move so quickly that my fingers touch his neck. My lips brush his unmasked jaw, and he shudders in a way so slight, only I perceive it.

We dance, striking our heels with more certainty than the languorous fairies. We beat out each step of this dance, making it so hard and insistent, it is our own, instead of the flitting thing the court has made it.

We dance, with such force the ground conveys the rhythm, and the fairies draw back.

Oberon steps forward.

We dance, ready for his rage. We have expected it. And for our defiance, he may turn us into doe and stag, or wolf and wife.

But he will never tear away this sight we have put before him. It will be woven into his mind as a tapestry, stitched in dyed thread and bitter detail. The girl he decided was his daughter, in the arms of the boy who defied him.

We prepare for the king's wrath.

But the music plays still, and Oberon does not part his fabled lips to command or condemn us.

Neither do Titania or Puck, on either side of him.

They all gaze into the sky. The chin of each fairy lifts to mimic them, masks of petal and feather inclining toward the heavens.

The moonlight revel halts. The musicians cease their playing.

But silence does not come.

A new song becomes heir to the one before.

It sounds as I would imagine the call of mermaids, high and clear as the rarest bird.

The first glint in the sky seems a falling star. Then another, and another after.

Narciso and I are still, hands paused on each other's waists.

With their descent, each falling star comes closer, each a moonbeam forged into a rod of silver. The bright head of each grows glinting edges.

Not falling stars.

Arrows.

It is a rain of Cupid's arrows. We recognize them by their gleam, as much light as metal, and for this, I do not fear them. The most harm they will do is give my heart to this boy and his brown hands.

I find Narciso's eyes, set within the half mask of amber leaves.

He is steady as the glass of a pond. He gives only a slight nod of his head, as though a falling sky sows no fear in him.

And so we keep still, the fairies hushed in awe. Peaseblossom and Moth and Cobweb and Mustardseed. Even Puck. Even Titania. Even Oberon.

The arrows, streaming down, set a rushing noise beneath the mermaid's song.

That far song rises, heralding the touch of arrow to earth.

But they do not strike us. They do not sway the motions of our hearts.

Instead, with each finding its ground, comes a bloom of color.

I expect purple, as with the flower Puck fetched Oberon, turned white from Cupid's mark.

But the shade that opens before us is not purple or any of her sisters.

It is brown, the soft heat and beauty of brown.

Every pale flower touched with an arrow's gentle weight becomes a rich and perfect brown.

Every pitcher of milk and cream dons an amber glow.

Every white gown is dyed to match the acorns and hickory.

The fairies startle back. Even Oberon, his wide eyes green as leeks.

For a moment, my heart is a weight pinning me to this patch of grass. Then I feel it shifting inside me, and I understand that is not my heart keeping me in the fairy court. My own fear has been the shell of stone around it, and my heart will forever be sealed inside if I do not take the bright star of this night between my fingers.

"Show me," I tell Narciso, soft enough that it's a breath between us.

"Show you what?" he asks, not as though he's confused but as if I have only to tell him and he'll do it.

"That there is a world in which we belong to ourselves," I say.

He looks at me harder, the fall of the arrows lighting the edges of his hair. "Are you sure?" he asks, and I know he understands that I mean tonight to be the last Oberon and Titania ever see of me.

"Yes," I say. "The world I know has grown as small as this court, so much that I've nearly forgotten my own blood comes from outside it."

Narciso takes my hand.

He draws me away from the fairy court, and I run with him through the woods, beneath the rain of arrows.

Still, they fall. Still, the palest things grow a warm color.

The magnolias crowning the trees and the water lilies adorning the ponds are cast in copper.

White cats and rabbits turn to brown, bewildered but not displeased with their new coats.

Swans find their wings burnished in bronze. The moon-milk on the ponds turns to fireweed honey. Even the moon herself grows a copper sheen.

I run with him until the trees open into a vale I have never seen.

Narciso stops, I alongside him.

He draws a deep breath, nearly a sigh, as though we stand before something he thought we might miss.

A meadow, the ground gently waving as a sea, wears a coat of rippling grass. Trees with leaves as deep as Narciso's shirt define the edges, hiding it from view of the woods.

Even through the rain of silver arrows, I know the place for what it is. I know it by the scent. The lilting perfume eases my heart open, even as I catch my breath. It is the damp green and early blossom of that which Narciso would not give up.

A wide, glimmering meadow of love flowers.

"And what shall I call you?" Narciso asks, his voice still soft with getting his breath back.

I look to him. The wind lifts the edges of his hair as carefully as the leaves.

Not *What is your name?*

Not even *What should I call you?*

But *What shall I call you?*

It happens as a quick, bright thing, how I cast off the name

Titania and Oberon have given me. And in its place I take up the earth from which the queen of the fairies stole me. It is a world away, that earth, but it is still mine. It lives in my skin and my blood.

"Tierra," I say. "Call me Tierra."

Beneath the rain of arrows, the shy, white blooms put on their coats of violet and brown and turn to face the glinting night.

> *The king doth keep his revels here to-night:*
> *Take heed the queen come not within his sight;*
> *For Oberon is passing fell and wrath*
> *Because that she, as her attendant hath*
> *A lovely boy, stolen from an Indian king;*
> *She never had so sweet a changeling;*
> *And jealous Oberon would have the child*
> *Knight of his train, to trace the forests wild;*
> *But she perforce withholds the loved boy,*
> *Crowns him with flowers and makes him all her joy:*
> *And now they never meet in grove or green,*
> *By fountain clear, or spangled starlight sheen.*

—Puck, Act 2, scene 1

AUTHOR'S NOTE

As tends to be the case with stories I reimagine, I both love and hate *A Midsummer Night's Dream*.

Love, because how could I, with my queer, magic-laced heart, not adore a tale about both fairies and desires ruling a charmed forest?

Hate, because I rarely found anyone talking about the "changeling" Oberon and Titania quarrel over. Had anyone else, I wondered, heard what I just heard? That this child, coded as brown and now in the arms of white fairies, had been stolen from his father? What else do the king and queen of the fairies feel entitled to?

It unnerved me as a Latinx reader who secretly wanted to be a fairy but didn't want white hands deciding my fate.

It's in this spirit that I code my narrator as Latina, a kind of brown these fairies likely would have called the same word as the original child in *Midsummer*. In some contexts, it's still the default term used to describe part of my family and my community's racial identity. These fairies, much in the spirit of English colonialism carried across continents and oceans, likely would have thought of her as the same, a chilling reminder of how interchangeable brown bodies—and brown identities—are so often considered to be.

While I was in these woods, you didn't think a queer

nonbinary author would leave without casting rainbows everywhere, did you? Alongside trans fairy prince Narciso, a character of my own making, I wanted as many pairings from the original text as I could manage. What if Helena and Hermia wanted each other far more than they wanted Demetrius and Lysander and the whole pining affair was just for show? What if Bottom enjoyed Quince bossing him around? What if Puck's devotion stemmed more from being Oberon's lover than his subject? And what if Titania's and Oberon's marriage is far more political than personal?

A note on the figurative language: Much is my own. Much is adapted from the Bard. It's the least he can do considering how many nightmares he gave me about being stolen by gringo fairies.

If bringing colonialism into the discussion of one of Shakespeare's most whimsical plays disturbs you, I invite you to consider why. And in the meantime, I send you off with the slightly altered closing words of fairy Puck:

> *If these pages have offended,*
> *Think but this, and all is mended,*
> *That you have but slumbered here*
> *While this retelling did appear.*
> *And this brown and queerest theme,*
> *No more yielding but a dream.*

WE HAVE SEEN BETTER DAYS

Inspired by As You Like It

Lily Anderson

Oliver: Can you tell if Rosalind, the duke's daughter, be banished with her father?

Charles: O no; for the duke's daughter, her cousin, so loves her, being ever from their cradles bred together, that she would have followed her exile, or have died to stay behind her. She is at the court, and no less beloved of her uncle than his own daughter, and never two ladies loved as they do.

Oliver: Where will the old duke live?

Charles: They say he is already in the Forest of Arden, and a many merry men with him; and there they live like the old Robin Hood of England. They say many young gentlemen flock to him every day, and fleet the time carelessly, as they did in the golden world.

—ACT 1, SCENE 1

It's worse than I imagined," I spat.

"But in a good way," my cousin said.

At a safe distance, behind the redwoods and only halfway up the driveway, we could tell this wasn't the camp we remembered.

It was horribly, painfully beautiful.

Each of the main buildings had a mural wall painted to

reflect its purpose in an explosion of color and bubble letters. The front lawn had grown back—lush green. Along the perimeter, sunflowers stretched toward the sky. The whole place looked brand new.

The sight of it made my blood boil.

"Do you remember when I wanted to buy a plot in the community garden and my dad said it was too expensive?" I pointed beyond the hammocks and horseshoe pit. "That's an outdoor kitchen! There's no way I have a college fund left!"

"Stay positive," Celia chided, shaking my arm the way she did when we were little and she used to try to "wake up my sillies." "We're back at camp! We didn't think we would ever see this place again."

"I was sort of hoping we'd never have to." I looked up at the WELCOME TO CAMP ARDEN sign. Repainted and sealed at a sun-reflecting high gloss, it was hard to look at.

"Rosie," my cousin chided.

"Cece," I stressed back, crossing my eyes at her. We were at camp, so I was no longer Rosalinda and she was no longer Celia. Camp was for nicknames.

"We wouldn't be friends if we'd never come here!" she said. She opened her arms and spun in a circle, distance-hugging every tree. "We would be cousins, but we wouldn't be *sisters.*"

"And I'd never know how sharp your toenails are," I said, fake swooning back at her. "Sleeping bag serial killer."

"Two sleeping bags!" Cece protested as though that was a normal amount of sleeping bags to tear open with one's toes.

The sound of a car pulling up the gravel drive made both of us turn around.

A silver sedan with multiple ride-share stickers in the

window pulled to a stop. The back door opened and out leapt a tall light-skinned Black boy in owlish glasses.

"Thanks, man," he called back at the driver. "And remember, you swore you'd give *Solo* another shot. Don't do it for me. Do it for Bradford Young!"

As the door closed behind him, he swung a backpack on and turned to see us. His face broke into a dimpled smile. "Sorry, I'm late. There's no clock in the forest."

The name on his luggage tags was Orlando Cohen-Kersey, but for the first few years we knew him, he'd been the smaller half of Ollie-and-Orly, the bickering brothers whose inane arguments kept their cabin up all night. When Ollie got promoted out of the communal bunks and into a counselor's twin bed, Orly had emerged as:

"Lando," I said, too quiet to be heard beneath the sound of the Uber-Lyft crunching its way back toward civilization.

Space buns bobbing, Cece ran to hug our old friend. "Look at you! You got taller again! I told you that you had to warn us when you did that!"

Lando laughed, and it was a rumble, not a wheeze. "You're just remembering me shorter because we missed a summer."

I gripped the straps of my overalls. "Aren't we lucky that summer is extra-long this year?"

Lots of people attempt the camp upgrade. Away from everyone who defines you, it's easy to show up in the woods with a new name and a statement wardrobe. Camp was the only place where Cece wasn't under constant parental surveillance and I tried to be a person who wore hats. But Lando had not only upgraded but stayed plused up.

Getting taller had a lot to do with it. Now, there was no mistaking him for a little kid. Instead of curls weighed down with grease, his hair was picked out. It stood up in a halo around his head as round as his tortoiseshell frames. His jeans were tight, and his socks were loud.

After camp ended, Lando had become decisively himself. It was such an unforgivably hot thing to do, I could barely stand it.

Cece beckoned him down to her level. "Come down here and let me admire your mane. I'm obsessed with the volume you're getting."

"I just do what you told me," he said, but he generously bent in half anyway so she could see every angle of his 'fro. Before she was the queen of the quickie hair tutorial, @CeliaCurlz, Cece had been known as the girl at camp with the hair product suitcase. A godsend to the other natural hair campers. Whether you needed shea butter, silicone-free conditioner, or someone with quick hands for a braid down, Cece was the person to know. Following that reputation had brought Lando to the door of Cabin 12, hoping to exchange cookies for cornrows.

We were camp besties ever since.

"Thanks for coming," I said. To save myself the awkwardness of trying to initiate a hello hug, I patted him on the shoulder. "I didn't know if you would."

Before this week, I'd never had to ask him for anything more than a movie recommendation or the finishing knot on a friendship bracelet. We were camp friends. Inseparable in summer, social media mutuals during the school year. We were untested in the off-season.

"My friends needed help," Lando said. "So I'm here to help."

"Right," I said. "Let's go find my dad."

I led the way, taking the first step into the wild, drunk yonder.

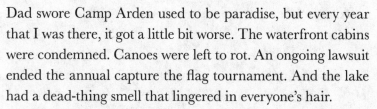

Dad swore Camp Arden used to be paradise, but every year that I was there, it got a little bit worse. The waterfront cabins were condemned. Canoes were left to rot. An ongoing lawsuit ended the annual capture the flag tournament. And the lake had a dead-thing smell that lingered in everyone's hair.

"Percy Jackson lied to us," I told Cece the year the ceramics hut burned down.

"Maybe camp is only good if your parents are gods," she said.

By our last summer there, camp was barely two weekends. Cece spilled an entire container of homemade flaxseed gel in the woods and cried for three days. Lando recapped the plots of Jordan Peele movies. I never even unpacked my swimsuit.

Not long after that, Dad sat me down, solemn-faced, to tell me that Camp Arden had officially closed. His autopayment bounced back to him. I was sad to know that I might never see Lando in person again. But we started a text thread and promised to keep in touch.

Dad, on the other hand . . . Dad rallied. He called other Arden alums, tracked down old camp directors, hired aquatic ecology experts and arborists, emptied his savings, cracked into his retirement twenty years early.

Because, to my dad, camp wasn't some old slice of the woods on the other side of a stomach-churning, two-hour bus ride. Camp wasn't its stinky mess hall or empty owl sanctuary or weird frozen food concoctions. To him, camp was home. Being a counselor was the first job he ever had, and he came back every summer, even through college. Until he and my mom had me and needed to move closer to family.

Camp Arden reopened, a little over a year after it closed. Except now it was a summer camp for adults.

And summer had been extended indefinitely.

※

The main office was the only building close to the parking lot. In the nearest space was the junky, old truck my dad had downgraded to when he had been raising the money for the camp renovation. I couldn't believe he'd traded in our Prius for something with no GPS, no Bluetooth for the stereo, and no backup camera. I was never going to be able to parallel park that behemoth.

Seeing the weeks of dirt accumulated on the windshield only fueled me forward, ready to pound my fist on whatever desk or door got between me and Dad.

But no one was in the office.

"At least they left the air conditioner on," Lando said, his eyes closed against the cold breeze coming out of the wall.

According to the dry-erase calendar on the wall, the bus had dropped us off in the free hour between lunch and afternoon activities.

I couldn't resist testing the handle of the camp director's office. Locked, of course. Through the smoked glass, I could only see the vague outline of a messy desk. I wanted to know what my dad looked like sitting behind it, what photos he kept in the frames on the wall. Had he changed the furniture in there? Everything on this side of the door was so eerily the same. The operations desk even had a bulky, old desktop computer that was way too clean to be disused.

Cece pulled down a printed map from a wall display of brochures and legal release forms. Tracing her index finger in a serpentine trail away from the camp entrance, she said, "If we walk fast, we should be able to do the whole walking trail in less than an hour. I want to run the wishing steps and ride the tree swings . . ." She gave me a weak smile. "And find Uncle Duke, of course."

"We're on a recovery mission, not a walk down memory lane," I said.

"I know," Cece said. "I can't help that I'm also just a tiny bit excited to be back at camp. With my camp friends. And I don't even have to spend the night! It's what I always wanted camp to be."

"I'm so glad that my parental abandonment is working out for you," I said coolly.

"What if your dad doesn't want to be found?" Lando asked me. "Didn't you say he turned off his phone?"

I extended summer by a week or so, Dad's last message had said. Like he had the power to control the seasons, to stretch weeks into an indefinite *or so.* Like it was an option to mistake one week for three.

"You know reception is spotty here," I said, chewing on the inside of my cheek. Spotty reception wouldn't account for him ignoring my messages. Or the lack of Wi-Fi signal in the office.

"Oh, we are going to find him," Cece said emphatically. "I did not spend eight summers here for no reason!"

"In a literal sense, you did," I said. "We didn't get college credit or learn a skill or anything."

"But in a figurative sense," Cece said, stabbing a finger victoriously into the sky, "I could find my way around here blindfolded. All of us could."

"You're just describing blackout tag," I said.

"Blackout tag," Lando repeated, with all the rough angst and gravitas of a brooding superhero. "That game is way too dangerous for kids! I almost cracked my head open on a tree branch."

"Must have been a low one," I teased.

"How are you gonna make short jokes when I'm taller than you now?" he asked, gazing down at me with an intensity that made my hairline sweat. I wanted to tear out my braided pigtails. They had seemed like a good idea when Cece suggested them but now made me feel like a giant toddler in overall shorts and too much lipstick.

"You can be taller than me all you want," I said, scrunching my nose at my reflection in his glasses. "But I'm here to keep you height humble. I won't let you forget where you came from. The top of your head used to be my armrest. You started at the bottom. Of my elbow."

He rolled his eyes. "You're ridiculous."

I smiled at him. "Yeah, but you must have missed me a little."

He smiled back. "A little."

Finding my dad on the first try had been a long shot, and yet we left the office without the gusto we'd entered with.

Outside seemed hotter, the buzzing bugs louder.

Following the signs for the lake, we passed the rebuilt ceramics hut and the health center.

"So, Lando," I said. "Are you totally loving being an only child?"

Cece sucked in an appalled breath, just like I knew she would. "God, Rosie! It's not like Oliver died. He went to college."

"Tomato, potato," I said, catching Lando's eye and sharing a private, silent joke through telepathy. Pretending not to know about Cece's endless crush on Ollie Cohen-Kersey was one of life's great joys. It was hilarious that she thought people didn't know when she was physically incapable of not calling him Oliver rather than Ollie.

"Fill us in on real life, Lando," I prompted.

"As opposed to fake life?" He chuckled.

"Exactly," I said. "I only know what you put online."

"Which means we have already heard your favorite movies of the year," Cece reminded him. "We want to know the fun stuff. Secret stuff. Did you get a girlfriend yet?"

"Your priorities are so specific," I told her. My cheeks prickled with secondhand embarrassment like she'd blurted out something rude, even though she hadn't. I tugged on the ends of my pigtails and tried to make my face stay still.

She stuck her tongue out at me. "Let me be nosy!"

Shoulders raised to his ears, Lando grumbled, "No, I did not get a girlfriend."

"Because you're too busy still pining over the embodiment of feminine perfection?" I asked him.

"Who?" Lando asked, taking this moment to clean his glasses.

"You know who," I said. "The Secret Camp Crush."

I drew out the last syllable so it whispered down the path ahead of us.

"It's Madison Poffenberger," Cece guessed. "Wait, no, *Tinsley* Poffenberger."

"No way," Lando scoffed. "Cabin Tenners? Please. The Poffenbergers don't care about art. I'd prefer someone who didn't think reality TV counts as cinema verité. Besides, I can neither confirm nor deny the existence of a secret crush."

"Two years ago, you said, and I quote!" I said, striking the end of each word like the hammer in a bell. "'I have always had the same camp crush.'"

Cece wriggled a finger at him, the tips of her fingers still dyed chocolate-cherry red from helping me with my roots last night. "It's the *always* that gave you away."

"You had a crush on one of the twenty-five girls who was here every summer, and you never told us who it was," I said to Lando.

"I bet it was Rachel," Cece said. "She was the only person short enough to three-legged race with you for a couple years."

"And she bullied me for not being fast enough the whole time!" Lando said. "Taking three-legged races too seriously is immediate crush disqualification."

"We're at camp for the last time," I reminded him. "I'm pretty sure that means you *have* to confess who Camp Crush is."

He snorted, looking at the trees that were starting to block out the sky. "First of all, she's *Secret* Camp Crush. And secondly, I would rather chug lake water than talk about who likes whom." He whipped his backpack around to the front and unzipped it in one motion. "Let's stop fishing for secrets. Have some contraband breakfast."

From within the well-stocked depths of his backpack, the three of us split a meal of 7-11 donuts and Takis. In the shade of the tree canopy, eating convenience store food on the walk from the cabins toward the lake, it was almost like the old days.

"Was junior year everything you wanted it to be, Rosie?" Lando asked.

"Pretty uneventful. Except, you know, my dad bought a summer camp." I kicked a pinecone off the path. "So far? Less fun than a zoo."

Lando scoffed. "Uneventful? You skipped another grade!"

"Sort of." I sucked spicy dust from my fingertips. "I was a sophomore with junior standing."

"What's the difference?" he asked.

"I actually did more work than I needed to, so I'm technically still a sophomore—they just ran out of classes for me to take. When I skipped second grade, I didn't have to do the work."

It was odd to talk about school here. The sharp, evergreen smell of the forest was the total opposite of the glass-and-cement high school I attended.

Camp used to be the one place I wasn't constantly reminded that I was younger than everyone else. People asked, shrugged their interest, eventually forgot. It didn't matter that you skipped a grade when there were no grades. There were only campers and counselors, opposite ends of a spectrum. And I had always clung to Cece, hoping people would assume we were the same age, instead of two years apart, an advantage that I definitely did *not* have in my regularly scheduled life.

"Who skips two grades?" Lando asked. He patted donut sugar from the front of his shirt. "You're a year younger than me, but you get to graduate the year before! That's wild, Rosie. You aren't even a little bit excited?"

"Sometimes we get to have the same homework now. That's exciting," Cece answered for me.

"That's true," I said. I fished out my water bottle and took a long drink. "But I'm mostly excited to be done next year. I can't wait to just work on classes that actually matter."

"It's not like it's all cinchy," Cece said, frowning at me with a sudden strange seriousness. She snagged the water bottle out of my hands. "You skipped to a grade so that it'd be a challenge. Now you have to study like the rest of us."

"I never said I didn't," I said. "But I'd rather be in college than in high school."

She thrust the water bottle back into my hands. "Stop wishing your whole life away. You'll get older just like every-body. You're rushing."

"I wonder why," I snapped back at her. "I don't see anyone else having to beg their parents to be parents."

The door to the nearest bath cabin burst open. A middle-aged guy holding a beer can came staggering out. Whether the beer had originated inside the bathroom was worryingly unclear.

"Lookit, some newbies!" shouted the drunk man to no one in particular. "You guys are just in time! They're tapping the kegs!"

Lando looked affronted. "Dude. We're underage."

Surrendering as best as he could without dropping his can, the guy held up his hands and started backing toward the ceramics hut. "Be cool, man, you're the one trespassing."

Lando started to speak but couldn't quite orient his mouth around an entire phrase, so I leapt in front of him, catching the drunk man's attention.

"We're looking for Duke," I said.

"Duke?" the man echoed. He was wearing a Camp Arden T-shirt. Dad hadn't changed the design, but he had printed them on better-quality shirts than the scratchy, straight-out-of-the-bulk-bag kind we used to get. These were prefaded olive green.

"Duke Castillo," I said. "The camp director? He's my—"

"Duke!" the man howled at the sky. It echoed through the pine trees and ricocheted back to us. When no one appeared, he said, "Guess he's not over here."

"I guess not," I said.

Cece and Lando both took a step back. Their eyes screamed at me to do the same. I didn't.

"The thing is," I said. "Duke also wasn't in his office, so—"

"Duke has no office!" the man said, throwing his arms out wide so all of his scraggly pit hair sneaked out of his sleeves. "The world is his office! And the woods are his world!"

"Okay," Cece said, smiling beatifically. "Thank you so much for all your help. Bye-ee!"

She turned and steered us away, muttering, "Go, go, go."

Once we were down the first small hill and out of sight, Lando asked, "Have we ruled out the possibility that it's a cult?"

"Everyone we've passed so far is wearing the same shirt," Cece said. "That's definitely cultish."

It seemed like a thousand years ago that I'd texted our group thread asking whether or not they thought my dad could be brainwashing people into paying hundreds of dollars to sleep in communal cabins. At the beginning of summer, it had been funny that Dad was going to camp and we weren't. When there had still been clothes in his closet. When he answered his phone.

I didn't find it funny anymore.

"We wore matching shirts when we were campers," I said. Our matching shirts had been an eye-watering shade of lime green that made us easy for counselors to spot. Half a dozen of them in different sizes lived in a box under my bed. Cece still slept in hers.

"We were children," Lando said. "We had no choice but to match."

He had a point.

We were coming up on residence row, where all of the

cabins had been upgraded. None of them had tarps covering holey roofs or boards eaten to dust by termites. Even with the cosmetic upgrades, I couldn't imagine my dad agreeing to sleep in a bunk bed in a room with strangers.

"Let's go check Cabin Twelve for our initials!" Cece said.

"Okay, but just for a second," I said.

She was already running off the path, toward the big-kid cabins. They were in the same order. The numbers still skipped unlucky thirteen out of tradition. The cabins themselves had been upgraded, painted barn-door red, and given new wooden railings.

The summer after I turned thirteen, I had done the honors of carving our names on the back of Cabin 12 with the pocketknife Dad thought I wanted for my birthday that year. I'd added Lando's name as an honorary member of the cabin after first pretending that I hated the idea when Cece presented it because it had seemed very important that no one think *I* wanted his name there.

And now, all of the boards were repainted or replaced, leaving no hint as to where we had started.

🌹

The deeper into the trail we got, the more attention we drew. We passed a group of campers lawn bowling beside a silver keg of beer and another group with a keg and no visible activity.

Like zombies scenting brains on the wind, the campers would stop talking and watch us pass. Near the archery field, a sunburned couple stopped making out long enough for one of them to ask, "Are those kids?"

I would have taken offense at that, but both of them looked to be older than my parents. Or at least more wrinkled.

As we crested the hill behind the archery field, we could see a large group of campers laughing and chasing each other.

Cece squealed and spun away, pushing us back down the hill. "Someone please warn me if I am about to see an orgy because my virgin eyes can't handle it! My mother said that there was a chance that this place was some kind of sex thing, and I never should have doubted her—"

"What are you talking about?" I interrupted her. "I didn't see any naked people!"

I started to go back over the hill to get another look, but my cousin stopped me, pulling me out of sight of the people below.

"I saw blindfolds," Cece whispered loudly. "Haven't you seen *Fifty Shades*?"

"No!" I said at the same time Lando said, "Yes!" Then he added, defensively, "It was shot by the same cinematographer as *Jurassic World*."

I goggled at him. "And that's a positive?"

Cece side-eyed us both and sniffed. "I saw a redband trailer. Blindfolds were part of it!"

Sometimes it was hard to believe that *I* was the baby cousin.

I marched back up the hill, braced to see something life-ruining. Instead, I saw campers, fully clothed in their matching olive-green shirts and bandana blindfolds.

"You guys," I said to Cece and Lando. "It's blackout tag."

Once we got closer, it was easier to tell that there were multiple teams of people playing. The blindfolded people who were "it" were chugging beers before each turn, making their tags lurching swipes that everyone else laughed at, easily dodging out of the way.

It didn't look fun. It looked mean.

"Do you see your dad?" Lando asked me.

My stomach churned at the idea of my dad being part of the mocking crowd, but I looked carefully as we walked by them. It was almost a relief that he wasn't there.

"Hey, kids, you're at the wrong camp!" someone called from the keg.

The product of strict and attentive parents, Cece was momentarily frozen in place by the sound of adult disapproval. To her, rules were rules, even when set in place by strangers at an adult summer camp. But we had practiced for this.

"Go home to your jobs!" I shouted back at them.

It broke the spell. While the campers jeered back at me, Cece burst into motion, running at full speed away from the adults. Lando and I followed, laughing too hard to catch up until we were around the corner and nearly to the arts and crafts pavilion.

"The wishing steps!" Cece said.

"Think of a good one," I said. "It's the last wish you'll get here."

The path was partially blocked by a huge fallen tree the camp had never paid to have moved. Instead, stairs had been nailed to the trunk so you could climb over it. When we were kids, the stairs were split boards so rickety that the only logical wish was "I hope the stairs don't break."

Now, it looked like part of an Aztec pyramid built over the fallen tree. Not only was there a railing and a platform at the top, but the new steps were painted to say, *Tell the tree your wish.* Running up the sturdy stairs didn't make you feel like you'd earned a wish. It felt like construction scaffolding redirecting traffic. But we wished anyway.

"I wish to find Uncle Duke," Cece said dutifully.

"Oh, good," I said, running up the steps behind her. "Then I can wish to find out who Lando's Secret Camp Crush is."

"Secret!" Lando repeated, chasing me down the stairs. "Wait, I missed my wish!"

"Too bad, so sad!" Cece and I giggled.

Lando paused on the bottom step, teetered on the tips of his toes, and swung back around. "Hold on! I'm going back over!"

His long legs took him up two stairs at a time.

"If your wish is to undo my wish, then I'm gonna double-wish it!" I shouted after him.

I followed him, trotting up the stairs and then leaping off the platform.

"You can't cross back over the wishing tree! It's a one-way wish!" Cece protested from the other side. And then she gasped. "Oh no."

"Oh no?" I asked, pushing Lando back up to the top of the platform so I could see the path again.

Lando froze at the top of the platform. "Oh no."

On the other side of the tree, a deep voice said, "Orlando? Celia?"

Lando's older brother was standing on the trail. The olive-green camper shirt matched Ollie Cohen-Kersey's eyes almost as well as it mirrored his little brother's queasy complexion.

Trotting down the stairs, I waved. "Hi, Ollie. I wonder who wished for you."

Cece flashed her eyes at me like warning lights.

Ollie didn't notice. He was pinching the bridge of his nose and shaking his head. "Of course. You're all together. None of you can be here!"

"Well, my dad owns the place," I said. "So, if he wants to throw me out, he can do it himself."

"Shouldn't you be at college?" Lando asked his brother.

"Shouldn't you be at home?" Ollie shot back.

"I'm here to find my dad," I said. "Camp was supposed to end weeks ago. What the fuck happened here?"

Ollie frowned at me like he was considering giving me a demerit for cursing. Remembering that he no longer had that power, he opened his hands and said, "Your dad gave us a do-over."

"Like when the whole class fails a quiz?" Cece asked.

"Something like that," Ollie said. Brushing past the three of us, he moved to sit on one of the new wishing stairs, the king of his little stage. It was the same pose he used to adopt when narrating ghost stories around the fire. "The first week of camp didn't work. Some people were here to party, some wanted to hike. And to save money, Duke didn't hire any counselors."

"Adults are supposed to be in charge of themselves," Lando said.

"True," said Ollie. "That means being in charge of hyping themselves up. Getting excited to do the camp stuff. Making bird feeders. Talent night. Playing guitar around the camp-fire. Capture the flag." He counted activities on his long fingers. "No one wanted to do everything, so lots of people did nothing."

"I do not blame them," I said. "That shit all sucks."

Cece cocked a hip and crossed her arms. "Rosie. You loved talent night. Remember your one-woman Peter Pan?"

I had been pretty proud of my hand puppets that particular summer. I pretended not to remember them.

"I wouldn't come back from college in the real world to do it all over again," I said pointedly.

Oliver's brow furrowed in offense. "Well, it was your dad who had the great idea to unplug. He bought those phone locks they use so people won't film concerts anymore. Duke said that anyone who put their phone in a lock sleeve could stay an extra week for free. To soak up the last bit of summer."

"To avoid going home," I said. My stomach ached as I imagined my dad feverishly looking for a way to push autumn away. The year of camp restoration had turned him into a shadow person, a ghost whose true self lived in the woods. I sucked my teeth. "So, what? Without your phones you forgot what day it was?"

"I guess they don't teach you to read the sun anymore," Lando added, arms folded in judgment. I knew he had a policy of being anti-Ollie, but it still felt nice to have someone on my team.

"No," Ollie said. "We didn't forget. It's just not important. Duke owns the land. There are built-in activities everywhere. We're hanging out and eating through the freezer. It's chill."

"Chill for you," I spat. "Not for the people you left in the real world. Just because you don't check doesn't mean there isn't news or that people don't need you!"

My voice broke, and I stared down at the scuffed toes of my hiking boots. Another pair of shoes appeared next to mine. Shoes with loud socks. Lando's arm wrapped around my shoulder. Hugged to his side, I tilted my face to look up at him.

He ducked his head down so that for one moment, we were temple to temple, his voice a hot hum against my ear.

"Secret crush," he said simply.

My heart lit up like a lantern.

"Where is Rosie's dad?" Cece asked.

Ollie stood up and dusted himself off, his ears momentarily blocking the sun. "At the lake. He's always at the lake."

❦

I had expected a small water park. Maybe an inflatable slide or tandem Jet Skis. But instead it was just a lake. Albeit no longer a lake that was also an EPA emergency.

Ollie followed us down the waterfront trail.

"You can't go to the lake without being properly buddied up," he said. "It's not safe."

"Aren't there people here your age?" Lando asked him.

His lack of an answer was answer enough.

The lake was greenish and still. Some campers splashed on the far shore, but near us, it was empty. There were canoes, but no one was in one. At the end of the dock, I could see my dad fishing. Alone.

Cece skidded to a stop in the middle of the trail. "Are you sure you don't want to go see the tree swings first? I bet your dad turned them into hammocks or a carousel or something."

"No, they're still tires," Ollie said. "But there are giant hammocks on the other side of the lake."

"We could do one more fun thing," Cece said, clutching my arm. She lowered her voice to a sleepover whisper. "Talking to your dad is going to make you sad. Why not do one more happy thing first?"

"Because I can't put off being sad," I whispered back. "I'd rather face it."

I took one more look at Lando and tried to imagine being the object of his constant crush. It filled me with an uncertain glow that brightened the more I believed in it. I tried to hold that feeling of being so impossibly *liked* as I walked away.

The dock was an untouched slice of camp, the round logs underfoot familiar.

Dad sat back in his chair. The sleeves of his green shirt were rolled up, exposing the pale hills of his shoulders to the sun.

"Evening out your farmer's tan?" I asked him.

He squinted up at me. "I thought you said you never wanted to come back here."

"I thought I'd have more of a choice."

There was an empty chair next to his. A matching Adirondack with a sharply slanted back and a cup holder built into the armrest. I took it without invitation.

A single yellow leaf spun on the green, glass surface of the lake, rippled along by a soft breeze. The horizon was misty white. Silence stretched between us, hammered thin with unsaid apologies and explanations.

"Last day of summer," I told him.

"Last day of summer," he agreed. He looked over at me with liquid eyes so like my own. "I'm glad you're here to see it, Rosalinda."

"Rosie," I said, stealing a glance at my camp friends over my shoulder. "At camp, my name is Rosie."

SOME OTHER METAL

Inspired by Much Ado About Nothing

A. R. Capetta and Cory McCarthy

Leonato: Well, niece, I hope to see you one day fitted with a husband.

Beatrice: Not till God make men of some other metal than earth.

—ACT 2, SCENE 1

strike up, pipers!" Benedick bellowed, taking Beatrice's hand and starting a riotous, streaming dance across the stage and down into the pit of delighted, drunken groundlings.

The performance was a success for certain, *The Globe* on fire this night, and even though both leads of this particular play had railed against the typecasting, the Ods Bodkins were on their way to becoming the best Shakespearean troupe in the damn galaxy.

Beatrice made her infamous move of twirling Benedick out of the dance and into an embrace that landed his face in her glorious cleavage. There he placed as many kisses as the cheers demanded before spinning them both back onto the stage and behind it, where the crowd's enthusiasm blurred to raucous white noise. The actors snapped out of their roles: no longer Beatrice and Benedick but Tegan and Taron.

Tegan let go of Taron's hand with a vengeance. "Why are your palms always so sweaty?"

"Stage lights and leather pants," Taron returned. "What's your excuse? My lips are all salty from your . . ." He motioned to their healthily exposed bosom, thoughts steaming. "You're hardly wearing clothes."

"Come to think of it, I am warm." Tegan hauled their muslin dress off the shoulder it still clung to, revealing at least 60 percent more breasts. "There. That's better."

"I' God's name; I have done!" Taron hollered, shielding his eyes with one hand and turning to his side backstage, where he wouldn't be bothered by the most unfortunate co-star of his promising young career.

Taron whipped open the reclaimed, old oak door to his dressing room, stepping into a small box of pristine stainless steel, which he'd buffed and polished to act as mirrors from every angle. Out the small porthole, the gigantic gas planet of New Vegas—famous for a highly debauched colony and the occasional diamond rain—filled the view with orange and teal stripes. Taron preferred a view of the stars, but then, this had not been a season of Taron getting what he wanted.

He stripped away his costume down to his sweaty boxers, filled the small sink, and stuck his head all the way into the icy water, banishing thoughts, washing away Tegan's soft touches and hard kisses and lines delivered so close to his lips. And not just from this night but the long and many months of this play's season.

When someone pulled him up by one shoulder, he didn't need to peel his eyes to know Hazem's hand. "I come to launch the merriment of our wrapped show and find you drowning your sorrows. You do know that's meant to be done with alcohol."

"As I don't drink, I must do it the old-fashioned way."

"I believe alcohol *is* the old-fashioned way," Hazem countered.

"Call me new-fashioned, then."

"Never." Hazem grinned and tossed a hand towel at Taron's dripping face. His good friend used the polished steel to examine his going-out look. Shirtless with gold suspenders, Hazem was advertising his lean, brown body this evening, still wearing his Don John eyeliner and knee-high boots. "You know I play each villain with glee, but the 'bastard brother' with a bizarrely anglicized name might be the lowest of the Bard's baddies. I spent nearly six months stomping the stage, indicating evilness until my eyebrows hurt. Evil eyebrows are a thing, did you know?"

"Do you honestly want to compare short straws?" Taron asked. "I had my literal breath cut off by Tegan's . . ."

"Glorious bosom?"

Taron flipped twin middle fingers. "Yes, do torture the demisexual mouse with your sex kitten persona. This game never gets old."

Hazem lifted Taron to his feet by both shoulders and kissed him on the cheek. "You know I jest from a place of deep love and a complete lack of understanding." His comfort turned wicked. "Plus, I, too, have lost my breath in Tegan's great asset. I wouldn't dare complain about it, though."

They struck up a mutual slapping spree that ended with Taron in a headlock beneath Hazem's muscular, bare arm.

"I yield!" Taron yelled, and Hazem released him.

"Come, get dressed. Let us move from pity party to cast party."

"What do you think I'm trying to do?" Taron pulled on a baggy sweater and the pants with the stylish rips up the leg.

Hazem frowned at the aesthetic. "After having spent so much time and energy on your chest, I'd think you'd show it off a little. You're healed now?"

Taron lifted the neck of his sweater and looked down. "It is a lovely chest. Next time, maybe. I'm always a mess of nerves after this damned play."

Hazem shook his head in disappointment. "We sold out the house, brother. As in, we're all getting paid this week, *and* you'll never have to play Benedick to their Beatrice again. Let us have an end to the punishment we all deserved from the moment we first conceived of slamming you two together."

"Don't fool yourself, Haz. We knew all along what mischief the company was doing, setting us up like that."

Hazem stopped perfecting the coif of his dark, curly hair, staring instead at Taron's reflection in the riveted steel wall. "You knew?"

"Of course we did! You used our—let's just say 'merry war'—for the profit of this troupe. You and Icon and the rest knew you'd get nothing short of our rich disdain, and *that* is the check we will be cashing tonight." Hazem gusted a sigh of relief, and Taron washed with suspicion. "That's not what you thought I'd say."

Hazem held up his palms, eyes closed. "We also thought that . . . mayhaps . . . you two might spark, like your roles." Taron's mouth fell open, and his friend pushed on, seemingly unaware that something fiery—and pissed—had indeed sparked in Taron. "We've learned our lesson. You two are as incompatible as oil and, well, a different type of oil."

Taron had lost all words, which was rare indeed. His brain was stuck on two separate hooks. The first was his friend's and their company's most sincere betrayal. The second was much more Tegan-based, which always sharpened his thoughts to the point of puncture.

"You're not mad," Hazem tried. "Say you're not."

"*Mad* is too few letters for my current feeling. Get out."

"Taron, curb your dramatic instincts for a moment. Nothing is damaged! You were an incandescent star these last months, and Tegan got to shout endlessly onstage, eyes fixed upon you, which we all appreciated. Their attentiveness can zap a person straight through and has done to so many of us, if you know what I mean."

Taron did. That was at least part of the problem.

And now if Hazem wouldn't leave, Taron would have to. He stormed out of his own dressing room, right into the rest of the company who'd merged the better elements of their costumes with clubbing clothes to take the shuttle down to New Vegas.

Iconoclast hooked Taron's elbow with hers, preventing him from going farther. "It's time to get our revelry on at your daddy's grand estate! Where are you huffing off to?"

"To spread news of your endless injustice," Taron hissed, flinging her off his arm.

The rest of the company quieted, laughter barely held in check by a series of quirked mouths. Icon turned on Hazem. "Oh, lords, did you tell him?"

"He guessed! Or maybe I cracked."

"Where is Tegan?" Taron snapped, avoiding the multitude of dubious faces. The Ods Bodkins were a motley and many-talented family, all part-owners of *The Globe,* the mighty ship they'd outfitted with a replica of Shakespeare's long-lost theatre, and like true family, he suddenly couldn't stand a single one of them.

Icon pointed to Tegan's dressing room, and Taron stomped onward, avoiding Hazem undoubtedly recapping this particular cat's escape from the bag.

Taron banged a fist on Tegan's door. "Open up, harlot!"

Tegan flung the door ajar, blocking the entrance. "Call me one more womanly slur, even one Uncle Will penned himself, and I will destroy you and the antiquated gender binary you rode in on."

"Harlots can be any and all genders. Now, we need to talk." Taron slipped inside their dressing room and shut the door, glancing at the familiar space that had been set up so differently from his own. The stainless-steel walls and floor were hidden beneath velvety curtains, tapestries, and small, brightly patched rugs. The long, soft curls of the Beatrice wig had been flung onto a rack, making Tegan's shaved head stand out. Gorgeously round and impossibly hard.

"I've discovered they set us up to be Benedick and Beatrice. We've been their toys."

"Of course," Tegan said, popping in the sparkly nose piercing stud that they wore whenever they weren't acting. Next they sat down to lace up the massive boots that had stamped a few overly aggressive suitors into fine powder. "The best actors in the galaxy couldn't conjure this amount of vivid tension. We're natural enemies."

"You misunderstand me. They set us up . . . to *live out* the story of Benedick and Beatrice. To fall for one another or some such nonsense. Hazem admitted it moments ago."

Tegan stood, now as tall as Taron, and got very close to his nose. "They were playing matchmaker with our roles? That's too meta, even for them. Besides, they failed spectacularly. I loathe you more now than when I played Horatio to your whiny-ass Hamlet."

"I was not whiny!"

"Thou doth protest *so* much," they said with a haughty laugh that cut off abruptly. "Plus, it's a direct quote from one of our reviews."

"I'll have you know—"

Tegan slapped a hand over Taron's mouth. "Before we banter into oblivion, if what you say is true, we need a revenge plan. Our so-called friends must be punished." They lowered their hand.

"Agreed," Taron said. "Which must be a first."

Tegan nodded once and began to scheme. Truly, scheming should have been in the Special Skills section of their acting resume, along with scansion, fight training, and speaking four interplanetary languages. "Now, what is the best rebuke for this foul act?" they asked.

Taron looked around the little room with skittish eyes as if the worst punishment imaginable might be hiding under one of Tegan's wildly flung dressing robes.

"Isn't the answer obvious?" they asked with a put-upon sigh. "We let them believe we *are* in a mountain of affection. Let their special hell be the one where they get exactly what they asked for. A couple." They *boop*ed Taron's nose with their finger. "The worst, most obnoxiously in love couple *The Globe* has ever seen."

"Why couldn't you just ask me to kill Claudio?" he muttered. "That would be easier."

"It would be easier to run Marius through with a rapier than pretend to be my boyfriend for a single night?"

"I should think you'd thank me," he said. "Marius is a jerk of the highest order."

"Oh, look, we agree on two whole things. Don't get cocky and try for a third." Of course, Tegan hadn't *always* disliked the company member who'd nightly overacted the role of Claudio. Post-breakup, it did help that Tegan's character hated Marius's so much in *Much Ado*. It gave Tegan an excuse for all of the eye-daggers they needed to fling at him. "Now do you want to punish the wayward Bodkins or not?"

Taron stood to his full height and inhaled, breath control so obvious that Tegan wanted to kill this soliloquy before it started. "I will create a tempest of flirtation. I will love you with such sloppy, unstoppable passion that—"

"Stop." Tegan let their not-quite-impressed face settle. "This might be too hard. I mean, it's acting, which is not exactly your strong suit."

"It is my only suit," Taron said with pride and affliction.

"Right, speaking of which, you need to change."

"If I change in order to woo you, no one will believe it," Taron tossed back. "If this ruse has any chance of working, I must be myself."

"I meant changing your questionable sweater, not your equally questionable personality."

Taron smirked. A most pernicious smirk. "I'm not sure I have anything tawdry enough. Do you still prefer stringy tank tops and hot pants? Or are you on to something more subtle, like invisible shirts and mood-changing underwear? I hear they are the rage in the Tanaka System."

Tegan rifled through a rack of outfits. "Stop talking and take off your clothes."

"See, it's like we're in love already," Taron said, so flatly, it was almost impressive. *Almost.*

Tegan looked for something that shouted "boy, newly in love." They kept their room stocked with clothes for every possible gender presentation. When Tegan took on a role, they rolled with the gender—held their body differently, bound their breasts or displayed them proudly, took on whichever pronouns suited. And when Tegan finished with the part, it was back to shaved head, murderboots, and they/them.

Tegan threw an armful of clothes, and Taron ducked like they'd just tossed a grenade. "Oh, you're fine," they said. "And you'll be *much* finer in a minute."

Taron snorted. Not quite a laugh. He tugged off his sweater and grabbed the shirt, pulling it on in a smooth motion that gave Tegan a single flashburn of seeing him. *Really* seeing him. Without that hapless sweater, Taron had a strong, dashing torso that stayed broad all the way until a notch before the hips then narrowed fast.

"Your scars are fading. That's good," they said matter-of-factly when Taron caught them looking. They'd seen him during countless quick changes. Why should this be different? "Hurry up." Tegan buried a pinch of breathlessness under a pound of impatience. "Pants."

They got on their knees, tugging at Taron's weirdly adhesive yet fully shredded pants. Tegan tugged, and he pushed, and they both kicked and—

Icon barged in.

"Everyone is leaving! Are you . . ." She took note of Taron's state of semi-undress and Tegan, holding his cast-off pants. "Wow."

"We're, uh, a tad busy," Tegan said, calling up the breathless intensity they'd dismissed a minute ago. "Meet at the party?"

Icon backed out, fast, flashing *oh my gods!* eyes at Tegan, and shut the door.

Tegan took a slight, rolling bow from the waist. "That's how it's done."

Taron clapped: a paltry bit of applause, especially from someone pantless. "We'll have to do better than that if we want them to *truly* suffer our love."

Tegan took a single unsteady breath; preshow nerves they hadn't felt in years were creeping back in for this special, command performance. "What do you have in mind?"

As it turned out, Taron's ideas were voluminous enough to fill the entire shuttle ride to the party. Now that they were both invested in the plan, opinions clashed about how it should play out. They bickered about blocking, backstory (how long they'd been hooking up, who instigated this tryst), and most of all about their lines.

"You'll have to compliment me until you're short of breath," Tegan said.

"I'll heap a horrible amount of praise on you," Taron mumbled, distracted by the view of the palatial estate orbiting New Vegas. Tegan glanced out too. When it came to cast parties, Ods Bodkins went all out, but this would be grander than usual thanks to Taron's parents' lavish, empty vacation house. Apparently he'd sent one message asking if the company could borrow the place for the evening, and his mother had written back that they'd forgotten they still owned it. This sort of vapid family arrangement had unfortunately put Taron's constant oddness into a new context. Tegan could see the lonely rich boy all grown up. Especially now.

"You're sure about the touching?" Tegan asked, to double-check. They didn't want this charade to make Taron uncomfortable. They wanted to make everyone *else* uncomfortable.

"Despite your need to slander me, I am an actor. We've been touching every night for theatrical purposes. Don't you remember my hand all over your . . . ?" He pointed vaguely at their entire backside.

"Indeed. My ass has only the fondest memories of your fingers," Tegan deadpanned.

Taron went a little pale, but when the shuttle door hissed open, he squatted gamely. "Time for our grand entrance."

Tegan crashed into the cast party astride their costar. Taron had sworn that the most distastefully coupled way to arrive was full piggyback, and despite the jiggling and jostling, Tegan had a good view of the company's reaction. Eyes turned their way, followed by grand cheers and a tipsy, lewd shout of "hey, nonny nonny!"

"Not working," Tegan grumbled. "They seem to think this is all good, drunken fun."

That's when they noticed a large fountain ringed with cups. Booze was the font of merriment for most—and Tegan wasn't above taking revenge by spoiling the company's drink. "Drop me in there," they whispered in his ear.

"If I must." Taron dumped them in the fountain. Tegan bobbed up, sticky and spitting.

They braced for cries of *party foul!* Instead, everyone merely laughed.

"To Taron!" Tegan shouted, grabbing a cup and holding a drink aloft, knee-deep and dripping toxic punch. "For making the Bard's best love story come true." The company didn't look nearly as grossed out by that sickly sweet declaration as they wanted. What kind of speech would snare the company? Acting was best with a drop of truth, right? "My Taron, who turns the color of a red dwarf star when he's nervous. Who sings to himself in the shower. Who has this blindingly cute expression every time I touch his chest." They raised their cup. "He is the only one of you I would bother fighting with!" Tegan took a deep, much-needed swig.

Taron pretended to nuzzle their neck. "Um, that's not what we scripted."

Tegan barreled on to the next step, squeezing Taron's hand and waiting for a squeeze in return before launching into a showy, handsy stage kiss. His lips grazed the barest corner of theirs—cheating the kiss as ever.

Tegan waited for the inevitable groans, but everyone roared, "To Taron!" and rushed to refill their drinks, even though the punch was now Tegan-infused.

So that hadn't worked either.

Icon pulled Tegan out of the fountain, whispering, "You don't date actors. Last week you literally carved it into your headboard with a knife. *No thespians allowed.*"

"Oh, you *do* remember?" Tegan asked, a drip of acid in their voice. "I vowed to be done with dramatics everywhere but on-stage." Dating in-company never worked out, and Tegan wasn't a fan of such misery, which their friends obviously knew, so the fact that the cast was behind this setup only hurt more. And now Tegan would eat all of their hearts in the marketplace.

"Just yesterday you told me, 'Love is a self-inflicted wound,'" Icon reminded them. "And today you're willing to fall on your sword for *Taron?*"

"You have no idea what I'm willing to do." They pulled Taron so close that their bodies welded together.

"What now?" he asked, his voice warm and familiar. A tone he saved for rehearsal when they were both too tired from bantering lines and actually spoke like humans to each other.

Tegan eyed the party. The alcoholic fountain, the feast of a banquet, the huge palatial home, and finally the patio square of loud, thumping music and swirling lights. "Next, we destroy the dance floor." They dragged him away.

"One moment." Taron swung Tegan by the table of treats, and before they could complain, he'd poured a jug of water over their shaved head and patted them down with a hundred small napkins.

Tegan was surprised enough to let Taron care for them without complaint. And it was better, not being so sticky. "Thank you," they said, mildly surprised and suddenly connecting this gratitude with the opening night of *Much Ado*. Marius had broken up with them ten minutes before the doors opened. Tegan had lost half of their lines in that heart-twisted surprise, and Taron had whisper-fed them the phrases like small bites, without a hint of frustration. "You're thoughtful."

"For you? With pleasure." And he must have meant it, because he truly was a terrible actor. Well, he was terrible when he had to stretch. Benedick was firmly in his wheelhouse, which said all sorts of things about Taron that Tegan didn't want to think about.

Right now Taron couldn't stop thinking about how much Tegan pushed themself. In every strong direction, all the time. Even now, he was ready to let this latest, greatest, torturous teasing by the company go, but Tegan would have their soulful regret and nothing less.

"You said something about dancing?" he asked, taking their less tacky fingers and leading them toward the dance floor, a marbled patio beneath the mighty crystal dome that separated the toxic gas of this planet from the floating palatial estate.

"I can't believe you grew up here," Tegan said, sparing a moment to take in the scenery.

"Not exactly. I came here only twice to memory." Taron managed not to admit that the last time he'd been on this patio, he'd been small enough to build a lonely tower of blocks, watching the diamond rain, wishing for friends. He wondered what that little kid would think of him now, body reclaimed, a ship full of mates, an electric person on his arm . . . even if they were only there to make a point.

He had to admit that most of the company was so far into their cups that this plan could hardly work. Icon was drawing everyone's eyes with her gymnastic dance style, walking on her hands, the music loud and throbbing over the company's cheers.

Tegan seemed to take this as just another challenge. They shimmied through, pressing their friends out of the way, tugging Taron along. Taron made the mistake of clapping eyes with Hazem, who shook his head and laughed in a way that made his too-visible abs clench, which was . . . annoying. Why *couldn't* he be in love with Tegan? Why was that the funniest, most audacious reality the company could imagine?

He swung Tegan tightly to him and started dancing. They were good, too good. Taron worked hard to keep up, biting his lip with the utmost concentration.

Tegan's eyes grew very big, very brown while they took him in. They tucked his head to the side of theirs and shouted over the music, "Why are you fighting the rhythm?"

"Is it not a battle?"

"No!" Tegan smiled and dropped two soft fingers over his

eyes, closing them, making themself the lead. Taron followed and moved, as in rehearsals. He found their waist, so familiar after the show, but this was not a stage, and they were not trading lines. His hands drifted lower to their hips, enjoying the way they moved so fluidly, sailing on the surface of a liquid beat. For the first time in a very long time, he let himself imagine Tegan's fingers on his lips, his hand finding the edge of their pants and all that waited beneath.

Taron's eyes shot open, and he was two steps away from Tegan before he thought to run, and then he wasn't anywhere near the dance floor, instead slamming through his parents' cold house into the bathroom full of polished, gleaming tile.

Too much, too much, too much, the words were a prayer in his mind. He filled the sink out of habit, but before he could drown these dizzying feelings, Hazem was there, perfectly sculpted eyebrows reaching for the ceiling, the imaginary brother Taron had wished for so long ago now come to life.

"My dear friend, you are a terrific mess. Tell me our gamble didn't pay off now. I want to judge your delivery."

"We mean to punish you for that gamble," Taron said, because that part still made sense. "And you did not succeed! But it may be that our plans to make you see how viciously wrong you were have . . . turned against me . . . most foully . . ."

"Don't write the Bard's lines, brother. That's not your art."

Taron turned to Hazem, the feel of Tegan's hips still in his open hands, a mental picture of them smoldering in his bed. And not for the first time, no. "Do you really want us together?"

"Do you really think it would be so bad?" Hazem's usual smile rested. He put a hand on Taron's shoulder. "Tegan does something to you that no one else does."

"I told you about those dreams in the strictest of confidence!" Taron roared.

Hazem grabbed Taron's other shoulder and spoke with punctuated enunciation. "I am not teasing you! You like Tegan. More than like them! We all noticed."

"Yes, and *they* do not like me, so you are worse than teasing. You're breaking my heart. It's been endless months of cracks. Every single show a new fracture."

"Taron." Hazem's eyes actually clouded, a small, disbelieving laugh slipping out. "I'm so happy for you. You're in love."

"How are you happy? After Marius . . . after you, even! Tegan swore off dating in the company. They will never have me."

"You have never tried."

And there, Hazem had Taron pegged. To try would be to unlock the door to his feelings, to unlock it meant that it could spring open, and while he might find pleasure in going out, Tegan could also come in and wreck up the place.

Not to mention, he honestly did not know where to start.

Taron eyed himself in the mirror. Even while goading him to be braver in his clothes, Tegan had redressed him in a tasteful outfit, always careful of his inner ledges. The vertigo inside of his sexuality. But Taron had more to offer them. More to offer himself, even. After years and years of binding his chest, his skin was free now beneath his shirt, his scars healed and handsome. And he was damn proud of that.

He glanced at Hazem, eyes taking in his neatly exposed body, those gold suspenders and pants that clung tight. "Trade clothes with me."

Hazem's grin lit up his face. "Brother, I thought you'd never ask."

As Taron strode out of the bathroom, crossing the long, pristine hallway, Tegan fell in love. While there were bright new parts of his body on display, it was Taron's dark, determined eyes that made Tegan catch their bottom lip with their teeth. They gave it a good, sobering bite. Taron had upped the stakes, yes, but this was still just part of the game. After all, he'd only lasted a mere half song of dancing before running away. People did that. Swore they wanted to be Tegan's love interest then half-assed it. *Actors.*

"I'm enamored with this look!" Tegan said, instantly questioning their overdone delivery. "Ready for phase three? I'm afraid the company has discovered your parents' grand hall."

Taron gave a smile that was mischief let off its leash. "I am ready for whatever the night could bring."

"Good, because your outfit is going to make the next bit a challenge." Tegan led him by the suspender into a voluminous room, filled with actors standing on golden chairs, brazenly shouting lines, lacking a notable amount of clothing. Strip Shakespeare was a proud invention of the Ods Bodkins. Marius had just doffed his hat, having missed a bit of doggerel from *The Tempest.*

"Amateurs," Tegan announced, standing atop a chair. Taron leapt onto one beside them.

They dueled lines from all over the canon, and Taron kept up. More than that—he drove the iambic pentameter faster, bouncing on his feet with each upward inflection. Tegan was the first to stumble, distracted by either the bold, new display of his body, or the wild edge of his personality, or was it a combination of the two?

"Strip! Strip! Strip!"

Tegan was known for not caring about nudity, so they did something far more scandalous. They slowly, deliberately removed one murderboot.

Taron clapped, delighted. "I've never seen your toes before!"

As the rules demanded, he started the game back up, surprising Tegan fully.

"Come, I will have thee, but by this light, I take thee for pity."

These were their lines from *Much Ado*. Tegan cocked an eyebrow. Taron always insisted that pulling from the current play was as good as cheating because the quotes were all freshly stamped in everyone's minds. The fact that he hadn't even tried to trip Tegan up with some obscure bit of a Dogberry scene that they'd cut from their production felt even more suspicious. What was he up to?

"I would not deny you," they rattled off, "but, by this good day, I yield upon great persuasion, and partly to save your life, for I was told you were in a consumption."

"Too easy!" Marius shouted.

But they were barreling toward a moment that hardly felt simple. A kiss that Tegan had thought they were done with. And why did it feel like Taron had *willed* them back here?

"Peace, I will stop your mouth," he said. Their bodies, so used to cheating out to face the audience, sealed together, and his mouth pressed theirs, full-on. This was categorically *not* a stage kiss. When Taron's lips warmed and his hands moved to the softly shaved nape of their neck, feelings Tegan had tried to banish for months were right there, waiting.

Taron kept his face close, cupping their cheek, and whispered softly, "How was that, my dear disdain?"

Zounds. Taron was trying to prove his *acting chops*. Whatever emotions that kiss had set free, Tegan was alone with them. Taron was merely playing along with Tegan's plotting.

They pulled him abruptly into the hall, shutting the door and the rest of the company's chaos out. "I'm going to say something I never thought I'd say to you."

Taron waited, looking hopeful. Bright-eyed. Sweet, even. It was too much.

"You're quite a scene partner."

"Scene partner?" Taron mumbled, expression folding up. "I thought . . . but it seemed . . ."

"You thought I felt something?" Tegan's nerves spiked. "No. Of course not. I mean, I felt you pop my nose ring up." Their finger went to the spot where the sparkly little stud had lifted after Taron's face collided with theirs.

Taron nodded with his eyes closed. "Right. Good. That's what I thought."

"I mean, *you* certainly didn't feel anything. Did you?"

Taron stared down at Tegan's one bare foot. "No more than reason."

The mighty doors of the grand hall blasted back open, a few crew members stumbling out along with Icon's screeching Viola delivery. Tegan shot back in to collect their boot, unnerved by being so uneven and ready to blame this weird imbalance of feeling on their feet. When they'd returned to their preferred and steady height, they couldn't find Taron anywhere.

And that was because Taron had made his escape.

"Fool," Taron whispered as he took the stairs to the third level, crossed the long, dark mezzanine to the room that had been assigned to him when he'd stayed here, although that hardly made it his. He closed the door and leaned against it, the only light coming in from the balcony, all orange and teal atmospheric stripes. No sunset or sunrise. A perfect place to echo Earth's infamously nocturnal city that he'd read so much about.

The room hadn't been touched since he'd last been here. He shrugged off Hazem's suspenders, trying not to remember the sweet shiver when Tegan had led him to those chairs by tugging on one. They were really good at not making Taron feel like an oddball for not wanting to grope everyone all the time like everyone else. They were really good at acting.

"Fool," Taron said again. "Idiot. Dreamer."

He crossed to the balcony and stepped out. Soon the company would be back aboard *The Globe*, voting on the next play, laying out the course for rehearsals and intergalactic travel. He wouldn't be a lead next time; it wouldn't be his turn. Maybe he'd take a break, leave them for a few months. Unlike the rest of the company, he had all the money in the universe. And unlike the lot of them, he knew intimately what money could never, ever buy. Maybe he'd go find an entire water planet to stick his head in and erase the too-pleasing memory of Tegan's mouth and hands and words and wiles.

This time the hand on his shoulder was not Hazem's.

He turned to find Tegan's mouth tipped open, looking out from the balcony across the view that was the actual winning facet of this forgotten vacation home.

"Oh, wow."

"It is something else." He leaned on the railing, folding his arms over his exposed chest. "You need something? I have to admit I'm burnt out. Sorry we weren't able to turn them inside out with regret." Heavens, his voice was the piece turned inside out. He felt sure that Tegan could hear it.

"You do like me, don't you?" they asked.

Taron looked away. He thought of about twenty things to say. He said none of them.

"Here's our own hands against our hearts."

Taron turned swiftly, puzzled. "That's my line. And *if* it were true, you . . ."

"I would what?" Tegan was sort of smiling at him. "I *could* swear you off in the name of all the fools I've kissed in the past. I could ignore these feelings now and bring them out on-stage, when it's safe and convenient. Or I could tally up all the moments that have fashioned the seemingly inextinguishable truth that we are incompatible . . . and toss them out. I could kiss you right now. Not the way we've kissed a thousand times before, but a real kiss."

Taron's arms dropped to his sides. "You're teasing me."

"No," Tegan said with a small shrug, hands slipping up his shoulders, his neck, cradling Taron's face in both hands. "I'm not."

They waited for him.

And it felt like a very long time indeed, from the moment he'd met them at theatre school years ago . . . to the day he'd agreed to make them a part of the company his parents had funded, despite their endless bickering . . . to the posting of the roles for this *Much Ado* and the scenes they wove together, which amounted to a love story almost against their wills. *Almost.*

Taron leaned down and kissed them.

And the sky rained diamonds in applause.

Authors' Note

So many things in this story actually happened. But we can't tell you which ones.

I Bleed

Inspired by The Merchant of Venice

Dahlia Adler

*To bait fish withal. If it will feed nothing else,
it will feed my revenge. He hath disgraced me, and
hindered me half a million, laughed at my losses,
mocked at my gains, scorned my nation, thwarted my
bargains, cooled my friends, heated mine
enemies—and what's his reason? I am a Jew. Hath
not a Jew eyes? Hath not a Jew hands, organs,
dimensions, senses, affections, passions? Fed with
the same food, hurt with the same weapons, subject
to the same diseases, healed by the same means,
warmed and cooled by the same winter and summer, as
a Christian is? If you prick us, do we not bleed?
If you tickle us, do we not laugh? If you poison
us, do we not die? And if you wrong us, shall we not
revenge? If we are like you in the rest, we will
resemble you in that. If a Jew wrong a Christian,
what is his humility? Revenge. If a Christian
wrong a Jew, what should his sufferance be by
Christian example? Why, revenge. The villainy you
teach me, I will execute, and it shall go hard but I
will better the instruction.*

—Shylock, Act 3, scene 1

ude, I am so goddamn depressed."

"First of all, Tony, you are not *depressed*," Sebastian Denunzio says without missing a beat as the two sidestep way too many overeager freshmen in the halls of

Venice High. "Are you ugly? Yes. Are you broke? Also yes. Did you bomb the physics midterm? Absolutely."

"You give the shittiest pep talks."

"You don't deserve a pep talk," Bas tells his friend, and this time, he does stop. "Your dad gave you a *Benz* for your seventeenth birthday, and you already totaled it. You know what my pop got me for my seventeenth birthday? A phone call. In February."

"Isn't your birthday in June?"

"Yup."

Tony is Bas's best friend (by default, as their last names, Devenzano and Denunzio, have had them placed together for years), and Bas practically has a degree in listening to his crap, but he's also a walking disaster, and sometimes Bas's patience for it wears thin.

For once, Tony takes note of his friend's annoyance, wrapping his arm around Bas's shoulders and changing the subject. "Message received. Enough about my troubles. Tell me what's going on with *you*, and specifically what's going on with The Girl."

Bas winces. "You know nothing's going on with The Girl. The Girl requires some expensive appreciation, and I'm broker than you are right now. Speaking of which . . ."

Tony holds out his hands dramatically. "I'm sorry, man. I know I still owe you for those tickets, but my old man is up my ass about the car. I mean, why even give me the machine if you're gonna make me spend the money to fix it myself, right? Shouldn't that be, like, part of the gift?"

Had Bas actually expected anything else from Tony, he might've been pissed off, but as it is, he knows it's pointless. "I figured. So, yeah, nothing happening with The Girl."

"Are you even gonna tell me who she is? This secret's getting old." Tony coughs. "I mean, I could probably help you figure something out, if I knew who she was and what she likes and whatever."

"And whatever." Bas rolls his eyes as they turn the corner to English and glances at his phone. They still have two minutes, so, what the hell. "Promise you'll keep your mouth shut? And don't you dare mention Scout's Honor."

"Swear on my entire collection of—"

"Stop. I know where this is going, and hard pass." He tugs Tony a few feet from the classroom door and looks over his shoulder. "It's Persia, okay?"

Tony snorts. "Persia *Belmont*? Like, 'my dad is a cop' Persia Belmont? Good luck with that."

"You see why I can't exactly take her on a date under the pier. So, yeah, if you've got a surprise influx of cash coming and can pay me back, maybe I'll have a shot. If not, you can chill on mocking me for not making a move."

"Sorry, bro. But someone's gotta have cash you can borrow." Tony squints and scans the room, and Bas watches his eyes land on a slight, bespectacled boy and light up as if Tony's seen God Himself throw down a spotlight. "Get some from the Heeb."

"Who?"

"Lauchheimer. The Jewish kid who gets a nosebleed every time we play basketball in gym."

"That's because you throw the ball at his face every chance you get, you dick."

Tony laughs. "Yeah, because it's hilarious. Anyway, kid deserves it, hiding his horns under that little Jewfro, acting like he's some poor 'minority' when he could probably buy and sell all of us."

"Man, I think you might be spending too much time watching Fox News with your dad." Bas looks at his phone again, wincing at the cracked screen he can't afford to replace, and slides it back into the pocket of his shorts. "Come on, we're gonna be late."

🌹

It isn't watching Fox News with his dad, is the thing. Well, he does that too, but mostly his dad sits and yells about how the Jews and the Chinese and the Mexicans are destroying the economy. He doesn't *do* anything about it, though, and Tony's tired of not doing anything. The White Knights—*they* do things. They understand the power of threats and violence, and the fact that they respect and embrace Tony in a way his father doesn't makes him powerful too. That said, considering the last thing he did with them was scratch swastikas into Lauchheimer's car, he knows it's probably gonna require a gentle approach to get the Heeb to cough up some cash so he can finally pay Bas back.

But it's either Lauchheimer or Tony himself, and since Tony just dropped a month's worth of allowance at the Ink Parade, getting tatted up with the other Knights, it's gotta be the Heeb. He knows the guy is loaded, not just because he's a Jew and they all are, but because his parents are both doctors, which seems to be another thing they all are. Charlie, his favorite Knight who also scares him a little, says it's because they want access to your organs so they can do weird medical stuff. Charlie's the one who taught him Jews mess with vaccines, when it was way too late for him to stop him from getting his own. Now every time he can't figure out the answer to a homework problem or the right way to talk to a girl, Tony knows exactly whose fault it is.

And he's done everything in his power to make sure the Heeb knows it too.

Clearly, Bas is gonna have to be the face of this request.

Then again, maybe a threat is all that's really needed here, and Tony definitely knows how to administer those. While Mr. Browning goes on with his useless lesson about whatever quadratic equations are, Tony rubs the new ink on his bicep through his shirt, his fingertips grazing the straight lines of numbers one and four, the smooth curves of the eighty-eight. For now, it's easy enough to hide it or to pass it off as something sentimental when it's found. Not like Charlie's matching version, written right across his knuckles.

Clearly Charlie's not planning on becoming an investment banker.

They'll corner Lauchheimer at lunch. Tony knows exactly where he sits with his paper bag of Jew food, too good to eat the cafeteria food because it's too "unclean" for his precious Chosen blood. Meanwhile, Tony's stolen it enough times to know it's just tuna sandwiches half the time like everybody else, and he'd laughed so hard and loud the first time he'd realized it.

Now he doesn't even check—it just goes straight in the trash.

Come to think of it, he hasn't seen Lauchheimer in the cafeteria in a while. Maybe he's cowering in the bathroom to eat his sad sandwiches.

The thought makes Tony laugh his ass off. Wherever Shai is, he'll find him.

Shai isn't in fact in the bathroom. Nor is he in the cafeteria, because he learned his lesson about that a long time ago. It's the library that's his solace, and the librarian, Mx. Tubal, who provides his salvation in the form of an office to eat in every day. "It really never gets less brutal out there, does it?" was all they'd said the first time Shai had shown up with his bagel and cream cheese under the pretense of needing a quiet space to finish an assignment. Now the two have a nice thing going, and it almost enables Shai to forget why he'd had to seek refuge in the library in the first place.

Almost.

Still, it's been protecting him well, which is why when he steps out from his lunchtime cocoon into the hallway, he feels a false sense of safety—disappearing from the cafeteria had become something of an invisibility cloak. But, no more than two minutes after emerging from the library, he hears his name called in a voice that is both unfamiliar and too familiar all at once.

He has never heard Tony Devenzano use his actual name before, and it's what makes him halt in his tracks for just a moment, and it's a moment too long.

"Lauchheimer!" Tony says again, clamping a meaty hand on Shai's shoulder, and it's all Shai can do not to violently twist out of his grip. "I've been looking for you."

"I already ate my lunch," Shai manages through gritted teeth.

Tony laughs, as if his continued trashing of Shai's lunch is nothing more than a joke between friends. Never mind that if Shai's mother knew of the food being wasted, she would unleash a firestorm of intergenerational trauma–induced rage that would burn Venice High to the ground. Never mind that it's been mental torture for Shai every single day. Never mind that Shai's been subsisting on vending machine fare and his belt can't be cinched any tighter. "No, no, I've just got a small favor to ask. See, you know Bas, right? About yea high? Great basketball player? General lady-slayer?"

"If you mean Sebastian Denunzio, yes, I know him." Not much more fondly than Tony. He never does the shoving, the yanking, the punching, but he's always there, laughing.

"Bas is in a little bit of money trouble, and being the incredible friend that I am, I've agreed to help him out of this particular jam." Tony begins steering him toward the corner by the garbage can, his grip tightening on Shai's shoulders for their leisurely stroll. "Unfortunately, I'm a little tapped out, which is where you come in."

Shai's eyebrows shoot up. "You want money."

"Yep."

"And you think I'm just going to . . . give you money."

Chutzpah isn't a remotely strong enough word for what Shai's hearing. It's shocking enough to root him into place, even though the idea of entertaining Tony's demand is so preposterous, it would make him laugh if he weren't programmed to be utterly terrified of the boy standing in front of him.

"Not *give*—lend! Isn't that what your people do? You lend money to poor suckers and then charge a million percent interest? That's all I'm asking for here. You lend me . . . let's say, three hundred bucks now, and I'll pay it back with interest."

"If you can afford to pay back a loan with interest, then why don't you just lend Sebastian the money?"

"Well, I don't have the money right *now*. But I will. I'll get it."

It's then that Shai understands: he is in the position of power. It's a position he's never once held over Antonio De-venzano, and it's exhilarating and daunting and makes his mind race with possibilities.

His heart pounds as he tests out this theory, sliding out from under Tony's grip and facing him. It requires tilting his head up, confronting for the millionth time the fact that Tony looks like he could crush him with one hand and eat him for breakfast with room for a couple of waffles left over. But Tony doesn't grab him back, doesn't threaten him. He can't, if he expects any cooperation.

For the first time between them, size doesn't matter. And even though Shai knows he should tell Tony to eff off, that he doesn't have the money and that he and Bas will have to go squeeze someone else for cash, he can't bring himself to say the words. This is the kind of control he's dreamed of for years. And while he knows there's no way in hell Tony would re-spect any kind of financial arrangement, it occurs to him that maybe there's a way to take this power a little further.

He conjures a silent prayer for the bar mitzvah money he's been stashing away for college, for the favors he'll have to call in for the plan taking a messy shape in his brain, and says, "Okay."

Tony's eyes widen in surprise, and it makes Shai feel a foot taller. "Okay? You'll give me the money?"

"I'll *lend* you the money," says Shai. "I just need some time to draw up a contract."

"A contract? What the hell? I just told you I'll pay you back with interest."

"Yeah, and what happens if you don't?" Shai folds his arms

over his chest. "I'll write up the contract, complete with repayment terms, and when you sign, the money's yours. Deal?"

Tony grins the careless grin of a boy who thinks he's getting away with something, because he always has. "Deal."

"'If the Borrower should fail to deliver the promised sum by the appointed time, the Borrower shall forfeit *the tattoo on his right biceps* to the Lender, by surgical means to be agreed upon—'" Tony shoves the packet of paper away and glares down at Shai, who, much to his extreme irritation, doesn't so much as blink. "This is insane. I'm not signing this."

"Wait, what?" Bas reaches for the contract Shai took three days to draw up, but Tony slams down on his hand. "Ow! What the hell?"

Tony ignores him, fixing his ice-blue eyes on Shai's calm brown ones. "You're crazy. You're literally crazy."

"Not crazy enough to permanently scar myself with hate," Shai replies with a calmness that feels like fire ants on Tony's skin. "You want to borrow money? That's the deal."

"Okay, I have to see this." Neither Tony nor Bas is quick enough to stop Persia from reaching for the papers. Of course, neither of them had wanted her to be aware of this deal to begin with, but naturally, Shai had come marching up just as all three of them were hanging out, and Tony had no doubt it was to make him look like a dick. "Well, that's a first," she says, her eyes scanning the pages. "So if you don't pay the money back in a month . . ."

"I get to cut that 1488 out of his skin," Shai confirms, as if it's totally normal. As if he isn't talking about *mutilating* Tony. "Seems fair to me."

"I don't get it," says Persia, wrinkling her nose. She looks up at Bas as if he holds all the answers in the world. "What's 1488?"

"Yeah, I actually don't know either," Bas admits slowly. "What am I missing?"

"Nothing." Tony's eyes flash danger at Shai, but the very same kid who used to tremble as he handed over brown paper bags of pita bread and homemade chocolate chip cookies is completely expressionless. *Clearly* the Heeb has forgotten who he's dealing with, and there's no way Tony would show an ounce of fear to that loser. "Whatever. It doesn't matter, because you'll have the money, and this stupid-ass contract will be completely irrelevant. But you know what? If I'm putting my body on the line, I want more money. Make it a thousand."

"You're gonna pay me back a thousand dollars? In a month?" Shai confirms.

"Hell, you said this is instead of interest, right? So, yeah, no big deal," Tony says with a confidence he wishes he felt. He wants to think the White Knights would come to his rescue if push came to shove. He wants to be sure Bas would. But truly, he doesn't know; he only knows that guys like him succeed and guys like Shai fail, and that's going to have to be enough for now.

Shai shrugs, makes an addendum to the contract, and then hands Tony the pen. "Give me another day to get the money. Tomorrow, you officially become a thousandaire."

Tony scrawls his signature on the appropriate line and then hands the pen to Bas to sign as a witness.

"Man, you seriously sure you wanna do this?" Bas asks, his hand hovering just over the paper.

"What's the big deal?" Persia twirls a strand of dark hair

around her finger, her gum cracking in the silent tension of the otherwise empty classroom. "He said he'll pay it back."

"How?" Bas asks. "How could you possibly pay back a thousand bucks in a month?"

"That's my problem, not yours," Tony says coolly. "Now sign the damn thing. Sorbello's waiting for us in the gym."

Bas sighs, but he does as Tony asks, his chicken scratch seeming weirdly out of place on such an official-looking document. "This is ridiculous, but okay. Let's go."

The boys amble out of the room without so much as a backward glance.

※

It feels like hours until the door finally closes behind them with a definitive click, but when it does, Persia picks up the pen, signs her name to the second witness line, and leaves.

※

Shai cannot believe it worked. He has utterly loathed that tattoo since he first spotted it on the home security tape that caught Tony and his Neanderthal friends defacing his car, arms bared by ribbed white tank tops.

It's the tattoo that's kept him in hiding, the knowledge that he walks the halls with a boy who holds enough hate in his heart to permanently scar himself with it.

It feels so fitting that it should be the beginning of the end of Tony's reign of terror.

※

A thousand bucks goes fast. Bas insists that Tony keep all but what he owes him, and they compromise on splitting what's left. Persia gets her nice, respectable dates at parentally approved movies, restaurants, and the Santa Monica pier. Tony fixes his car, drops some cash on White Knights dues. His new ink starts to itch as the deadline nears, the beginnings of a reddening infection from constantly forgetting to clean and moisturize it, but the Knights blame it on a Jewish curse and Tony is only too happy to agree.

Still, no one offers a solution—not a way to call off the curse nor a loan to tide him over.

They do offer to visit Shai at home again, do damage to more than his car, but Tony knows that means pipe bombs, and it's a little hard to keep those quiet. Considering word of the loan has already spread around VHS, it's not worth the speed with which he'll become the number one suspect.

The skin festers, and one way or another, he will make the Jew pay for it.

He'll have to, because the deadline is looming, his wallet is empty, and he is out of options.

❀

Bas is the only one of their friends showing any concern for Tony, but then, it's partly because of Bas that he's in this situation in the first place. "Do you really think he's gonna carve into your arm? Your dad would be all over him."

"Yeah, and my dad would also tear me a new one for signing a contract with a shady Jew in the first place," Tony spits back. "I knew it was a mistake to try to deal with one of them. You can't trust 'em."

Bas murmurs in silent agreement, biting his tongue so he won't point out that the only one to violate trust in this agreement was Tony. He's Bas's friend, even if he makes some stupid choices. Shai's just some dork with deep pockets. "We should just tell him to get off your dick because it's not gonna happen," Bas suggests. "Come on."

"Hard pass," says Tony. His infected tattoo seems to blaze at the mere suggestion. "I'm not letting him curse me again."

"Dude, the curse is not real. Jews are cheap and sneaky, not magical."

"Not worth the risk." Tony digs his nails into his forearms, just barely avoiding the blistering red skin above.

It's maybe the most ridiculous thing Bas has ever seen, and as much as he wants to stay out of Tony's drama, this is just too much. "Okaaaay," he says slowly. "Guess I'll have to take care of this. You're welcome, loser."

He half expects Tony to catch up by the time he's halfway down the hall, but there's nothing other than the sound of his own sneakers squeaking on the floor.

🌹

It's Shai's bad luck that he stopped at a water fountain on the way to Mx. Tubal's office, that he took thirty seconds longer to get to the safety of the library. There's no chance Sebastian would've found him in there; Bas would probably burst into flames if he walked into a room with more than three books inside. But despite the relative calm that'd come into his life since Tony had stopped harassing him every day, choosing avoidance rather than looking his debtor in the eye, Shai knew it was bad news as soon as he saw Bas's hulking form lumbering in his direction.

"My bank is closed," he says to Bas, hoping that cuts matters off there. "It was a onetime loan. Unless you're here to repay it on Tony's behalf?"

"Man, why are you even bothering? You know Tony can't pay you back. Who cares? You've probably got a billion dollars more where that came from."

"I don't, actually. Tony came begging—*begging*—for money he needed for a friend. This whole money-borrowing thing was supposed to be some sort of honorable mission. And he's the one who's always bragging about his car and his clothes, so honestly, isn't it a little embarrassing that he can't pay me back?" Shai shrugs as if it's truly the most pitiful thing he's ever heard. "I wouldn't have thought he'd want the entire school knowing he's completely broke, but what do I know?"

It's accurate and brutal, and Shai knows it, knows from the way Bas winces that he's hit his mark with his framing. "Christ, you really are a dick. Tony wasn't kidding about Jews being shady, heartless pricks," Bas mutters under his breath. "All that and you still want to carve him up. What are you even gonna do with that tat? You know you can't just stick it on yourself, right?"

And just like that, Shai, who had never raised his voice within the walls of Venice High, who's made himself so small that he can disappear into the confines of a librarian's office and be entirely forgotten, who's been riding the bus to school for weeks because he can't bring himself to take his hatefully defaced car to the shop, whose wrist still aches when it rains because of the time Tony thought it would be hilarious to trip him down the stairs, whose brain still echoes with a thousand hurtful nicknames . . . cracks.

"You think," he spits in a voice cold as steel, "that I want that hateful shit anywhere near me, let alone touching my body? You think he hasn't already carved *me* up into a thousand little pieces? You think he hasn't bled *me* dry? Broken *me*?

Made *me* look and feel pathetic with whatever means he has? You think it's nothing that he uses my faith against me, my religion, my trauma? You think you're all better than me because what—I have a difficult name? A bump in my nose? *That's* what makes it okay to push me and trip me and humiliate me and steal from me, even now, even when you sign your names to dotted lines as proof of your honor?"

"They're just jokes, man." Bas's voice has never been so quiet.

"Well, fuck you, and fuck your jokes." Shai's dark eyes flash fire, and it gratifies him to see Bas recoil as if all his and Tony's suspicions have been confirmed that he's the devil himself. "I may not have your muscles and I may not have your ego, but as long as you're rifling through your Jewish stereotypes, here's one that's true for me: my entire family is full of lawyers, all as sick of this anti-Semitic bullshit as I am and all prepared to help make sure that contract is executed to the fullest if Tony doesn't pay up in three days, as promised. You might want to let him know."

And then Shai steps around him like he's nothing more than an inconvenient ant in the path of an elephant's paw and lets himself into the library, where Mx. Tubal awaits with the shadow of a smile on their lips and ears full of earbuds that play nothing at all.

🌹

Deadline day comes and goes. The money doesn't. A practical plan doesn't. But a court summons does. Begrudgingly, Tony asks Persia to read and translate it, and Tony feels himself turning fifty shades of purple as she does.

"It's definitely binding," she says, handing the papers back with all the authority of a police chief's daughter. "You're out a lot more if you don't show."

"You can't possibly think I should let this kid carve me up like a Thanksgiving turkey!"

"Hey, don't yell at her," snaps Bas, but Persia puts a restraining hand on his arm, her sharp, red nails leaving the slightest indentations.

"Of course I don't," Persia says with a calm that borders on irritating. "The contract is absurd. But it's legal, and it's signed, and right now the best thing you can do is just show up and deal with it in person."

"So you'd go to court," Tony confirms.

"Well, first I'd confront him. See if there's another way. Court fees are a bitch." The sympathy in her voice sounds real, at least.

Bas looks at her in surprise, probably hearing his precious angel swearing for the first time. But Tony nods, strokes the chin he's neglected shaving for days. There has to be another way, and he will find it.

Shai glances at his watch then back at the front doors of the school. There's a chance Tony would exit another way, but Shai has eyes on his car, and anyway, he's confident Tony's the one who'll come looking for him, once he thinks out the publicity and expense of a lawsuit.

It takes another three minutes, but then, there he is, summons in hand. "I can't go to court. This can't be on my record. You know I can't afford the fees."

"That is extremely not my problem," Shai says coolly. "You want to avoid court? We can take care of this at my house with my excellent plastic surgeon cousin. We both know you don't have the money, so those are your options."

"Fine. Your house," Tony bites out. "And I'm gonna need to see your surgeon cousin's credentials."

"Of course."

"And no one else comes. I don't want an audience for this shit."

"Well," says Shai, his hand patting his messenger bag, "the witnesses to the original contract have to be there. But that's it."

Tony sets his jaw. "Witnesses? You mean Bas?"

"And Persia. I did need a second witness, after all."

"I didn't see her sign the contract." Tony's teeth are grinding now.

"There's a lot you don't see, apparently." Shai pulls out his phone. "I'm texting my cousin to meet us at my house in half an hour. Considering you've already been in my driveway, I assume you know the way?"

He doesn't wait for a response before walking off to his own car, leaving Tony visibly nauseated in his wake.

🌹

"You don't have to do this, man. Don't do this." Bas's mantra is practically background noise at this point, and the words take turns targeting both Tony and Shai. But neither one is listening; both of their eyes are fixed on Shai's cousin Raphael, who's laying out a terrifying, sharp, and gleaming array of instruments. Now it isn't only Tony's tattoo that's itching; the feeling of his skin trying to burn itself from his bones is traveling to every limb. Sweat beads at his brow, and suddenly he has to pee worse than ever before in his life.

His eyes dart between the scalpel and Shai's face, which shows no sign of fear or remorse. It hits Tony then that this is really going to happen, that he's really going to be sliced open, that his very *skin* is going to be torn from his body, that there will be no last-minute rescue. His father isn't going to charge in and stop this, and the Knights aren't going to be his saviors. He has to get out of here, has to get out, has to get out—

Before he can move a muscle, a brown leather strap closes around his wrist, holding him fast. "What the—" Another joins it a moment later, circling his forearm. He hadn't even seen these guys walk up, tall and lean and so much stronger than they look.

"You said no one else!"

"Don't worry," Shai says calmly. "They're leaving." He says something to them in Hebrew, and one ruffles Shai's hair, nearly knocking his kippah to the ground, and walks off.

"I don't want to do this." The edges of fear lace Tony's voice, and he hates himself for it. He tries to jerk his arm out of the strap, but it's stuck tight. His left hand is useless at the complicated buckles. He's well and truly trapped.

Raphael walks over and pushes up the sleeve of Tony's shirt, his reaction to the ink a grimace that he quickly hides under a critical eye. "I was going to start with anesthesia, but maybe we should just go right in."

"What! No! Fuck no!" Tony yanks harder at the straps, digging in with his left hand, praying for something to click under his increasingly useless fingers. "You're a surgeon! Don't you have to do no harm or some shit?"

"You're not exactly a traditional patient." Raphael has the same calm demeanor as his cousin, which is something

Tony's come to realize he has sorely misread as weakness. "Besides, I'm doing you a favor."

"Like hell you are! Bas, help me!"

"You let him go, and I'll sue you too, Sebastian," Shai says coldly.

"You can't do that." The wavering in Bas's voice suggests he isn't completely sure about that, though, and neither is Tony.

"Pretty sure I can. You signed the contract. You're a witness that he owes me this. And before you get high and mighty about it, why didn't you just use your own money to take out Persia? I mean, it's kind of your fault he's in this position in the first place, isn't it?"

"I'd have *had* money if he hadn't 'borrowed' it from me for a concert ticket he couldn't afford," Bas snaps. "You're not the only one he screwed over."

Tony slumps where he stands, strapped to the table. So much for help. Sure enough, Bas rejoins Persia, who's been sitting stone still on the padded bench on the side of the room in Shai's enormous basement this entire time, every bit as cold and unmoved as the treacherous, devilish cousins about to massacre his flesh.

He takes one last look at the black ink upon his skin, the four numbers that mean nothing to some and everything to others, and both hates it and believes it with every fiber of his being. The fourteen words: "We must secure the existence of our people and a future for white children." The eighty-eight, each one standing for an H, code for "Heil Hitler." Part of him doesn't know what he was thinking getting his body inscribed that way, and part of him feels more hate than ever, anger and rage at being bested and tortured. This tattoo was supposed to be proof of his supremacy, and he will leave here with a wound that will scar into proof he is no white king, not even a knight.

Then he closes his eyes, squeezes them shut against the tears that threaten to fall, and says, "Go."

The scalpel is cold against his skin, and even before it takes its first cut, any bravery Tony felt slips away. His deep breaths devolve into panicked gulps, and the tears come freely. "Please don't please don't please don't please don't please please please please." The room smells like sweat and fear and pee, and he cannot do this, cannot do this, will not survive it, will not—

"Stop."

The sound of a girl's voice is so unexpected in the stillness of the room that Tony wonders for a brief moment if he's slipped into a hallucination. He'd completely forgotten Persia was there, having assumed no salvation would come from her corner, especially after finding out she'd signed the contract without his knowledge.

"What is it, Persia?" Shai asks, his voice matching the scalpel in its sharpness.

"The contract you had me sign—it says you get his tattoo. But if you cut him open, you'll be getting more than that, won't you? Think how much blood you'll be spilling. Pretty sure that'll qualify you for assault even if taking his tattoo doesn't." She turns to Raphael. "And that probably wouldn't be conducive to keeping your license, would it?"

Raphael locks eyes with Shai, dark brown piercing dark brown, and for the world's longest minute there is nothing in the air but stink and silence. "It would not." He puts the scalpel down. "Sorry, cuz. You're on your own for this tattoo removal, though I wouldn't recommend it."

Tony can hardly believe what he's hearing. His face is so full of snot and tears that he actually isn't sure he *is* hearing correctly, at least until Shai walks over and takes hold of one of the straps.

"You asshole," Tony blubbers, because he wants to be triumphant in this moment but is still shaking. "You tried, but you'll never—"

"I'll never what?" Shai spits back. "I'll never make you piss your pants in fear the same way I almost did when I came home to those swastikas? I'll never make you cower, afraid you're about to feel a world of pain, the way you've done to me a million times for no reason other than that I wear a kippah? I'll never make you beg and plead the way you've had me do from inside my locker over and over again? I'll never make you feel completely friendless and alone? I'll never make you wish for death because you know it'll be a lot more pleasant than whatever you're about to endure?"

Shai unbuckles the first strap, and they both watch the blood flow back into Tony's arm, though his face remains white. "I did it, Devenzano. I made you feel the way that brand on your arm is intended to make everyone like me feel—everyone with less power than you in a world that rewards you for being a blank slate. I want you to remember that every single time you look at that number in the mirror, every time you tag someone's car. I want you to think about everyone you'll be terrorizing with that tattoo, everyone you'll be making feel the same panic you felt today, everyone who's unsure just how deeply you mean what your skin says."

The second one is unbuckled, but Tony is unable to move, unable to internalize that he's actually free. Finally, he rasps, "So now what? You didn't get my tattoo, and you didn't get your money."

"Now you go home and tell your dad. You show him your tattoo. You tell him you want it removed or covered—I don't care which. And I won't know which, because I never want to see you in my face again. Do not come near me. Do not say a word to me. If you do, I will tell everyone every single thing that happened here today, right down to you desperately needing a change of pants. You hear me?"

Tony nods, and finally pulls his arm back to himself.

Shai takes a deep breath. "Go."

Tony runs, barely making it outside before he pukes in the grass.

It's only after everyone else is gone that Persia stands from the bench, having watched Raphael wrap up his tools and Bas beg off to go hide in his house and play video games until this entire afternoon disappears. Her outside demeanor is calm as always, but Shai sees the storm still surging behind her dark eyes, knows a part of her feels sick about this but a bigger part is glad to have played a role after staying in the shadows for so long. "Well, that went about as well as it could have."

Shai smiles wryly. "Got the job done, I think. Thank you for playing your part so well. Let no one say Jews do not excel at theatre."

"Raph was pretty great too. You're lucky to have such a

talented stable of cousins," she says with a curtsey. Then her face grows serious. "Listen, I'm sorry—"

"Don't." Shai squeezes her hand. "You've got your reasons for hiding your Jewishness, and I've got my reasons for wearing mine on my sleeve. Or, more literally, on my head, I guess. We both know the world isn't exactly kind to us."

"No, it's really not. I hate how grateful I am that my dad has the least Jewish name ever."

"Well, you made good use of that here, and it was cool and brave as hell." Shai grins. "Mi yode'ah im la'et ka'zot higat l'malchut?" *Who knows whether you came to the kingdom for a time such as this?*

"Did you just quote Esther at me?"

"Good ear."

"The devil can cite Scripture for his purpose," says Persia, cracking her own smile. "Nice job, cuz."

He doffs his kippah, and together they climb the stairs.

The quality of mercy is not strain'd,
It droppeth as the gentle rain from heaven
Upon the place beneath: it is twice blest;
It blesseth him that gives and him that takes:
'Tis mightiest in the mightiest: it becomes
The throned monarch better than his crown;
His sceptre shows the force of temporal power,
The attribute to awe and majesty,
Wherein doth sit the dread and fear of kings;
But mercy is above this sceptred sway;
It is enthroned in the hearts of kings,
It is an attribute to God himself;

And earthly power doth then show likest God's
When mercy seasons justice. Therefore, Jew,
Though justice be thy plea, consider this,
That, in the course of justice, none of us
Should see salvation: we do pray for mercy;
And that same prayer doth teach us all to render
The deeds of mercy. I have spoke thus much
To mitigate the justice of thy plea;
Which if thou follow, this strict court of Venice
Must needs give sentence 'gainst the merchant there.

—PORTIA, ACT 4, SCENE 1

AUTHOR'S NOTE

There was never any question for me what story I would be retelling from the moment I conceived this anthology. One of the most notable things about *The Merchant of Venice* is its classification as a Comedy, which it earns due to its protagonists getting their happy ending, finding love, et cetera. Of course, for Shylock—the Jew—the story is tragedy upon tragedy, especially to those who see Shylock's ultimate punishment through the same lens he does.

I originally read *The Merchant of Venice* when I was in (Yeshiva) high school, which was, in retrospect, something of a "safe space" for it. Certainly I wasn't surrounded by people who bought into what might be the most enduring anti-Semitic depiction in the history of Western literature. It wasn't until I was an adult that I would see its effects, and so, given the opportunity to mold the story in a different way—one that wouldn't erase Shylock's very real emotions of anger, isolation, resentment, and desire for justice, but would give him both more agency and more community—I leapt at the chance to rework it into a version that wouldn't make light of either its consequences or its "villain."

This isn't to say that as a Jewish reader, I find no merit to the original; Shylock's "Hath not a Jew eyes?" speech is one of the most humanizing monologues in Shakespeare's canon.

But it is, of course, telling that Shylock is in the position of needing to humanize us in the first place, and it was just so biblically familiar that I had to mesh it with one of my favorite Jewish stories of complex heroism: the book of Esther, in which family and revenge win the day.

(With thanks to the Pixies for the title.)

A SONNET

His Invention

Inspired by Sonnet 147

Brittany Cavallaro

My love is as a fever, longing still
For that which longer nurseth the disease,
Feeding on that which doth preserve the ill,
The uncertain sickly appetite to please.
My reason, the physician to my love,
Angry that his prescriptions are not kept,
Hath left me, and I desperate now approve
Desire is death, which physic did except.
Past cure I am, now reason is past care,
And frantic-mad with evermore unrest;
My thoughts and my discourse as madmen's are,
At random from the truth vainly express'd;
For I have sworn thee fair and thought thee bright,
Who art as black as hell, as dark as night.

—Sonnet 147

They drove down to Big Sur, down the California 1 from Marin. Sophie was eighteen then, a young eighteen; she counted horse farms out the window. Michael agreed to pull over halfway down the road to Pfeiffer Beach. Sophie fed a dapple gray her lunch, a comforting memory from one of her favorite childhood novels—*The Secret Garden*, maybe, or *Little House on the Prairie*. He leaned against the hood of his car, taking pictures of her with his father's camera. She knew better than to look straight into the lens.

Instead, she let her dark hair fall in front of her face, biting her lip as she stretched to pat the horse's whispering nose.

Michael had met her at boarding school at the start of her final year. She had escaped her Minnesotan hometown with a scholarship, something he had guessed from the way she carried a purse to class, by her thin legs in knee-high socks, by the long braids she coiled around her head. When she spoke, her words were full of soft *r*'s and long *o*'s that hung sweetly in the air, and that voice and those braids left him with the confused sense that she was some sort of milkmaid, some mountain girl who'd found herself by accident in his Borges seminar. Though his friends made fun of her hick accent, he took every possible chance to ask her the time or what she thought of that night's reading just to hear the strange cadence of her answer as she nervously crossed her legs.

He took her to California for the first time that winter during the long January between semesters. He had always had a girlfriend, and so his mother paid little attention to Sophie, even in the mornings when she would pour orange juice in sock feet, one of Michael's shirts falling down to her knees. They kept to themselves in his downstairs bedroom, though they always had the house to themselves, as Michael's mother was sequestered in her office on the top floor. At night, Sophie would look out at the lights from the bay spilling over each other down the cliffs to the sea. Michael was amazed that she hadn't seen the Pacific before. He bought her pastries from the market down the street, a camel coat from an upscale store in San Francisco. He found her one night in one of the dozen chairs around his dining room table, and when he brought her back to bed, she asked quietly why they had so many seats for just two people.

His bed, too, was oversize, untidy, the sheets stirred up like foam under the silky coverlet. She scuttled away from him at night, her legs kicking uselessly in the immensity of the covers; even though he slept soundly on the far side of the mattress, Sophie couldn't put her limbs to rest. One morning, her body exhausted, she woke to both his hands moving under her shirt, soft and skittish like birds. She stood up in a rush and walked quickly to the sliding door to the garden. Through the window, she watched Michael move fitfully in bed, then slower, slower, his face finally slack in sleep. He hadn't once glanced after her.

She turned away from the house and, ignoring the ocean below, sat straight down in the daylilies. Her mother hadn't wanted her to take the week off from work to come to California: Sophie who never sulked about long weeks of waiting tables in her family's restaurant when she was home; who let her mother dress her in old German school uniforms, tall stockings, loafers; who wore one-piece swimsuits to the beach and wide hats in the sun; who never made the ten-minute drive into the Twin Cities on a Friday or Saturday night; who never touched even a neighborhood boy. Sophie who had won the money to come across the country to school. Sophie who escaped.

She went inside once Michael heaved himself up off the bed. He stood stretching in the center of the room, his feet buried in the soft chenille rug. He said nothing about that morning as Sophie slipped past him into his bathroom. As she stripped to take a shower, she could feel the heat from her body warming the cold tiles, clouding the full-length mirror behind her. This damp, rolling landscape, the fog, the open palm of the sky. At home, her family was all still in snow boots.

Some mornings, after her mother came in from checking the mail, she broke the ice out of her hair in little sharp pearls.

Sophie set the taps to cold and stepped in all at once. Then she kept herself still for a long moment in the freezing water. All at once, she felt a welling in her mouth, the sudden desire to spit. She parted her lips and let a long bloom of blood spread down her chin and to the floor. Sophie touched her face with both hands and took them away warm and stringed with red. Outside, she heard Michael singing along to the radio. She stood with her mouth open.

🌹

They had planned the trip to Big Sur for this weekend, the last three days before they flew back East. Michael packed the car the night before with a picnic basket and cooler, three suitcases, his father's camera on its leather strap. That morning, Sophie hurried out before him, wedging herself between the luggage in the back seat; when Michael came outside, she said that she needed to nap, that she hadn't slept well the night before. As he pulled onto the 101, she pulled a tissue from her jacket pocket, winding it into a paper worm. She stuffed it between her lower lip and teeth to staunch the blood. In the shower, she had examined her tongue, the roof of her mouth, had explored the landscape of her throat until she gagged under her desperate fingers. She still bled, more slowly now, in long cords that crept out the sides of her mouth, but she couldn't find the source of the bleeding. Now, in Michael's car, it kept her from speaking as he tried to make small talk to ease that morning's tension. She answered his questions with syllables instead of words, the blood hissing and pooling and hissing again with every sibilant sound she made.

Michael fell into silence in the seat in front of her as he searched for a radio station. Now and then, he tried to point out a town, a rock face; he took a hairpin turn quickly and waited for her to squeal. He stopped finally at a gas station in Monterey, intent on reassuring her face-to-face, but she ran past him into the convenience store and paid for cotton balls at the self-checkout. In the restroom, she spat hard, then pulled the balls apart and nestled them against her gums. She hesitated, then glanced in the mirror. Static from the car seat had pulled long, crackling hairs from her braids. No trace of blood showed on her mouth. She walked outside to the parking lot.

He had the fuel nozzle locked tightly into his car. He touched her face. "Are you okay? I can't tell if you're asleep or awake back there."

She nodded, ducking her head so he couldn't see the bulge of gauze in her mouth.

"We don't have to talk," he said, "but will you just come sleep in the front seat?"

"Okay," she whispered, and the tension went out of his shoulders.

The rest of the drive wound through forests and breaks in forests, through pockets of towns in roadside pullouts, wound past stretches of cliff, massive arches crumbling in the water, rocks broken and mossy, licked by the surf. Sophie distracted herself by searching for signs of civilization: general stores and grade schools, station wagons strapped down with surfboards, farms for alpaca and for horses. In Minnesota, her family's land backed up next to that of an elderly couple who kept ponies for their grandchildren. On walks in the summer, Sophie would sometimes stop to hold an apple over the fence for Granger or Sally, but both would stand suspiciously on the other side of the paddock, Sally flicking her dirty, white tail.

But the horses on the road to Pfeiffer Beach took her carrot sticks and even bits of her turkey sandwich. She had asked Michael to pull over, a tissue against her nose and mouth as if she were about to sneeze, but he was so engrossed in driving down the dirt road that he didn't notice the flecks of blood she caught against her teeth. He snapped photos of her, hands cupped in offering to the horses' quick lips, her shoulders wrapped in his gray sweater for warmth. He snuck up behind her and undid her braids with quick hands and snapped photos of her hair whipping loose against her face and neck, against the lens of his camera. He framed her leaning against the split-rail fence and snapped her again, now her hand to her lips, now his lips against her cheek as he held the camera high in the air to take the picture.

"We can get to the beach from here," he said, hoisting his backpack from the trunk. "It's just a minute's walk. We can have a quick lunch and then check into the hotel."

She caught her knapsack when he tossed it to her. Two dunes and a negotiation through bramble and grass and they found themselves feet from the water. Farther down the beach, two boys ran shirtless into the surf. Shivering, Michael pulled up the hood of his sweatshirt and sat down next to the smoking remains of a firepit. "I'm going to get this thing started," he said, pulling matches from his bag. "You can go back to the horses if you want to."

She nodded and turned away.

"Sophie," he said, straightening. "Sophie, look at me." When she didn't speak, he groaned, and through her lashes she could see him drag his hands down his face. "God," he said. "Right now, I don't even think you like me, and I—I do so much for you. So much, Sophie. Don't you know that?"

She shook her head.

"I can't sleep sometimes, thinking about you," he said, stepping forward. "Sophie. *Look* at me."

And with that, he moved as though to kiss her, but she shied away on her long legs. He reached for her with both hands, but she turned to run, the same way she had run the first time he had chased her, across the long lawn at school on an October morning until he caught her in a thicket of trees and kissed her over and over, chastely, his lips pressed gratefully to hers. She did not want his mouth near hers, not today, not with all this mysterious blood pouring down her chin, faster now, thick and tin-sweet, blood he did not seem to see as he backed her against the fence, prying her mouth open with his.

TRAGEDIES

Partying Is Such Sweet Sorrow

Inspired by Romeo and Juliet

Kiersten White

Why, such is love's transgression.
Griefs of mine own lie heavy in my breast,
Which thou wilt propagate, to have it pressed
With more of thine. This love that thou hast shown
Doth add more grief to too much of mine own.

—Romeo, Act 1, scene 1

3:14 PM

Ben

Romeo

Romeo

Yo where u at Romeo

ur mom texted me

Wish that was a dirty joke but it's not man they r worried

When was the last time u left ur room

Romeo

Romeo

BEN would like to videochat with you

ROMEO is not available for videochat at this time

Romeo

stfu

you woke me up

My dude its 3

How r u still asleep

Sleep is my only solace

Too many hours in the day

So many hours

Empty empty hours

Let's go out

I'm already out

U r?? where, I'll meet u

Out of my mind

And not on hers

She doesn't even hate me

I wish she hated me, hate would be something

But I get nothing

I'm as cold as a fire

Heavy as a feather

Healthy as death

Awake only when sleeping and sleeping when awake

I feel everything and nothing and I hate it and I love her

Lol oh my god man

Sorry I'm not laughing, ur just so weird

I'm actually worried

I'm coming over

No that will only make it worse

I know I'm pathetic

I don't need you feeling sorry for my stupid ass

Bye

What's her name

Rosaline

She's so hot

And like crazy smart

Smart hot

Hot smart

And she goes to Capulet

noooooooooo

u want a Capulet girl??

They're messed up

She said she's not dating until college

College

That's a lifetime away

Seven hundred lifetimes

I live and die a lifetime every single day just thinking of her

And she won't even follow me back on insta

Is she loaded

She's rich in beauty

More like rich period, that school is $$$$

Bunch of rich ass snobs think they're too good for us

Not good enough to beat us on the field though
Forget her

How

Come out, meet other girls
So many other girls, man
What is one girl??

Everything
You don't get it
Fifty says I find someone hotter than ur crapulet crush
Hotter and without a chastity belt made of money and pride

You can't afford that
Get dressed weirdo
And get cash
Because ur gonna owe me before the night is over
Romeo
Romeo I'm serious man I'm on my way

5:46 PM

Mom
Just got off the phone with my sister.
What a mess. How is Juliet?

Ros

How would I know
Don't you see her at school?

No
She's a freshman
And she's always at like dance or whatever
Isn't there a school party tonight? Invite her.

What?? no
It wasn't a request.

She doesn't even like parties, mom
She never goes out
She probably has some ballet thing
If you want to go out tonight, you are taking your cousin.
That is final. Also wEIL hEILo ThErE bUtTfAcE
What was that? Why did my phone do that?

Fine can I have money for tonight
Of CoUrSe I lOvE mY sOn ThE mOsT
Why did my phone do that?? What is wrong?
I wanted to type Of CoUrSe I lOvE mY sOn ThE mOsT
Of CoUrSe I lOvE mY sOn ThE mOsT

THIS IS NOT WHAT I AM TRYING TO TYPE.

Talk to the son you love the most

He programmed autofills

It's easy to turn off

I disagree with your definition of easy.

Tell your brother he's grounded until he fixes my phone.

And invite your cousin. It'll be nice.

Ugh fine

I can stay out past curfew right

Of CoUrSe I lOvE mY sOn ThE mOsT

6:52 PM

Father

Do not mess this audition up.

Juliet

Are you coming?

Your mother is.

She is?

She should be there.

Is she not there? I swear to god . . .

I see her now! I'll text you when I'm done.

Juliet

Mom?

My audition starts in five minutes.

I'm in the second dressing room.

On the right, sorry. Second on the right.

Maybe you missed me.

I'll look for you in the audience.

I didn't see you. The lights were bright though.

It went well.

I'll text father that it went well.

I need a ride home.

My private lessons are canceled.

Mom, I'm done.

Mom?

Mother

Don't text you r father

Call a

Cab

7:48 PM

Cousin Rosaline

Hey
there's a costume party at 8 at the school greenhouse
It was boring last year

Juliet
. . .
. . .
. . .

Anyway I can pick you up if you need a ride
But it's fine if you don't want to come

I had a big audition today.
I just finished, actually.
Normally I'd have lessons, but they got canceled.
Cool just let me know

It was for a ballet school in Paris.
My father really wants me to go.
neat
Anyway it's fine if you can't come

It's so far away though.
Paris, I mean, not the party!
But my father REALLY wants me to go.
To Paris. Not to the party.
It's really prestigious.
Paris, not the party

LOL. You're so funny! Yes. Paris. Not the party.
I don't think he'll let me go to a party.
K oh well maybe next time

But he doesn't know my lessons got canceled!
Oh my god. I could come.
I shouldn't.
That's fine then

I really shouldn't!
K see you around

Oh my god. OH MY GOD.
I can lock up the studio and just go. Okay.
I'm going to do it.
Are you sure

YES. Yes. Oh my god. My heart is racing.
What should I wear? What are you wearing?
I only have the costume I'm wearing right now.
well it's a costume party

so that's fine

What are you going as?

Prince

Seriously? Wow! I can't wait to see!

Which prince? Like, Harry or William?

Prince like PRINCE

the singer

Oh right! Yes. Prince the singer. He's so great.

Is he on tour right now?

Just text me a pickup address

Okay! See you soon!

We are going to a PARTY!!!!!!!

I'm so excited!

Thank you for inviting me!

It's a school party

You are already invited

Right! Cool! C U Soon, Cuz!

8:07 PM

Montague Mavericks group chat

Ben

Hey we need to get Romeo out

Tio

Right now?

Ben

Soon

He's in the shower

It was needed

Extremely needed

Tio

Whats your flavor

Ben

Anywhere with girls

He's obsessed with a crapulet

Goes on and on about how she's a swan

Tio

More like a crow

Ben

More like a cow

Tio

Ah ha ha ha haha wait

Creeped on some instas
Capulets having a party tonight
We could crash

Ben

Can u pass for a crapulet, because I can't

Tio

it's a costume party

Ben

Who
Who does that

Tio

Private schools apparently

> *Romeo*
> She's a swan
> You two are swine
> Look her up
> No one is hotter
> She's like the sun
> No
> The sun wishes it was like her

Tio

Oh my god dude I love you but you are exhausting
Speaking of exhausted last night I had the craziest dream

Ben

NO

> *Romeo*
> No man please

Ben

nO DREAMS TIO WE DO NOT WANT TO HEAR IT

Tio

dicks

Ben

Let's go to this party
u can see her and we can judge
And find u someone hotter

> *Romeo*
> An impossible task
> But if it means I get to see her
> It will be enough
> Yeah let's go

Tio
And I can tell you about my dream
It had a fairy queen in it
Romeo would be hard for her
Ben
I will push you out of the car
Tio
good luck since I'm driving

                     8:39 PM

Tio
Tonight

                                              Ty
                                       Can't
                                       busy

I know
Look for a fairy queen

                         Tf are you talking about
You always say I'm secretly a queen
Just wait

                                     . . .
                                     . . .
                                     . . .
                         Man don't do anything stupid
Stupid is my middle name
I'll be the one in glitter and wings

                                     Don't
                         We talked about this
                 You know how I feel but I can't
                             Not yet
            You don't understand what my school is like
It's a costume party
Everything is a secret
It's perfect

                 TY would like to videochat with you
              TIO is not available for videochat at this time
I'm driving
see you soon

                     8:42 PM

GIRL TALK group chat
Ava B

Umm did everyone see Black Swan come in

Who is that skank

Ava C

OMG RIGHT?!??!!

Ava B

Like ur skinny we get it thanks

Who is she

> *Ros*
>
> Juliet
>
> My cousin
>
> She's a freshman

Ava B

Lol whoops sorry

I'm sure she's nice

> *Ros*
>
> Whatever
>
> She came from ballet
>
> Where are you

Ava B

By the back gym doors

Come find us

I'm dressed as a sexy RBG

> *Ros*
>
> Cool so it's okay to be a sexy supreme court judge
>
> But not a ballerina

Ava C

Yes because feminism

> *Ros*
>
> Lol
>
> Let me ditch my cousin I'll be there in a min

Ava B

OMG

DO NOT COME BACK HERE

HE'S HERE

> *Ros*
>
> Who

Ava B

YOUR STALKER

> *Ros*
>
> Are you kidding me??

How did he get in?

Ava C

They broke in the back door

He just came in with two other guys

One is dressed as a fairy queen

Actually he's hot I'm into it

Ros

Romeo? NO he's terrible

Ava C

No the fairy queen

Romeo is dressed as

I don't know actually

Depression?

Ava B

We'll come to you

8:48 PM

CAPULET'S GET IT ON group chat

Ava B

Three montague pubic school boys are here

Jaden

Lol pubic

Chris

What where

Ava B

They came in the back

Chris

Oh we're gonna kill them

Liam

They're dead

Jaden

Hey Ava I have something 4u

In my pants

Ava B

How is he still on this chat

Liam

LET THE BODIES HIT THE FLOOR

Ty

Leave them alone

Chris

What why

Ty

If we start a fight we'll be the ones who get in trouble
And I am barely hanging on with my gpa
I can't give them any excuse to bench me

Ava C

I'm not opposed to slumming it with montagues
A little fresh meat

Jaden

I have a little fresh meat 4u

Ava B

Yes in your pants we are all aware
I swear to god I will castrate you

Ros

Not worth the fight Ty is right
Just leave them alone
But if you see them heading for me, intervene
One of them has been full on stalking me

Jaden

Dick pics?

Ros

Worse
Poetry

Ty

Which one

Ava B

emo one

Ros

He's in all black, hoodie up
His friends are dressed as a luchador and a fairy

Jaden

A fairy are you serious
We need to beat them up

Ty

I said leave it

9:05 PM

Juliet

Hey, Cuz! I lost you! I'm over by the drinks.
I love this song they're playing!
Do you know what it's called?
I only really know classical music.

Because of ballet.

It's really loud.

Everyone looks so pretty.

I think I saw someone from my science class.

I know I go to school here, but I feel like I don't know anyone.

I'm always so busy with ballet.

And my father doesn't like me going out.

Anyway, where are you?

9:07 PM

Montague Mavericks group chat

Ben

Romeo whered u go

I thought u were gonna show us the sun

Where is this supreme hotty

Romeo

Oh my god

Who is she

Tio

Wait you don't even know who your crush is

Romeo

No you were right

Rosaline is a crow

And now I've seen a dove

Ben

What is it with u and birds

Tio

Maybe he's secretly british

Romeo

How can you not see her

It's like every light in the room is on her

Or she is the light

I have to talk to her

Ben

Am I to take it that

u r over the chick

who I promised u would get over

AND U OWE ME $$$$$$$

Romeo

God, look at her hands

I would die to hold her hand
Touching her would be like praying
I'm going in

Tio

Yeah man we'll catch up with you later
This song is calling my name

Ben

Where r u going tio
Ur gonna get us caught
GET OFF THE STAGE
Why do I take u two anywhere
Oh look snacks

10:16 PM

Ava B

OMG ros
Where are you
911 emergency where are you

Ros

Too worried about running into romeo
I'm in the far bathroom with Ava C
We are self-medicating
Come join us

How old did you say your cousin is

I dunno like fourteen maybe fifteen
She's a freshman
Why

Because she's in the darkest corner of the gym
Holding hands
And wrestling tongues
With YOUR STALKER

THE FUCK

Also the fairy montague is on stage now
And he's singing Whitney Houston
He's good actually
Omg
OH MY GOD
OH MY GOD
HE JUST DEDICATED IT TO TY

10:18 PM

CAPULET'S GET IT ON group chat

Jaden

Wtf man

Did the montague just dedicate his song to you

Thats super gay

Ava C

Don't use gay that way you dick

Jaden

Sorry that's super homosexual

Ava C

Die in a fire

Chris

Do u know him Ty??

Ava B

And his friend is macking on Ros's INFANT COUSIN

Ava C

Wtf is happening

Ros

I'm on my way

But stop them!!!

Chris

Ty? Do u know him?

> *Ty*
>
> . . .
>
> . . .
>
> They're on our turf
>
> Let's show these pricks we're capulets
>
> It's on

Jaden

HELLLLLLLL YEAH

10:32 PM

Montague Mavericks group chat

Ben

Where r u guys

I'm two blocks away

I think half the football team hit me

Cant see out of my left eye

Why does walking make my ribs hurt

Tio did u get out

what the hell man this is ur fault

Why did u do that on stage

Tio

Why do you think

Romeo

I have to see her again

Did I breathe before tonight

Did the sun shine before today

Was there beauty before I saw her

My hands

I swear my hands are different

Holy

Purer for having touched her hands

Ben

Romeo I love u but stfu

Tio

Man r u gay

Because it's totally cool if u r

Tio

Oh its cool huh

Ben

U know what I mean

I don't care

Ur my friend

My brother

Why didn't u tell us

Tio

You've said stuff

Ben

But I didn't know!

Tio

But you still said stuff

Ben

But it's u now

So I don't care

Tio

awesome

you don't care

wow this changes everything

Ben

Ur right

I'm sorry

I'm really sorry
But I'm also mad
Tio
You have NO right
Ben
I'm not mad about that
I'm only mad that u and Romeo BOTH HAVE BAD TASTE
CAPULETS
BOTH OF U
GOD WHAT IS WRONG WITH U
WHY R MY FRIENDS SO STUPID
Tio
Doesn't matter now
Ben
Sure it matters
And ur right I care in like a good way
I want u to be happy
Wait
Was he one of the ones who chased us
Tio
I'll talk to you guys later
Ben
Wait man
Where r u
I'll come to u
Let's talk
Tio?
Tio?

Romeo
Did you see her though?
I never saw before tonight
I really didn't understand
I thought I knew what love was
But now
Oh god, now I know

Ben
My dude
Not the time
Tio needs us
Where r u

Romeo

I'm staying

Ben

Whatever

I'm going to find tio

10:42 PM

Cousin Rosaline

Where the hell are you

Juliet

I'm still here.

I'm on the second floor balcony.

The air was too stuffy down there.

I met someone.

Yeah no shit you did

He doesn't go here

He's from the public school

And he's a creep and a weirdo

He only talked to you because he's obsessed with me

He's been stalking me

Come down we're leaving

. . .

Oh. I see. That's okay. Thanks for telling me.

I don't need a ride anymore.

My mom is picking me up.

10:44 PM

Juliet

Hey, Mom! You're probably wondering where I am.

I should have been home by now, I know!

But don't worry. I'm safe.

I'm with Rosaline. She asked me to spend the night.

Isn't that nice?

Aunt Willa says hello.

Anyway, so don't worry about me.

We're having pizza and painting our nails.

Okay, well, gotta go! The movie is starting.

Love you! Hope you're having a good night.

10:46 PM

Juliet

Romeo?

Are you okay?

Where did you go?

Romeo

I can see you

You're like the sun

I could find you anywhere

Wait, you can see me? Where are you?

I'll come to you!

No, stay there

I want to look at you

God, you're so beautiful

It makes me want to die

I could honestly die happy tonight

Having met you

Looked at you

Touched your hand

Um. This is awkward. But I talked to Rosaline.

. . .

. . .

. . .

Why would you talk to her?

She's my cousin.

She said some weird stuff about you.

How well do you even know her

Not that well, actually.

I think she only invited me because her mom made her.

She ditched me as soon as we came in.

Yeah, that sounds like her

We hung out a few months ago

As soon as she found out I wasn't rich she ditched me

I haven't even thought of her since then

Weird that she'd say stuff about me

So you don't like her?

I mean, like-like. Like romantically.

Nope

And she really ditched you just because you go to
Montague?

People get so stuck up about going to Capulet.

Like they're roses in a garden of weeds because of the
name.

They tried to beat me up just for talking to you

But they don't care about me!

No one is friendly.
No one even sees me. No one ever sees me.
Not really.

> They're jealous
> I wish you could see yourself the way I saw you tonight
> You're like the sun
> And everyone is the moon
> Pale and cold and sad

They really tried to beat you up?
Can you really see me? What am I doing right now?

> Leaning on the balcony
> Stealing my heart and my breath
> Now you're covering your face
> As though that could dim your beauty

But what if they find you?

> I don't care
> I couldn't leave without seeing you again
> Besides
> If you don't feel the same way I do
> I'd just as soon they beat me to death

Oh my god, don't say that!
. . .
. . .
. . .
I do.
I do feel the same way.

> Then nothing can hurt me
> Not ever again

But . . .
But how do I know you really feel that way?
And I . . .
Well, I've never had a boyfriend.
But I do feel the same way! And we only just met.
Am I a fool?

> I swear by the moon

Oh, the moon you just said was pale and cold?

> No! I mean, I swear by the sun

So you're swearing to me, by me?

> You are impossible
> What should I swear by?

What will you believe?
Because I have never been this serious
This sincere
I feel you in every inch of my soul
I don't care that we just met
There are some things you can never know
Until you know them
Never feel
Until you feel them
And I was changed the moment I saw you
Swear by yourself, then, because it is yourself that I love.

. . .

. . .

Oh my god. I didn't mean to say that.

It's okay
I feel the same way
I could fly right now
No, don't turn away!
Let me look at you

I should go.
I shouldn't have said that.

Are you taking it back?

No.
But I'm scared.
I've never felt this way before.

. . .

. . .

Tonight was my first kiss.

That can't be true

I dance all day. Every day. It's my whole life.
My father wants me to be the best.
And my mother does what my father wants.
Everyone does what he wants, because he's rich.

That sounds lonely

It's complicated.
They had three other kids.
They all died as babies. My mom still cries a lot.
And she drinks.
I shouldn't have said that.
And my dad—well, I'm his only daughter.

Sometimes he doesn't know how to love me.

I mean, he loves me!

He just doesn't always express it in normal ways.

He wants me to be the best.

To reflect well on them. You know?

> Not really, no
>
> My parents don't care what I do
>
> But anyone who doesn't love you
>
> Doesn't deserve to know you
>
> Juliet, are you crying?

No.

Maybe.

Listen, I should go.

> When will I see you again?
>
> I have to see you again

11:03 PM

Father

Where the hell are you

> *Juliet*
>
> Hi, Daddy! I'm at Rosaline's. My cousin's.
>
> I texted Mother. She knows. She said it was okay.
>
> She dropped me off.
>
> To celebrate the audition, because it went so well.
>
> We went to dinner after.
>
> We missed you.

I heard from the school.

> I'm sorry. I tried. I really did.
>
> I promise I tried.
>
> I worked so hard to make you proud.
>
> I'm sorry, Daddy. Please don't be mad.

Why are you being stupid?

They accepted you. They had a student drop out.

They can take you immediately. You leave in two days.

> . . .
>
> . . .
>
> . . .
>
> Oh. Wow. Two days.

Have your cousin bring you home. You need to pack.

> But . . . Paris. It's so far away. I'll miss you.
>
> And Mom.

Maybe we could just wait until the next semester?

Are you kidding?

Do you know how much money I paid for your lessons?

For that stupid school your mom insisted on?

How much it cost to get you in front of those French bastards?

Can we at least talk about it?

11:06 PM

Mother

What did you say to your father

Fxe it

Fix it

Juliet fix it now

11:07 PM

Juliet

Okay, sorry. You're right.

I was just overwhelmed.

Thank you for this opportunity, Daddy.

I'll be home soon.

Thanks, Daddy.

11:07 PM

Romeo

Why are you crying?

What happened?

Juliet

I got into a ballet school.

That's great though

It's in Paris.

No

No you can't go

We just found each other

I know. I don't want to go.

My father's making me. I don't want to leave.

But he controls everything.

And he hurts

Sorry my finger slipped. He pays for everything.

I can't say no. He'd just send me anyway.

And once I'm there, what could I do?

You can't leave

You can't

He'll make me.

Don't cry
Please stop crying
We can fix this
We can

How?

Marry me

What???

Marry me!
If you marry me, you have legal rights
You're emancipated

Is that even legal?

I'm googling
Just a sec
Oh my god
We could do it
In Utah the minimum age is 14
But there are some rules
You have to
Uh

What?

Well, if you were pregnant

. . .

. . .

. . .

I leave in two days.

Okay that's out
Ha ha I was kidding anyway
But if we have a parent's signature

They would never.
Actually . . .
I could trick my mom.

And I have an uncle who's a judge in Utah
If we explained the situation
But he might not do it just to keep you here
Unless there was another reason

. . .

. . .

. . .

My father isn't a nice person.

Oh god, Juliet

I'm coming up

We'll figure this out

Not tonight.

I have to get home.

He'll get worse the longer it takes.

Come and get me tomorrow.

I'll have my mother's signature.

Okay

Okay

God, I know you're scared

But I want this

And I swear I'll take care of you

We'll be together and I'll take care of you

You promise?

I swear it

Tomorrow then.

Tomorrow

I feel like I could burst

Tomorrow is infinitely far away

And yet I float through the night toward it

Tomorrow, my love

Tomorrow, my love.

Wait, what time?

9 am

I can't possibly wait longer than that

Okay.

I wish we could be together now.

I don't want to be apart from you.

It feels like a dagger in my chest.

I can't breathe.

Tomorrow!

Tomorrow.

Wait, can you give me a ride?

Oh dammit

Let me see if my friends are still here

We kind of got chased out

11:18 PM

Montague Mavericks group chat

Romeo

Hey tio can you give us a ride

Ben
U asshole
U absolute asshole

Romeo
What???

Ben
U left him on his own
They beat him up

Romeo
Who

Ben
Who do u think
The capulets
Because that's what they do

Romeo
Where are you now

Ben
In his car
I can't find his keys
I think they know where we Oh god they're here
Tio's in bad shape
He's barely conscious

Romeo
I'm coming

11:20 PM

Juliet
Romeo?
Can you give me a ride?
Romeo?

11:25 PM

Juliet
Hey. Can you give me a ride home?

Ros
You said you didn't need one

I was wrong. Come get me?

Just call a ride

Who?

Uber. Lyft.

I don't have either of those.

Can't you come get me?
Please?

Isn't there anyone else you can call
Like no offense
I know we're related
But I barely know you
And suddenly I'm your only ride

Oh. Sorry. I just thought, since you invited me.

God it was a school party
It's not like I invited you to a sleepover

. . .

. . .

Sorry I'm a little high
It was a weird night
Listen I can't drive right now
But I'll get a lyft for you
You're still at the school right

Oh, no, it's okay. I found a ride.
The girl from my science class.

Ok good
See you around

11:32 PM

Juliet
Romeo?
Where did you go?
Can you give me a ride?

11:34 PM

CAPULET'S GET IT ON group chat
Ava B
Omg the cops are here
So many of them
Ava C
What's happening?

Ros
Yeah we're not there anymore
what's going on?

Ava B
Big fight
In the parking lot
Guys?

Jaden

Shiiiit

Shit shit shit

Did you guys get out

Ava B

What do you mean?

Jaden

Not you

Chris? Ty? Liam?

Dudes tell me you got out

Ava B

They're carrying someone out on a stretcher

Wait two people

Omg

It's Ty

He's not moving

Jaden

Who else

Goddammit ava who else

Ava B

The fairy kid

Oh shit

The cops are looking for the guy who did this to ty

Ros

Who?

Ava B

Give me a minute!

Jaden

Come on

Ava B

That Montague stalker

Romeo

Romeo stabbed Ty

11:38 PM

Romeo

I need help

Uncle Laurence

What? Do you know what time it is?

I'm in trouble

What kind of trouble?

I got in a fight

. . .

. . .

. . .

It was bad

Were there any injuries?

Yes

Did you start the fight?

No

I was defending my friend

They ganged up on him

He was unconscious when I got there

And I just

I just went crazy

I don't remember exactly what happened

And then the cops came and I ran

You shouldn't have run.

If you were defending an unconscious minor, that's good.

Go into the station and give a statement.

I can't

They're rich

The people in the fight

They'll have good lawyers

I'll go to jail

I know people. I'll get you a good lawyer, too.

It will be okay, Romeo. Just go into the station.

My friend's in a coma

What about the other boy?

I don't know

Do as I said. Go into the station.

There's something else

A girl

She's in trouble

Because of the fight?

No

Because of her father

I think she's being abused

She's my girlfriend

But we can't get her away from her father

Not safely

Unless we get married

You want to marry her.

Yes! Yes yes yes
I know it's crazy but I love her
And it's the easiest way to protect her
Her mother gave permission
We just need a judge
And a state where she's old enough

Romeo.

Please
God, please
You know how things have been lately
I love her
I love her so much
I need this
She needs this

Text me after you've spoken with the police.
And then I don't know, we can talk about the girl.

Thank you
I don't know what I'd do without you
You're the only adult in my life who listens or cares

I love you, kiddo. Please keep me updated.

11:45 PM

Romeo

Juliet I'm so sorry
There was a fight
It was bad

Juliet

Oh my god, are you okay?

I'm okay
But my friend is hurt
And a Capulet
I'm scared

Where are you?

A few blocks away
I can't go home
My uncle says to go to the police
But what if they arrest me
Then you'd get sent to Paris
And we'd never see each other again

My studio!

My dance studio. You're not far.

I have a key. I'm there so often, they gave me one.

I have to go home and get the signature first.

But I'll meet you there.

You'll be safe there.

How long?

An hour.

It feels like twenty years

Be careful!

11:58 PM

Mom

Have you seen your cousin?

Ros

About 5'3", big eyes, wearing a tutu

Yeah

I've seen her

Don't be a smartass. My sister just texted.

They're worried. She's not home.

She said she had a ride!

Where did you last see her?

I don't know, at the school

She was with a boy

There was a fight

Police and stuff

Maybe she got stuck there

There were police? You got your 14

year old cousin arrested??

God mom you're the one who insisted I take her!

She told me she had a ride!

I couldn't exactly drag her out!

She's very small. You could have.

Her father just called. How my sister lives with that man.

But Juliet is a child! You should have kept track of her!

I don't

Know where

She is

And I'm pissed that you're making this my fault

Call her.

Rosaline?

Fine yeah whatever
I'm calling
She's not picking up

12:03 AM

Mother
Where are you
You bitch
You selfish little bitch

Juliet
I'm sorry, Mommy.
I love you.
I'll be home soon.

12:10 AM

Romeo
I love you
I'm sorry tonight got so out of control
You're the most important thing in the world
And I swear I'm going to protect you
Hurry back to me

1:35 AM

Uncle Laurence
Oh my god.
What are these photos?
Who is that?

Romeo
Juliet
So will you help us or not

Her father did that?

Yes
Because she got home late
That's why her mother signed the permission
Go to the police! And the hospital!

She's a minor
The hospital would call her parents
And if he finds her again tonight after she left
We don't know what he'll do
He knows the police too
He owns half the town
She'll never be safe here
Please

Uncle Laurence

This is life and death

Are you somewhere safe now?

Yes

Okay. This is insane. That poor child.

Do you have the signature from her mother?

Yes

How did you get mixed up in this?

I love her

That's the only thing that matters

When you get older, you'll see it differently.

But I'll do what I can to help.

1:43 AM

Juliet

I need to borrow your car.

Cousin Rosaline

Oh so now you're answering

Also last time I checked you're 14

I tried calling you so many times

I'm in trouble because of you

I'm with someone who can drive.

We need a car.

Who are you with?

It doesn't matter.

Omg

You're with him aren't you

Romeo

Juliet he's a psycho

Where are you I'm coming to get you

Juliet?

Listen I know your parents have issues

but you have paris to look forward to

Far away from all this

Alone.

Yeah exactly alone

No parents to worry about!

Thanks for taking me to the party, Rosaline.

I appreciated you reaching out.

Bye.

1:45 AM

Montague Mavericks group chat

Romeo

I need your car

Ben

Where tf r y

U

Where tf r u

The police r looking for you

I'm at the hospital

Tio's awake but

It's bad

It's really bad

Romeo

I know

I'm sorry

But I need your car

Or Tio's

Tio

Fuck you

And fuck capulet

Fuck everyone

Ben

we never should have been there

we should have been there for u

Romeo

I came back!

I fought for him

Ben

I love u but u scare me

u made everything fucking worse, man

Romeo

I didn't make any of this happen

Blame the costumes

Blame the stars

Ben

Why did u even have a knife

Tio

A knife?

Where is ty

Is ty okay

Guys answer me

1:46 AM

Tio

Ty?

Ty?

Ty?

Im sorry

1:47 AM

Romeo

Look I really need a car

It's life and death

Ben

. . .

. . .

. . .

They had to sedate Tio

I cant make tonight about u

1:55 AM

CAPULET'S GET IT ON group chat

Ava B

Ty's going to survive

Chris

Thank god

Jaden

Oh thank god

Ava C

I can't stop crying

Ava B

But they think he was dating that other guy

The one you beat up

Why wouldn't he tell us?

Jaden

No way

No fucking way

We talk all the time

Chris

Yeah we text like a hundred times a day

We would know

Jaden

We know him

We talk

Ava C

You text you mean

Ros

Have the police found Romeo

Ava B

Not that I know of

Ros

Shit

2:05 AM

Ros

Mom I think Juliet's in trouble

I think she's with this creepy guy

He stabbed someone tonight

Mom

What?????

They're asking for a car

She wanted mine

They won't be at his house or hers

The police are looking for him

Oh my god. That poor girl.

Where would they be?

Omg

She has a key to the ballet studio

She said she was locking it up

I bet that's it

I'm calling the police right now.

You're a good cousin, sweetheart.

She's lucky you're looking out for her.

We'll get her home so she can go to Paris.

We won't let this criminal ruin her life.

2:16 AM

Ty

I'm sorry

I'm so sorry

I'm so sorry

I was so scared

I'm sorry

2:37 AM

Juliet
Oh no.
There are so many cops outside.
You were right.
They haven't seen me.
And they don't have a key.
But we don't have a car.
We can't get away.

Romeo
Come back

But what are we going to do?
I can't go home.
I can't.

I know
I won't let that happen
Come back to the dressing room
We'll be together
No matter what
You're so beautiful, Juliet
I love you so much
Nothing is going to separate us
3:14 AM

Mom
They found Juliet.

Ros
Oh good
I warned her!!
Did they arrest Romeo

. . .

. . .

. . .

Dreaming of the Dark

Inspired by Julius Caesar

Lindsay Smith

> *O mighty Caesar! Dost thou lie so low?*
> *Are all thy conquests, glories, triumphs, spoils,*
> *Shrunk to this little measure? Fare thee well.*
> *—I know not, gentlemen, what you intend,*
> *Who else must be let blood, who else is rank.*
> *If I myself, there is no hour so fit*
> *As Caesar's death's hour, nor no instrument*
> *Of half that worth as those your swords, made rich*
> *With the most noble blood of all this world.*
> *I do beseech ye, if you bear me hard,*
> *Now, whilst your purpled hands do reek and smoke,*
> *Fulfill your pleasure. Live a thousand years,*
> *I shall not find myself so apt to die.*
> *No place will please me so, no mean of death,*
> *As here by Caesar, and by you cut off,*
> *The choice and master spirits of this age.*

—Antony, Act 3, scene 1

Briony and Cassie are too busy making eyes at the boys' lacrosse team to pay attention to the memorial assembly for our dead best friend. But no one will look at us too closely—they see the skin we wear. Their whispers drift around us, their fear crackles like dead leaves. When Julia was here, she was the lightning rod for their fear. But now, I fear so much more.

"Westbrook Romans," Principal Carthage intones, because

a memorial assembly is clearly the time to remind us of our sports mascot. We're crammed into the drafty field house that usually hosts pep rallies, basketball games, and homecoming dances—I'm half expecting the marching band to storm in. "We are gathered here today to say farewell to one of our own."

As if there's much of Julia left to say farewell to. I still see it when I close my eyes. I've got the strongest stomach of any of us—I had to, to hold my own with her—but the smell of burning rubber and the sight of intestines draped over a steering column proved hard to scrub away.

But now—right now—I don't want to scrub it away. I need that power. I need that hate. And Julia—god, if there's one thing she knew how to do, it was *provoke*. Briony and Cassie rub their thumbs over rough crystals, readying for tonight, dreaming of the Dark. Gathering their strength. But watching them gives me the strength I'll need to see this through.

The initial slap of Julia's death has stopped stinging, and what's left behind is different for us all. For Briony and Cassie, it's the void now at the dark heart of our summoning circle and the question of who will fill it. For me, it's the weight of everything Julia left undone.

"Julia Simmons was a bright girl," the principal continues. "A pillar of our student body."

Bitch, most would say. *Tyrant*. They wouldn't be wrong. It was never about who Julia was, though. It was what she made out of the rest of us.

"Her kindness and generosity should be an inspiration to us all."

Julia had claimed Westbrook's greatest treasure for herself, and it got her killed. There was nothing generous in it. Nothing kind about her leaving me behind.

But the worst part is that Cassie thinks Julia's place is something that she's *earned*.

"The Shade won't regret this," she mutters to Briony. "We can actually use her gifts for good."

Briony's eyes catch on mine as she leans forward to answer; she quickly looks away. "I guess we'll find out tonight what the Shade thinks."

The lost cemetery outside Westbrook Township at night is a study in negatives: the vast star-strewn sky blotted out by the looming blackness of uneven mausoleums and worn-down statues and dark veins of bare tree branches. But it's sacred and silent, save the sounds of seven pairs of boots stomping through dead leaves. Like we all sense, somehow, how soon everything is about to change. Over my shoulder, Cassie bitches about stubbing her toe on a headstone because she can't see, but Julia hushes her.

"No lights until we're there," Julia says.

Cassie flicks her phone screen on with a sneer but kills it just as fast and shoves it away.

"Okay. Here."

Julia stops, and I nearly crash into her—steady myself on my arm. Risk a nervous squeeze. I can't see her face, but I feel her smile in the flex of muscle and shift of her shoulders, and that small allowance is enough to fuel me for tonight.

The hurricane lantern sputters to life with an oily stink. Julia kicks at the leaves, unearthing a square, stone platform sunk deep into the ground. "Gross, what is it?" Eun-Min asks. "Like, some sacrificial altar?"

Cassie snorts. "Well, now it is."

"That isn't funny," Briony says.

"Shut up. All of you." Julia's glare is whetted by the harsh light and shadow as she turns to look at me. "Anamaria?"

I shrug the duffel off my shoulder with a clank of thick glass.

The thing about the gift is, it doesn't matter how you call on it, not really. What matters is believing. What matters is knowing yourself and what you have to bargain with. And Julia—there is nothing she wouldn't give.

"They call you the Westbrook Shade," Julia intones, once we've gone through the intricacies of lighting the candles and incense and flecking the stone with our blood. "We know, though, that you are much older than Westbrook itself."

The tar that binds the stones. The darkness that swallows the light. If the words are in our hearts, our ears, or our heads—we have no choice but to let them in.

The seven of us have forged an uneasy bond of shared hunger: hunger for the power of the Dark that lives beneath the town. Hunger to make use of this shiver in our blood and whisper in our hearts, convinced we're all capable of more than what the town of Westbrook wants from us. But seven people wanting the same thing—how could we expect it to end any other way?

"You were here before Westbrook, and you will be here long after this town devours itself with hate," Julia says. "We come to you with ourselves as offering. We will be the vessels for your will."

They say the Westbrook Shade was once named Philippa; that she was just a girl like us. What she bargained with and why is lost to time, but her anger echoes throughout the town. No one speaks her name if they can help it. No one questions the fortune she's brought. Westbrook is hers to toy with as she pleases, and whoever gains her favor gains Westbrook.

And if her words and her shadow follow you through a bitter Westbrook night—the worst thing you can do is run.

The candles gutter like a chord playing out. "Oh, hell, no," Shemella mutters to my left as the flames shift.

"Westbrook Shade?" Julia says, and I like to think I'm the only one who hears the uncertainty beneath her tone. "I am here to bargain. Grant us all your power, and I will bring you what you ask."

A dark laugh rings like a stone thrown in a pond. *Such a lovely, pampered life you lead . . . Is Westbrook not already yours?*

My throat clenches. Julia's parents own half of Westbrook, it's true. All Julia would need to do is nudge things with one manicured nail to get whatever she wants.

But the seven of us are here for a different kind of power. The kind even money can't command. It isn't enough to make this town our own. We want the same thing the Shade sought—an eternity to savor and forge.

I want to taste surrender, the Shade purrs. *Give up all your comforts. Show me that you would sacrifice everything for each other, and then we can converge.*

Someone chokes back a sob at the other end of the circle—Eun-Min, maybe—but no one else moves or speaks. I suck in a deep breath, realizing I could barely breathe before; it's like a heavy blanket has been ripped off us.

"She's gone," Cassie says, as if it's not obvious.

"Sacrifice," Briony sputters. "She wants a *sacrifice*."

"It's the same as any of the bargains we make to use the darkness." Julia stands, and I can just *hear* her eyes rolling. My hand is cold and clammy where she's dropped it. "Don't be so dramatic."

"It didn't sound like that's what she meant. It sounded like she wanted a *life*."

I don't like the way Cassie turns to Julia just then, sleek, pale-blond hair glowing in the candlelight. "I guess we just have to decide if we want this power enough, then."

"Of course we want it enough." Julia nods to herself. "I'd think you of all of us would, Briony."

My stomach tightens like a fist. It's the first time Julia's ever really acknowledged how she wants to use the Shade. We all have our tiny vengeances to enact—but Briony's is at the top of all our lists.

Briony's shoulders fall, and she gives Julia a solid nod. "Okay," Briony says, and the tension breaks.

Because we are stronger as a circle. No matter how we struggle and chafe against that yoke—we are stronger together.

But the Shade's whispered promises are stronger still.

"This is such bullshit," Briony mutters now, as the principal keeps droning on about all these half-glimpsed ideas of Julia that are terribly, painfully wrong. "She deserves better than this."

"Did she?" Cassie asks. "Seems to me like we trusted her more than she deserved."

It takes all my willpower not to slap the smirk right off her face. What I want to do is wrap one hand around the crystal in my pocket and use the other to shove her to the wall. Squeeze that pale throat. But I have to wait, I have to wait—I can be as patient as the Shade.

"Did we get everything we need for tonight?" Cassie asks me instead.

"It's all packed and ready."

She's already fiddling with the hidden zipper in her purse where she keeps her loose cigarettes. "Then I'll see you ass-holes then."

She stalks off, and I watch her face transform instantly into the sweet, appeasing good girl she likes to play, pretending she's on the verge of tears as she begs the gym coach to let her step outside the field house. Julia taught her well. But Julia kept all her bile-etched turmoil and honesty and passion locked be-neath a powerful shell. Cassie's simply empty inside.

"It's hard for Cassie, too," Briony says softly to me. Always the peacemaker. "Just because she and Julia fought all the time—"

Her hand lands on my sleeve, and I yank away. Heart hammering against my ribs. My skin burns, corroded, under my coat where she touched it.

"I don't give a shit what she feels."

Briony sighs. "She cares about you."

"No." I laugh. "She only cares what I can do."

🌹

Julia cuts through the indoor pool like a blade, long limbs honed from Pilates and tanned from her family's holiday trip to Monaco and Cinque Terre. The underwater lights shift from purple all the way to red and back, and for a moment, they perfectly frame her billowing hair like it's a golden crown. Then she surfaces in a rush and swims to the edge where I'm sitting. Her waterproof mascara hasn't even budged.

"You haven't said a thing about the other night. What the

Shade asked us for." Julia frowns up at me, a practiced jut of her lower lip that I can't look away from. "I know you have an opinion."

I shrug. There's no use talking Julia out of something she wants, and it's not like I don't want her to take the Shade's power. I just worry about how much of her will be left. But that's nothing she wants to hear.

"Cassie wishes it was her," Julia says, when I don't answer.

"Cassie wishes *she* was you."

Julia gives a horrible dry laugh. "That's not true."

But it always has been. In grade school, long before anyone in Julia's orbit knew I existed, Julia and Briony were inseparable, dorky best friends like any other. Cassie came later when she and Briony grew close heading up the homecoming committee in junior high, and in retribution—I never believed it was anything but—Julia plucked me out of the background of the newspaper staff and made me into her newest project. Eun-Min was Cassie's friend from a soccer team they'd both long since left behind, but she was always on the periphery.

Then there was Shemella and me. They were my accomplice in learning to draw from the Dark for years; we'd bonded over our shared fascination with it—them from scribbles and notes their mom had at the historical society, me from the dribbles of half-remembered dreams. We hadn't gotten very far, though, and weren't that keen on pushing for greater power—satisfied with small curses and tweaks—before Julia decided she wanted to command it, too, and I brought her into our fold.

But there's only so much that one can dabble in the Dark before wanting to bargain for more. It wasn't enough to give Eun-Min's stepdad food poisoning or make Mrs. Gearig forget about a pop quiz. This town is built on secrets, lies, and shadow. If you want to break the first two, you'll need more and more of the last.

Julia's hunger has always been there. Cassie's, too, though she's always lacked the wits and the will. But Julia—her, I love in spite of her darkness. Maybe because of it—the way it stretched her, tested her, made her even better and worse.

I love the darkness in her, too—that's what no one else can understand.

She grabs my wrist and tugs me downward, nearly yanking me into the pool. "Hey!" I yank my hand free then flick her with water. As if that'll do anything.

"Come in with me."

"I've got my feet in the water. That's enough for me."

She shakes her head. "All the way."

I look at the void of churning water as the lights shift to nothingness before the cycle starts again. "No thanks."

"Fine. A kiss, though."

And that I can never deny her. I lean forward, let her damp, water-slick lips press to mine, and I savor the taste of chlorine like every taste of her.

It's almost enough to tempt me to fall in beside her and sink. Almost enough to drown myself in the darkness, too.

※

The six of us who remain are crammed into Briony's SUV. And I should've realized we'd have to take this same road to the old cemetery—of course we'd have to wind around Piney Hill and the salt marsh and the barn where Shemella and I used to first draw on the Dark together, before I stabbed myself on a bent nail and had to get a tetanus booster. But more importantly, it's the road from the Piney Hill Estates to just about everywhere else worth going in Westbrook—the storybook main street and old mill and school and the soggy, vinyl-siding shacks where people like me live.

It's the road Julia took from the party. The mangled-up bit of useless steel railing and old oak that took her life.

Cassie and Briony are arguing about music in the front seat—Briony wants something to cover up the silence of us in our grim task; Cassie says she needs the silence to prepare herself for the ceremony. Then Shemella's screaming at the two to focus on the road, and Eun-Min's begging for everyone to get along, and I hate them all, I wish the whole car would catch fire right now, burn while Julia laughs, winning as she always does—

"Pull the fuck over," I shout.

And Briony, at least, is scared enough of me not to argue. As soon as she's stopped, I throw open the door and practically fall out onto the highway. My head is pounding, spinning. My conversation with Julia is a dark, taunting drumbeat in my veins, and everyone else's frenzy smells like the stink of someone else's weed.

But I was right—I could find this spot in my sleep. Not that I need to. There's a bright-white painted cross and the heap of flowers and long-dead candles and stuffed bears, as if Julia gave a fuck about stuffed bears. It's all piled high like its own kind of offering to the Shade.

It's exactly what I need.

"Anamaria?" Briony says. I jump—I hadn't realized she'd followed me. Her hand lands on my shoulder. "Hey. Sorry." Softer: "I know you miss her."

This is not a conversation I'm willing to have. With Briony, most of all.

I crouch down. Select a sad little snow globe someone left—the Westbrook Old Mill, signature autumn leaves swirling around instead of glitter and white flakes. It's perfect for what I need.

I slip it into my pocket, right alongside the dead crystal I stole from Briony's backpack during the memorial assembly.

"Okay." I stand. "Let's get this over with."

🌹

The truth of the Westbrook Shade is this: she was just a woman, and sometimes even that can be too much.

The Westbrook settlers knew there was something living beneath the town; they felt it humming in their fields with an untapped energy and plucking the harp strings of their dreams with promising chords. The Dream, some called it. The Dark, others muttered. It was always just around the next corner, shimmering around the next tree, and trying to grasp it only made its absence more acute.

But Philippa offered herself up. It spoke to her differently, or so she swore. She didn't want any great power, she claimed, because what was power to a single woman back then? All she wanted, she said, was to help however she could. Channel the Dream for the town, in whatever way served it best—to drag the isolated village from destitution into opulence.

What they offered her instead was too much power. More power than she could resist. They wanted her to become the Dream, the thing that could cure all their ills.

Three times, she said no.

A fourth was more than anyone could bear.

No one knew quite how to invite the Dream to them, though the town's leaders seemed confident. Philippa, though, she went below the funeral altar, to the chamber where the whispers echoed most. Where the air turned gossamer and hungry. Where she heard the Dream scream her name.

She would do everything it asked.

She would give everything of herself.

And when her bargain with the Dream was finished, the person who emerged was Philippa—but not.

It was the townsfolk who claimed to see the difference. Her stares that lasted a little too long, words a little too clipped, fingers sharp and stretching. The whispers followed her same as the dreams once had—of stolen husbands and sacrificed cows and girls led into sinful ways.

Easy to ignore, at first. What with all the good she brought as well—crops flowering into the dead of winter and fat live-stock and babies who never once cried. The Westbrook heal-ing springs and the piney hills drew money from all around as tourists came to pay tithe. No one warned them of the Dream, and most of them never acknowledged the way it murmured to them during their stay—because who would want to break the spell of money and prosperity and survival that bargain-ing with the Dream had brought?

But—and no one is sure just what the tipping point was in the end—the scales slid.

This monster they had made, this creature knotted up in the Dream, or more accurately, the Dark—she had to be un-made, too.

They tried to snare her. Break her spirit. Run her out of town, though they didn't know what it might cost. What would become of Westbrook if the power underneath it collapsed? In the end, it came to fire. Nothing so deliberate as burning at the stake. Just a fire set by wronged villagers (so they claimed), all-consuming, the orange flames turning green and black as they licked at her Dark-touched bones.

All they did was strip away the husk that the Dark had donned. What was left behind was a new master of that power, an eternal one in search of new forms: the Westbrook Shade.

Power only lasts for those who don't seek it. And it lasts longer than any of us can stand.

Cassie leads us through the old cemetery, past the overwrought mausoleums of all the men who tried to burn the Shade, her cell phone's flashlight sweeping crudely over battered headstones of everyone who wanted her dead. We are as loud tonight as we were quiet under Julia's guidance. I can barely hear the leaves crunch under Briony's constant nervous chatter to my left.

"Do you think Julia would understand?" she asks me. "I mean—it isn't like she's the only person who's been able to bargain with the Dark. We've all pulled on it before. She'd want us to use it for good."

"The fuck are you asking me for?" I mutter.

Briony's stare crawls over my skin. "She trusted you more than anyone. In the end."

I resist the urge to make a fist. "But you're her oldest friend," I say. "You tell me."

"Yeah, but." Briony's voice drops. "She liked you more."

And we are *not* having this conversation, this is *not* what I'm here to discuss. Briony doesn't get to know me. She doesn't get to know what Julia meant to me. All I want is for Briony to feel it, the weight of all they've done.

What I want to do is reach over, grab her neck, and squeeze.

Rip that crystal off the cord around her throat.

But I already know what I need to know, and I have what I need from it. It is, after all, a twin to the dead one in my bag.

"Okay." Cassie draws us up when we reach the altar stone and throws down the two shovels she's been carrying. "Time to dig."

I volunteer, and Briony gets voluntold, and we dig through dense layers of moldering leaves until the top of an archway begins to emerge from underneath the stone. It feels like it takes forever to clear away, but it must only be an hour; by the end, my hands are blistering and bleeding, and Briony can't stop whining about the same. But all we need is enough for the six of us to squeeze down into the ritual chamber under the slab. Which we do, and only Eun-Min's fishnet hose are a casualty of the jagged doorframe.

"One last time," Cassie says, as she busies herself with lighting the candles. "You all will let me bargain with the Shade?"

Shemella nods. Briony says yes, just a little too loud. Eun-Min hesitates but agrees. It all comes down to me.

I close my hand on the velvet bag dangling from my side and don my sickly-sweetest tone.

"It's what Julia would have wanted," I say.

※

It's the middle of March, and we're christening the start of spring break at the Ogden barn. It's about the last thing I want to be doing, but Julia insisted, and she always gets her way. She's offered to DD—a shock that I'm still wary to trust—but rather than cling to my side, which I was absurd for hoping she might, she's been snarking at anyone unwise enough to cross her sober path.

"God. Get her drunk already or something." Briony slumps next to me against one of the hulking hay bales, the golden bonfire light painting strange shadows across its form.

"Nothing for her tonight." I shake my head. "And you say that like I can tell her what to do."

"More than the rest of us, anyway." Briony watches me over the lip of her red plastic cup. "You're sure there's no way to talk her out of this 'binding with the Shade' thing?"

I frown. Something in her overly familiar tone is putting me on the defensive. As if this is something we've talked about before. Like I'm automatically going to take her side that this is a bad idea.

"It's time someone harnessed the Dark for good. Especially for all we need to do."

"Yeah, but." Briony huffs. "Don't you think she wants it too much? The power, I mean. Doesn't it scare you, what she might do?"

Everything about her scares me, I think, but that's not for Briony to hear. "The same any of us would do with it. We take care of our own." And because I'm drinking gin and extra bitter, I add, "She's going to clean up your mess for you, isn't she?"

"Hmph. Maybe." Briony shoves off the hay. "But she seems to think she stands alone."

An hour later, she and Cassie and Julia will pile into Julia's car, Julia driving them back toward Piney Hill. I will be left behind. And in that car, something will break: darkness bubbling up like an oil well. Julia's car will lurch, jumping across the median, and slam into the guardrail and cliff along the inside of the road. The driver's side—crushed. Ravaged. Shredded. The driver along with it.

The passengers—both seated on the right side—make it out with nothing but bruised ribs and one broken nose.

A tragic accident, everyone says, especially when the autopsy shows no alcohol in Julia's blood. But there are darker things that can lurk in people's veins. Especially in Westbrook.

※

"Westbrook Shade." Cassie speaks loudly, crisply—she's been waiting for this for a long time. "We are ready to fulfill the bargain you offered us to tap into the Dark in full."

The candles dance on a phantom breeze in the musty chamber. Someone—Briony?—whimpers, but Cassie stands firm, squeezing my right hand.

"You made an offering to one of our own. Julia. She is no longer with us, but perhaps, in death, she has made herself a worthy sacrifice for your needs."

There is a strange tingling sensation all over my body; like the dizziness after giving blood. Like I'm not even here, just watching this from afar—but also like I'm rooted, surrounded by the flood.

". . . Westbrook Shade?" Cassie asks. "We've brought you an offering for your request. Are you with us now?"

And then the tingling shifts. The shifting weight of someone stepping into my skin.

The snow globe, the crystal, the binding spell I cast— exactly like Julia begged me to, just days before she died.

"The Shade has accepted your sacrifice," I say, my voice thick as clotting blood.

Shemella's head whips up first, their brows furrowed—recognition or concern. They know the Dark better than most. Then Eun-Min glances to me with the flame dancing in her eyes. Briony's expression is the one I seek, though. She delivers, that wide-eyed terror turning her inside out, and it's the most delicious sight.

I turn toward Cassie, still gripping her hand. "Two girls who thought they were worthier than Julia. That's what she wants you to pay."

"What the *fuck*," Cassie shrieks, trying to wrench away from me. But the shadows are like claws growing from my fingertips, wrapping up her forearm, pinning her. The Dark is like thorny vines reaching out for Briony.

"How did Cassie convince you to do it?" I ask Briony. "Did you really think Julia would be drunk with power?"

The Shade is speaking with me—but she is not me. She is in my blood, like spiced wine, but I am my own. I can see the Dark that lives underneath Westbrook. And I can see the darkness others can do to possess it—a darkness all their own.

"She was going to abuse it," Briony cries. "She wanted it too badly!"

I crook my fingers, and both Cassie and Briony wrench toward me, screaming, strangling on the oily black that surrounds them. "So do you."

Cassie's eyes fill with blood, the blood she spilled when she wrenched on Julia's steering wheel to smash them into the tree. The blood she'd shed if she'd taken control of the Shade instead. It pours down her face as she chokes and coughs, as her lips go blue and her face turns gray.

And Briony—she didn't want to take Julia's place. That much, I understand. She thought by stopping Julia, she was stopping something worse.

I'll be the something worse, since Julia can't.

"You shouldn't have listened to Cassie." I stand over Briony as she shudders and shakes, wheezing as her lungs refuse to fill. "She only ever wanted to be like Julia, but she was so much crueler. So now you're all stuck with me."

The Dark called each of us, and we each wanted it in our own way. But with the deaths of Julia's murderers underlining the power pulsing in my veins—

The Dark is mine now.

THE TRAGEDY OF CORY LANEZ: AN ORAL HISTORY

Inspired by Coriolanus

Tochi Onyebuchi

Volumnia: O, he is wounded; I thank the gods for't.

Menenius: So do I too, if it be not too much. Brings a' victory in his pocket? The wounds become him.

—ACT 2, SCENE 1

THE TRAGEDY OF CORY LANEZ: AN ORAL HISTORY

There are no monuments to Cory Lanez in the Rose Park neighborhood of Long Beach, California. Briefly, on Ohio Avenue, a poster of the rapper/singer had been taped to a palm tree and, over the course of a few days, several bouquets of goldenrod and roses had been laid at the makeshift memorial. Within the week, the whole thing had been dismantled, but not before the poster had been vandalized, a red X spray-painted across the seventeen-year-old boy's face. On a wall of Corky's Market, on East Fifteenth Street and Junipero Avenue, a mural to the musical artist had been painted in similar shades of goldenrod and crimson. It had lasted a few weeks, guarded by some of Lanez's most ardent fans and childhood friends, before being similarly defaced and, ultimately, painted over by the proprietor of Corky's.

"It brought too much trouble," he told me in a later interview.

🌹

It's like this all over Rose Park: on storefronts, in alleyways, along freeways, portraits or some other pictorial record of the boy, sometimes with details of what happened to him, will appear somewhere in Long Beach and remain for some time, his face haunting that corner of the city before evanescing into the ether. A ghost trawls Rose Park. The violent tearing down of these memorials tells the story of a figure almost universally hated in the neighborhood.

🌹

Cameron Marcus, more popularly known as Cory Lanez, was stabbed outside the Executive Suite nightclub on Redondo Avenue in the Belmont Heights district of Long Beach on April 2, 2019. He died six days later. Weeks of news coverage and remembrances followed. At his memorial service, those who spoke told stories not only of Mr. Lanez's musical career but of his vision for his Rose Park neighborhood and for the larger Long Beach area: his plans to build a clothing shop in a lot not far from his childhood home, the entrepreneurial center he had started to help neighborhood kids get involved in the tech industry from an early age, as well as the skate park he had planned on turning into a gallery for art installations displaying local talent. Notoriously, in attendance at that memorial service were members of both local Crip and Blood gangs as well as local elected officials and many of the music industry's most powerful titans. To look at the audience was to see evidence of a young man whose life had a widespread impact, his presence felt everywhere from local gangland rivalries to the affairs of those walking the halls of the local political establishment. To hear Cory Lanez spoken of like this, one would be mistaken for thinking those in the audience were preparing to bury a grown man who had lived half a dozen lives and not a seventeen-year-old boy.

The passing of Cory Lanez was felt widely throughout the music industry, with tributes from the likes of Kendrick Lamar and Billie Eilish. Everyone seems to have a Lanez story. As widely as his loss has been felt, it has been felt most deeply by those who knew him not only as a successful recording artist but as a son, a father, a lover, and a friend. This is his story, as told by those who knew him best.

Terence Stevens (member of the local CitiZens rap group): We was at school together, but we hated that nigga at first. Cory was always so standoffish. Or, at least, that's how it came across. He was quiet, never talked to nobody unless it was to hurt they feelings. (Laughing) Even then, he had bars. I think that's what made him such a good battle rapper later on, you know? One afternoon, in the cypher, I overheard him call the dude he was battling a "fragment." That's it. Fragment. (Laughing)

Herbert McKenzie (member of CitiZens): He *was* quiet. It could read as standoffish, but he also had this self-possession about him. We was in middle school and he seemed to already know who he was. Principles.

Menachem Adler (childhood friend and Lanez's longtime producer collaborator): I saw that, but it was weird. We got close very early on. Grade school. I was the only Jewish kid in the neighborhood. It was quiet for me. Always gettin' jumped, all of that. Cam was the first kid who would get in the way of the bullies. Long time, he was the only one.

Stevens: Yeah, y'all were thick as thieves.

Adler: Me being Jewish had nothing to do with why he sorta became my protector. It was like this barrier between me and everybody else, but it didn't matter with him. Matter fact, he was the one always asking about it. He wanted to learn.

Violet Marcus (mother): Self-possession. That's what it was with him. It was a tough childhood for him, but I made sure there were always books in the house. He actually used to be a pretty gregarious child. As a baby, he was always crawling around. I called him my little explorer. He wanted to know about everything. I think he really looked to his daddy in that regard. It's no secret Van was a Panther. Van wanted to make sure the boy knew where he came from and what it was like out there. I would watch them sometimes, and it looked so often like he was grooming a soldier, not a son. I did what I could to give him a childhood, but after Van was killed, I couldn't be around as much. I had to work three jobs just to keep the lights on. And that did something to Cameron. Suddenly, he has to eat his cereal with water, and I can't cook meals anymore. And when he does see his mother, she's always tired.

The night of January 12, 2009, Van Nathan Marcus was at the office of a local nonprofit and food bank—Breadren—when LAPD officers raided the building on suspicion that there were narcotics and guns on the premises. Marcus was armed at the time (he had a concealed carry license). In the ensuing confrontation, several volunteers were wounded, and Marcus was shot and killed. The district attorney declined to press charges against the officer who shot and killed Van Nathan Marcus. A subsequent wrongful death lawsuit against the city of Los Angeles went nowhere in the courts and nearly bankrupted the family in the process.

Adler: Cam never talked about his dad. But you could tell there was a seriousness about him.

Titus Lawrence (former member of the Piru Street Bloods): Lotta cats got involved in gang shit because they dads was locked up or dead. Some of them, it was like a family business. You know, your daddy's a Piru, so you're a Piru. Your daddy's Rollin 60s Crip, so you're Rollin 60s, feel me? A lot of us, it *was* like being made into a soldier.

Cornelius Thompson (former member of the Piru Street Bloods): And you had a lot of gangbangers was loud, you know? You post up on the corner with your chain, your kicks, and your strap. You ain't even have to open your mouth to be loud. But Cam was quiet even when we was bangin'. Everybody knew he was a Piru, but they also knew that if he was called in to deal with somethin', it was a wrap for you.

Lawrence: Bro was a warrior. Name rang bells all throughout Bompton. Imagine bein' fourteen, fifteen, and havin' the scars that he had.

Violet: It seemed like every day, he came home with some fresh wound. It became a ritual. He never said what happened, and I learned, after a while, to stop asking. I was just happy my baby was surviving. Still. I knew he was destined for something greater. I made sure there were always books in the house, but I also took him to the record store. We played a lot of Motown at our house, and some house music from Chicago from back in the day. But one day, he came up to me with an N.W.A. album. I think it was their first. And he asked me to buy it. I'll never forget the look on my Cameron's face when he came up to me and held it out to me. It seemed like such a strange thing. He could have stolen it, that wouldn't have been unheard of. He certainly had enough money to buy it himself. But we never played rap in the house, and I think he knew why. He knew I thought there was enough gang nonsense outside that I didn't want to bring it back into the house. But he was earnest. And there was a look in his eyes. Like he'd found something magical. So I bought it for him. If I'd known what would happen . . .

Adrian Young (senior VP of A&R at Volscian Records): A few years prior, we'd signed Aufset, and he'd come out of the same battle rap tradition that Cory Lanez seemed to come from. There's lore in music circles that says the two of them used to battle at school.

Stevens: Those battles were epic. In another time, they woulda been on those Smack DVD tapes everyone in the hood used to be passin' around. And that's when you really saw Cory shine. The gang shit was one thing. But, yo, when it came time to hurt someone's feelings during a battle? Forget it.

McKenzie: Legendary. They musta battled like four, five times while we was there.

Young: Aufset was making a name for himself on the mixtape circuit. He had the neighborhood behind him and pretty quickly picked up some sponsors. Ross wanted to sign him. Jay wanted to sign him. Even Em wanted to sign him. He did his own independent thing for a while, worked with local producers on this very grimy sound he wanted to perfect. It sounded like someone who'd listened to a lot of '90s New York hip-hop.

Stevens: A lot of cats was feelin' it, I'm not gonna lie. But it wasn't West Coast, feel me?

McKenzie: There's a special West Coast sound. Dre, Snoop, 'Pac, E-40, and the rest of those cats from the Bay. Game. All of them. You could be gangsta, but you could also be at a party. Auf had that East Coast vibe, and if you listened to him, you couldn't tell he was even from Cali. You could always tell with Cory.

Adler: So when Cam finally came to me and was like, "I wanna make music," it was the same thing as before. He already knew who he was. Wasn't just in his rhymes either. We spent I don't know how many hours in the studio I rigged up at a mutual friend's basement putting that sound together. Like, it wasn't just the hood. It was *this* hood. And that's how we made the *Rosa Parks* mixtape.

Lawrence: Yo, the *Rosa Parks* mixtape shook the entire hood. The birth of Cory Lanez.

Thompson: The whole hood rallied around him. He had us puttin' up posters. We were payin' out of our own pocket for radio advertisements.

Adler: We'd produced the album independently with what money we had or whatever people we knew would front us. Lotta folks didn't even ask for their money back. That's how much they believed in him when that first tape came out. Cory Lanez was this larger-than-life figure that the hood could put all their hopes and dreams in. It was a Serena Williams situation. Someone from your hood makes it to such a big stage and every time they win, it's like all of us win.

Thompson: But every time they lose . . .

Adler: That's the thing. We almost never lost.

Vera Gibson (partner, mother of Lanez's son, Mutasa): We'd been seeing each other for a little over a year by then. Our son, Mutasa, had been born. Cameron had suggested the name after hearing about this place in Zimbabwe.

Violet: Cameron's father could trace his ancestry back to Zimbabwe. Ultimately, it became a point of pride for him. For us. Everything in the house was Manicaland.

Vera: Mutasa was a few months old when *Rosa Parks* came out. Cameron and I met just as Cam was getting out of the gang life. I knew how it wearied him. He wouldn't show that to anyone. He needed you to know that he was ride-or-die, but it aged him. And I think having Mutasa helped him realize some things that made him ultimately leave that life behind. Over the next few years, Mutasa heard how everyone spoke about his father and even started calling him Cory. (Laughing) Cameron would try to get mad at it, but it was always our joke.

Julius Brown (former city councilman): And then the hood turned on him.

Silas Vale (local law enforcement community liaison): We'd been working on gang prevention initiatives, and I think there was tension between his burgeoning musical career and his efforts on the ground trying to better his community.

Adler: Nah, don't talk about Cory like that. There wasn't tension.

Thompson: You were the Feds' eyes and ears in Rose Park, and when Cam's star was bright enough, y'all swooped in. But you couldn't just shoot him or whatever, because the hood loved him. Wasn't no tension.

Brown: Cory Lanez was not a universally loved figure. As a city councilman, it was my job to be out there on the streets and know the concerns of the people. And, to a T, they felt when they listened to his music that they were being talked down to. They felt they were listening to a guy who couldn't be bothered with them, who thought they were lesser than him. Call it standoffishness, call it him being quiet and taciturn, but *that* was the mood on "the streets."

Stevens: Wasn't a problem for y'all until he started talking that Panther shit. When it was all stick talk, nobody had no kind of problem. But he started making music to elevate us, like N.W.A. did when they first came out, started really dishing the truth about our situation, then shit changed. He was just a regular hood nigga with a mixtape until he turned into someone that could do your job for you, Councilman.

Adler: So much was goin' good for Cory. That's when someone from Aftermath reached out and we started putting a terms sheet together for Cory to link up with Shady Aftermath. He woulda been their biggest West Coast artist since Game.

Thompson: He even had me in the room with him and Menz. Just goin' over terms. Now, I'm just a hood nigga from the block. I don't know shit about contracts, but it was always, "Yo, Com, this look right to you?" or "Com, what you think about this?"

Lawrence: He wanted all his people to make it. If he was movin' up, he wanted all of us to move up with him.

Thompson: Woulda been easy to sign the Aftermath deal and be done with it.

Adler: They were givin' us everything we were asking for.

Thompson: But Cory was so hardheaded. Couldn't put his principles to the side, not for the little shit, and *certainly* not for shit this big.

Vera: It really felt like everything was happening at once. Yesterday, he's this quiet boy who loves putting jalapeños on everything and who I'm having a baby with, and then the next day, he's a Grammy-nominated rapper and the police are constantly comin' by our house.

Stevens: I'm sure the councilman had nothin' to do with that.

Vera: When it got to be too much, we moved. He bought us a house in Calabasas. That's how much money he'd made off his music at that point as an independent artist.

Lanez's eagerly awaited debut album, Common-Wealth, *was years in the making, its origins tracing back to the* Rosa Parks *era. Released in October 2018, after he inked a partnership with Volscian Records,* Common-Wealth *was acclaimed as one of the year's most audacious, genre-bending, and impressive musical albums and, along with a Grammy nomination, launched Cory Lanez into the mainstream. Lanez would go on in the months that followed to collaborate with ScHoolboy Q, Bryson Tiller, JID, and Burna Boy.*

Young: It was so strange to watch this kid who'd put out a critically acclaimed mixtape and who'd just snagged a Grammy nomination move through the world like he didn't enjoy any of it. I mean, I got to know him a little better, and it was a little more complicated than that. It's always a little more complicated with him. But—

Violet: He was missed. I think he felt betrayed by his city. By Long Beach. By Rose Park. Almost everyone he'd loved and who'd been around him when he was low had turned against him. I'm sure part of it was envy. But I'm sure there was more. Rose Park is protective of its own. Whatever its problems, they're *our* problems.

Young: We were cognizant of all of that when we signed your son to our label. There's this widespread notion that we tried to soften his sound a little, have him stand in contrast to Aufset, but they complemented each other very well. They had a mutual respect for each other.

McKenzie: Lot of us felt betrayed by that. Aufset was someone else. He wasn't us. Lotta people looked at Auf and what he represented as the enemy. Like he was the death of West Coast rap. Then when he started singing, that was it.

Vera: Things did change when we moved to Calabasas. Cam spent more time by himself. He would vanish for days at a time. He became more closed off. It began to affect his relationship with Mutasa. Didn't feel like we was raisin' a kid the right way. So I moved back to Rose Park to be with Violet. It hurt me to leave him like that, but . . . it felt like he'd already left me.

Young: We worked to make sure that we could provide as welcoming an environment as we could. It wasn't just about the music. We take care of our artists. I know Cory and Aufset spent a lot of time together. They grew very close. It's easy to forget they're both kids. Cory turned seventeen, Aufset's a little older, but they were both working through things. Figuring each other out.

Adler: Rose Park wasn't the same without him. It was almost like he had to leave in order to really blow up. *That* hurt. We'd built something beautiful here.

Stevens: The hood holds on to hurt.

Lawrence: The guy we saw in videos and on TV, that wasn't our Cam. Cory Lanez was someone else. Dressin' different. The people he was hangin' with now. Totally switched up.

Violet: But he didn't look happy. He was coming back to do a show at Rose Park, him and your artist. And . . .

Adler: He'd called me about a week and a half before the Rose Park stop on his tour to tell me about meeting DJ Khaled. He was so hype, and the two of them really hit it off. He and Auf had a recording studio on one of the tour buses. And that night, Cory wrote a whole-ass record based off that one convo with Khaled. He was always a workhorse.

Lawrence: The Rose Park show felt, to a lot of people, like the ultimate disrespect.

Thompson: There wasn't a lot of love for Aufset in Rose Park. And I know it was supposed to be on some dead-the-beef shit, but after everything we'd watched Cory go through the past couple of years, the whole transformation, lotta niggas wasn't ready to see him again.

Vera: I told him not to come. (Crying) I told him not to come. Because I knew. I knew something bad would happen.

Violet: It was one of the toughest conversations I've ever had to have. The three of us—me, Vera, Mutasa—we went to Calabasas, and we prayed with Cameron that he skip the Rose Park show. It was too dangerous.

Vera: There was one moment, that afternoon, when Aufset came in, and I could feel the change in Cory's body. He was tense when we were in the room, but once Aufset was there, he loosened. There was an ease with them. And I saw it. So much made sense when I saw that.

Adler: During that phone call, I told him it might not be a good idea to do the Rose Park show. And we got into it. It got pretty heated. I was in tears by the end. Because I didn't want to lose him. I didn't want him to come back and for something to happen. I felt like I'd be responsible.

Vera: He and Aufset. People joked about it before when they would perform together. You'd see videos of them on Twitter, and pretty soon there'd be homophobic TikToks. It was like that. The replies in some of those tweets were just too horrible to look at sometimes. How could they say that about my partner? The father of our son? We loved each other. But I saw him and Aufset, and it wasn't a joke anymore. That . . . that distance I felt growing between us when we lived in Calabasas together, I thought that was because of the music and everything that came with it, but . . . (Crying)

Violet: He loved you, Vera. He always did. Cameron and I never had any talk about his sexuality. Whether he was gay or bi or . . . He behaved like the boys around him behaved, then he closed himself off, and he went somewhere I couldn't reach him.

On April 2, 2019, Lanez was reportedly seen waiting outside the Executive Suite gay, lesbian, and transgender bar and lounge. He'd recently visited several of his childhood haunts in Rose Park before riding with an associate to Belmont Heights. Earlier in the day, he'd taken pictures with fans and signed autographs.

According to unsealed transcripts of the grand jury proceedings, he was allegedly approached by several men claiming to be associates of Aufset. According to further testimony, they had asked him whether he planned on doing the Rose Park show. When he answered in the negative, they shook hands and Lanez turned to leave. After he did, one of the men stabbed Lanez in the back several times before three of the others joined in.

A nearby witness called an ambulance, administering aid as the 911 operator instructed before the paramedics arrived. But Lanez could not be saved.

Tyson Aufson, also known by his stage name Aufset, announced the cancellation of the Rose Park show on Twitter and Instagram, explaining, "I am struck with sorrow." He alluded to possible gang involvement in saying, "Though in this city he hath widow'd and unchilded many a one, which to this hour bewail the injury, yet he shall have a noble memory."

Aufset subsequently released a track in remembrance of Cory Lanez titled "Assist." Within 24 hours of its release, it was the highest streaming song on all platforms.

Out of the Storm

Inspired by King Lear

Joy McCullough

> *Shut up your doors, my lord; 'tis a wild night.*
> *My Regan counsels well. Come out o' the storm.*
>
> —Act 2, scene 4

(CORA, 15, and her sister GABI, 20,
in an ICU hospital room, the curtain drawn around the bed.)

CORA: She'll come.
GABI: She won't.
CORA: You think the worst of her.
GABI: With good reason.

(Beat.)

CORA: I get that it was hard for you when she
    left—
GABI: You don't know. I'm sure she seemed like
    a hero to you, blazing some new trail,
    striking out at sixteen, but it wasn't
    like that.
CORA: I do know.
GABI: She left and didn't look back.
CORA: Still. Our father's on life support. How
    could she not—

GABI: No warning, just gone. And now it's been two years. You don't know her like I do.
(Beat.)
Marybeth, hi. Yeah, there's no update, just read the same statement from the morning livecast. Prayers welcome, donations to the ministry. It is not tacky. It's what he'd want.
(She hangs up.)
What? Don't judge. We haven't hit our quarterly goal yet.

CORA: I didn't say anything.

GABI: You never do.

(A commotion in the hallway.)

ROWAN *(off-stage)*: I *am* family! How do I convince you I'm his daughter?! Just because I'm not on the livestream every week, I swear to God. Check the website. Pretty sure I haven't been cropped out of the photos yet.

GABI: She came.

CORA: Told you.

ROWAN *(off-stage, sweetly)*: Thank you so much. And God bless.
(ROWAN, 18, enters with a suitcase.)
What's up, bitches?

GABI: Oh my gosh, Rowan! Keep your voice down!

ROWAN: Is that any way to welcome the prodigal daughter?

GABI: There's press everywhere. The nurse's father is a major donor! You can't just waltz in here, all foulmouthed. Is that a tattoo?!

ROWAN *(to CORA)*: Look at you, baby sister. I wouldn't have even recognized you.

CORA: Hi.

ROWAN: Hi.

CORA: How was . . . Yemen?

ROWAN: Somalia. Yemen was last week. But I didn't file any stories from Yemen; my contacts weren't as good as I hoped.

CORA: Oh.

GABI: How are we supposed to know where you even are?

ROWAN: Follow me, like Cora does. I'm @RowanReports.

GABI: So I can watch you thrill-seeking in war zones? No thank you.

ROWAN: I'm doing important work.

GABI: Fine. I'm just saying, it would be a lot easier if you called occasionally.

ROWAN & CORA: Nobody calls.

ROWAN: Jinx. Buy me a Coke.

CORA: Um. Okay? There's a vending machine—

ROWAN: Not for real. It's a thing we say, don't you remember?

CORA: . . .

ROWAN: Sugar and caffeine only make my jet lag worse, anyway.

GABI: Your body is a temple. And yet you're still smoking?

ROWAN: Why are you going through my bag?

GABI: I'm looking for a charger.

(ROWAN grabs her bag, finds a charger, and shoves it at GABI. GABI plugs her phone in. Silence. At one point, CORA almost speaks, but then chickens out. Finally:)

ROWAN: So do they wait to read the will until after we pull the plug?

GABI: Rowan! What is the matter with you?

(GABI bursts into tears and runs from the room.)

ROWAN: Oh my god, the drama.
(CORA stands.)
Don't go after her. It's what she wants.

CORA: That's why I should.

ROWAN: You're too pure. She's manipulating us. Wonder where she learned that.

CORA: Gabi's not like Dad.

ROWAN: No? She made my entire sixth birthday party about her because of a skinned knee.

CORA: She was only eight.

ROWAN: Tell me she hasn't done something similar to you in the last year.

(Beat.)

CORA: This isn't a skinned knee.

ROWAN: No. It's not.
(Silence.)
Are you dating anyone?

CORA: Seriously? You can't just show up after literal years away and make chitchat. And what are you even talking about? I'm only fifteen. Were you allowed to date at fifteen?

ROWAN: Why do you think I left?
(Beat.)
Look, what am I supposed to say? I didn't abandon you—I knew Gabi would never leave. But I reached a point where

it was clear: if I didn't make a break
for it, I'd get sucked in and lose myself
completely. Maybe it's different for you.

CORA: You don't know what it's like for me.

(Beat.)

ROWAN: Gabi was the one who used to dream about
getting out. She was going to be a traveling preacher, leading revivals all
over the world. Of course, that's before
she bought into Dad's whole thing about
women in leadership.

CORA: She basically runs the ministry.

ROWAN: Through Anthony. She's still engaged to
that loser?

CORA: Anthony's nice. Mostly. And she has official duties of her own.

ROWAN: Does she ever get to preach?
I'm not trying to be an asshole, Cor.
It's just easier with some distance to
see . . . Honestly, I hope you get out
the first second you can. I'll even help
you. It'll be easier now, with Dad—

CORA: Are you rooting for him to die?

ROWAN: He's already dead, hon. It's just the ma-
chines.

CORA: I know that. I'm not a baby. But I don't
know how you can sit there and tell me
things will be better when he's dead.

ROWAN: Not better. Easier. And obviously I don't
mean everything. Just your choices about
what to do with your life—you won't have
to weigh his opinions or face his wrath
if you have some of your own. You can
date, if you want to. And oh my god,
college! You're not locked into going

	to Spurgeon. You could go to a state school. Or take a gap year!
CORA:	Sorry if I'm not thinking about my own future right now.
ROWAN:	Fine. Sorry I brought it up.

(Beat.)

> It's just, there's nothing wrong with thinking about your own needs.

| CORA: | There's also nothing wrong with considering others'. |

(Silence.)

> It's like you don't even understand how many people will be devastated by his death. The memorial's going to be nationally televised. World leaders will be there. I know he wasn't perfect, but do you even care how many people will mourn him?

ROWAN:	I've met people literally across the globe who know his name, who quote his books. A woman in Nairobi found out who I was and wanted me to touch her dying baby.
CORA:	Tell me you didn't give her an earful about the real Ray Lawrence—
ROWAN:	I touched the fucking baby, Cor. And sat there with the mother while he died. I may have sung.
CORA:	*Amazing Grace*?
ROWAN:	What else? But how many brilliant sermons, how many uplifted lives do you suppose it takes to outweigh each one he destroyed? My mother, your mother—
CORA:	Stop. Just stop it.

(CORA exits.)

| ROWAN: | Rowan Lawrence, clearing rooms since . . . forever. |

*(She checks her phone, sends a few
texts, then leaves a voice mail.)*
Hey, love. I made it. Just wanted to hear
your voice, but . . . Anyway, I'm here.
I miss you. I would rather be in a war
zone right now. A different war zone than
this one. Just . . . call me if you can.

*(GABI enters with a clipboard and
some paperwork.)*

GABI: I already read these, but you have to.
Welcome to adulthood.

ROWAN: You already know my vote.

GABI: Pull the plug and go out dancing?

ROWAN: Or drinking. I'm flexible.

GABI: This isn't a joke. This is your father's
life! There's a reason he stipulated
that we both have to sign—

ROWAN: A final fuck you to his oldest daughters?

GABI: If you don't care about him, at least
think about Cora. We're all she has now.
If you could attempt to not be a complete narcissist—

ROWAN: Do not call me that.

GABI: Truth hurts?

ROWAN: It's unfair and you know it. Tell me you
know it.

(Beat.)

GABI: Fine. You're just phenomenally selfish.

ROWAN: I can own that. But I came, didn't I? It
wasn't for him.
*(ROWAN studies the paperwork while
GABI responds to messages on her
phone.)*

It's pretty messed up, don't you think?
Requiring us to be the ones to decide
this? To agree? He could have just . . .

GABI: What? What were his other options? For
all the people around him, he wasn't really close to anyone.

ROWAN: Except for whoever was sharing his bed.

GABI: Don't start.

ROWAN: It's true.

GABI: But it's not. Of course there were women,
but he couldn't confide in them. Have
you ever thought about how lonely he
must be?

ROWAN: There's a difference between lonely and
power hungry.
           (Silence.)
           Do you think he ever—with Cora—

GABI: No. I made sure of it.

           (CORA enters with a Caffeine-Free Diet
           Coke for ROWAN.)

CORA: I still think you're the worst.

ROWAN: No arguments here.

GABI: Ro's had some time to look at the paperwork. Maybe we should—

CORA: You wanted to preach, Gabi?

GABI: What?

CORA: Rowan said you wanted to preach. When
you were younger.

GABI: Oh, no. I mean, I also wanted to be a
unicorn.

ROWAN: We went on that revival tour when Cora
was tiny, remember? The crowd was getting restless, and you marched up to the
pulpit and started preaching!

CORA: How old was she?

ROWAN: Like seven. I was so scared what Dad was going to do when he found out, but he just laughed it off.

GABI: Well. Yeah, then, in front of everyone. After was a different story.

(Beat.)

ROWAN: What did he do?

GABI: It doesn't matter.

ROWAN: Of course it matters!

GABI: I don't want to talk about this stuff, with him right there—

ROWAN: Maybe that's exactly why we should. A chance to speak when he can't silence us? I never thought that would happen.

GABI: It wasn't what you're thinking. Physical or whatever. It was just words.

ROWAN: Words are never just words.

GABI: Just, you know. I was so tired and wanted to go to bed. But I had to keep standing there while he lectured me about my place, made me quote scripture about women keeping silent. When I cried, it was proof that I'd never be strong enough to lead.

ROWAN: Did he say that? Or did you think it?

GABI: I don't . . . I don't remember.

CORA: It doesn't matter anyway.

(Silence.)

ROWAN: Okay, so if I understand these documents—

CORA: You should preach. At the memorial service.

GABI: Don't be ridiculous. He already planned everything. He wants Pastor Matt—

CORA: So?

GABI: So . . . it's what he wanted! Last wishes and all that!

CORA: He always got what he wanted! Just because he wanted it doesn't mean it's right.

ROWAN: Amen to that.

GABI: Anthony wouldn't like it. The deacons would never allow it.

CORA: Forget the deacons.

ROWAN: Definitely forget Anthony.

CORA: Would you do it? If you could?

(Pause.)

GABI: Maybe? I don't know. I'm not sure if that's the way I want to finally stand up there and speak.

ROWAN: Fuck, yeah. You deserve a pulpit on your own terms.

GABI: Like it's that easy.

ROWAN: Sure it is. Start a podcast, a YouTube channel. Write a book. I guarantee there'd be an audience for what you have to say.

GABI: I'm not sure what I have to say. I'm not you.

ROWAN: Lucky. Being the one who blurts out every thought isn't always fun.

GABI: It looks fun, to be honest.

ROWAN: I always put on a hell of a show.

CORA: So what's the real you, then? If this is an act?

(Pause.)

ROWAN: I don't know. The honesty is real. The bluntness. I guess it's just the part where it seems like I don't care how

people respond to it . . . that's the
act. Like, I gave this giant middle finger to Dad and the ministry by leaving,
but he still follows me everywhere I go.
His voice in my head.

You're lucky, Cor.

CORA: How?

ROWAN: I know you think I'm an insensitive ass-
            hole to be saying this now, but you'll
            get to make choices, decide your truth
            without risking the judgment or manipu-
            lation or fallout . . . I envy you.

CORA: I grew up with him too, you know.

ROWAN: I know, but—

CORA: Anyway, I don't even know my truth.

ROWAN: But that's okay! That can be your truth!
            What will you do, without Dad to stop
            you?

GABI: Maybe lay off her, Ro.

CORA: I want to find my mom.

ROWAN: Wow. You had that ready.

CORA: No, I . . . I hadn't even thought about
            it. It never seemed like a possibility
            before.

ROWAN: It wasn't.

GABI: It probably still isn't, just realisti-
            cally.

CORA: I know. I don't even know if she's alive.

ROWAN: But it's sweet that you want to try.

CORA: It's not sweet.

ROWAN: No, I—

CORA: I'm not sweet! Or pure! Stop saying things
            like that. You're not only saying I'm
            young. You're calling me naïve and . . .
            and untouched, like I've somehow lived
            this idyllic life. You've been gone for
            so long, Ro, or wrapped up in running

things, Gabi—neither of you know. Neither
of you know what it's been like for me!

ROWAN: Cora. Fuck. Did he—

CORA: No, don't. Don't ask if he touched me,
like it matters. Like it's worse if he
hurt me with his body. How is it worse? He
still got inside me. You know what that's
like. You just said, Gabi. Standing there
as a child, sobbing to go to bed and having to listen to him tearing you down?
None of that was different for me!

GABI: You're right. I'm so sorry. I just, I
thought you were special.

CORA: That's the worst one. Nobody ever say I
was special to him ever again, please?

ROWAN (to GABI): I thought you were watching
out for her—

GABI: I did everything I could! Maybe if you
hadn't left—

CORA: Please. Don't do this here, with him there.
Still breathing, still sucking the oxygen
out of the room. Still tearing us apart.

GABI: You're right. I'm sorry. I'm so sorry.

(Pause.)

ROWAN: In his own twisted way, he brought us
together with all these hoops he left us
to jump through.

CORA: That's not why he did it.

ROWAN: I know. But fuck his why, because we're
here now, together.

(Pause.)

GABI: What if . . . what if we didn't let him
have the last word?

CORA: If we didn't let him tear us apart.

ROWAN: What if the way we honor the good in his
         legacy is by standing up for the truth?

GABI: But the truth—

ROWAN: I know.

         (Beat.)

CORA: Together.

GABI: Together.

*(ROWAN takes the clipboard and
signs the paperwork then hands it
to GABI. GABI signs then sits with
CORA on the love seat. ROWAN drifts
over to the window, where she begins
to sing softly, Amazing Grace.)*

End Scene

Elsinore

Inspired by Hamlet

Patrice Caldwell

First Clown: Is she to be buried in Christian burial, when she willfully seeks her own salvation?

Second Clown: I tell thee she is. Therefore make her grave straight. The crowner hath sat on her and finds it Christian burial.

First Clown: How can that be, unless she drowned herself in her own defense?

Second Clown: Why, 'tis found so.

First Clown: It must be *se offendendo*. It cannot be else. For here lies the point: if I drown myself wittingly, it argues an act. And an act hath three branches—it is to act, to do, and to perform. Argal, she drowned herself wittingly.

Second Clown: Nay, but hear you, Goodman Delver—

First Clown: Give me leave. Here lies the water. Good. Here stands the man. Good. If the man go to this water and drown himself, it is, will he nill he, he goes. Mark you that. But if the water come to him and drown him, he drowns not himself. Argal, he that is not guilty of his own death shortens not his own life.

—Act 5, scene 1

28 April 1892

arkness sweeps across the graveyard as my heart pounds with fear. The remnants of the gravediggers' words—that Camilla, my best friend, didn't deserve a Christian burial—fill the silence. The gravediggers sang and riddled as they prepared her hallowed ground. All the while telling tales about the late duke's daughter, Anne—the late duke's *crazy* daughter, Anne, whose madness—they claimed—was the cause of Camilla's death.

If only they knew the truth.

But how could they? They wouldn't believe it. I barely do myself.

The church clock chimes, and my attention turns to the full moon. I shiver as a breeze rustles through my hair and crawls down my spine. None of it matters, not their words, not my mother's conviction that my uncle (turned stepfather) is innocent. Soon we all shall know the truth.

Besides, maybe I am mad. Maybe Camilla and I are mad to believe what we do. After all, is not madness just what others do not understand? Believing in things that shouldn't exist. Seeking revenge, not justice. As I have learned, you must redefine what is right and what is wrong when those who are supposed to be just are anything but.

And so, I deceived my mother—I deceived them all, playing the fool while Camilla played with her life. Why, just an hour ago, I climbed in her grave, danced about it, and begged to be buried alive with her until they all left, certain of my madness. My mother hesitated as she walked out of the cemetery. For a moment, I thought she'd turn back. Ask me what was really going on. Promise me that this time she'd listen, that this time she'd believe me. But she merely adjusted her coat and followed my uncle back to Elsinore. Reminding me once again that she would always choose him, and thus her status, over me. I must—I will—end this pestilence upon Elsinore, the hall I used to call home, a home this place is not and will never be for as long as my uncle holds power over my family and friends.

The twelfth chime rings, echoing across the graveyard. Two fingers peek through the dirt, then an arm—pearlescent in the moonlight—then a face, then a body, until all of her is revealed. White dress clinging to her limbs in the breeze, still in the gown she wore when she'd supposedly drowned.

When she looks at me, she wears the wickedest smile. Camilla faces me, the near product of the monster we now face. Now I know, now I am certain: my father was killed by a vampire.

LETTER FROM THE DUCHESS OF ELSINORE TO LADY ANNE

18 April 1892

DEAR DAUGHTER,—You are a woman of seven and ten. It is my wish that you and your ~~uncle~~ stepfather, Andrew, can see past your differences, for your dear mother's sake if not your own. I know you miss your father, but even he would not want you to mourn so—it has been two months. It is unbecoming for one of your upbringing to carry on like this. Come home, my daughter. You spend too much time studying. Even with your handsome dowry, your fondness for books over peers will make you very unattractive to potential suitors.

I urge you this time not to leave.

Your Mother,
Penny
Duchess of Elsinore

LETTER FROM THE DUKE OF ELSINORE
TO LADY ANNE

19 April 1892

MY DEAREST NIECE,—Your mother tells me that you shall arrive in three days' time. I am anxiously expecting you. I do hope that we can put ~~my brother's~~ your father's untimely death behind us and move forward as a family. For your sake if not your mother's. I trust that your journey from the Wittenberg school in London will be a happy one and that you will enjoy your time back at home.

Your Stepfather,
Andrew
Duke of Elsinore

22 April 1892

LADY ANNE'S JOURNAL

Left London at 8:35 p.m. Should have left earlier, but the train was an hour late. And then, of course, there were even more delays on the tracks.

Arrived in Elsinore a couple hours later. The strangest thing happened. A woman, around my mother's age, begged me to stay with her and her husband for the night. They claimed it wasn't safe for a young lady to be out at this time. Not because of worries about my virtue. But because of a ghost that has been roaming these parts.

Yes, a ghost.

I tried not to laugh. I don't think I hid it well.

I politely declined. I couldn't imagine what my mother would say if I told her I was delayed because I feared ghosts. She'd think I was lying to get out of coming home. Of course, I'd prefer to not come home, but telling falsehoods wouldn't aid me.

Besides, I truly did miss my mother. It was my uncle I could do without. Especially since they'd married before my father's body was even cold.

My mother's marriage to my father had been a loveless one. That was obvious to anyone. "Good morning" and "good evening" were the only words they ever exchanged. The two were introduced when my mother was younger than me, by a friend of her mother who was known for pairing "dollar princesses" (rich and beautiful American women) with indebted and titled English men. My mother, the sole daughter of an American financier, had the biggest dowry my father had ever seen. A dowry that led his family to overlook my mother's heritage—her mother, my grandmother, was a Black freedwoman—in favor of her family's ability to put forth enough money to allow them to fully repair their decaying estate, among many other things.

Of course, her marriage to my uncle seemed like just another transaction. Because I was a girl, my father's title passed to his next male relative: my uncle. Therefore, by marrying my mother, he kept access to her money, and by marrying him, my mother retained the status she'd grown to love.

Still, she claimed she was in love with my uncle—words she'd never once uttered about my father—and so for her I would return home.

Oh, look! I see it now. Finally, the coach is coming!

Left the station at 11:42 p.m.

The journey to Elsinore Hall was darker than I remembered. The sliver of moonlight reflected in the swelling hills of the surrounding village, painting them in wonderful shades of purple and blue.

I leaned out the window, and the driver looked back at me. Be careful, he said, once again touching—no, gripping the cross on his chest. The night is chilly and many ghosts roam, he said.

The villagers have always been a superstitious bunch but now seemed even more than usual.

I murmured something, humoring him as he continued to ramble.

It is said that even the ghost of the dead duke roams.

At that I perked up. I'd been away at school for years; he likely didn't recognize me. Glad I had not revealed myself, I posed a question. *What do you mean the duke's ghost?*

*It is said that the duke is restless and cannot yet be at peace. That he walks these parts looking to—*Just then, he stopped. Down the road, maybe in a distant farmhouse, a dog howled. A howl so loud, I thought it wolves. But wolves do not live in these parts.

I shook my head. The man's tales were getting to me, making me hear things that clearly weren't there. What would my mother say? That it was unbecoming for a young lady of my status to believe in such childish things as ghosts.

But then the howl happened again. The man jerked; he clearly heard it, too. And the horses strained and reared. The driver spoke to them in a low tone, but they kicked at the dirt as if fending off something in their path. When I looked out the coach, I saw a faint blue light that disappeared as soon as it came.

The horses reared up again. The driver yelled, but it did no good. The coach tumbled onto its side, and I fell out. Quickly, I scrambled up. *Are you okay?* I asked the driver. The horses bolted away into the dark.

I squinted as a figure approached in the distance. My blood grew cold. It was clad in military regalia that had once hung in my father's office—an outfit he'd always say to me that he wished to be buried in. The figure looked me in the eye. At once, I was filled with dread.

Papa? I asked.

As I took it in, there was but one thing I knew: the driver had been right—it was my father's ghost.

He leaned into me, and then he whispered.

One, that he had been murdered.

Two, that his brother, my uncle, had himself done the deed.

23 April 1892

LADY ANNE'S JOURNAL

8:31 p.m.

It's been a day since that dreadful night in which my father's ghost came to me. Since then, my sleep has been restless, my dreams plagued with the words he whispered to me.

One, that he had been murdered.

Two, that his brother, my uncle and now stepfather, had himself done the deed.

And so, I did the rational thing. I told my mother. Well, not entirely rational, as she didn't believe me. She went so far as to claim I had lost my mind.

But I know what I saw.

I'll never forget what I heard.

And so, I left her room, swallowing my tears like I used to all those years ago, back when my mother cared more about impressing society ladies who'd never accept her than spending time with me. My father was the one person who understood me, who supported my dream of going to Somerville College, who convinced Mother to let me go to boarding school rather than be tutored at home like most girls my age. Now that he was gone, she would force me into a society lady in order to secure a proper marriage—one that would finally give her the acceptance she wanted.

Clearly, I was on my own again.

I paced in my chamber, trying to sort everything out. I didn't know much about my uncle. He had always been distant growing up. Taking trips constantly here and there. Never before desiring to marry and settle down. He had never been kind to me, but never cold either. He treated me simply as if I didn't exist.

My dead father would have nothing to gain from blaming his brother for his death. But my uncle would have everything to gain from killing his brother. And if he really did kill him, then he didn't just rob me of a parent, he took away my future—my dreams of college—too.

My mother thinks me mad.

I must keep this to myself.

I must find evidence to convict him. I need proof.

And I shall chronicle every moment here lest my mind do deceive me.

10:03 p.m.

I was sitting at my desk, looking out the window into the courtyard, when a lady in white walked by. She was in the courtyard holding a candlestick. The wax was dripping down her hand, but she didn't flinch, she didn't shiver—even though she was wearing but a nightgown. It was as if she herself were a ghost. A fact I might've further considered if she hadn't turned her head, just so, in my direction. The moonlight hit her pale skin, and I knew she was very much alive. For it was my childhood friend, Miss Camilla.

Last I heard from her, she was visiting her brother at Oxford. What was she doing here?

But when I looked back up from my journal, she was gone. I must investigate. I shall return.

LETTER FROM MISS CAMILLA WHITBECK TO MR. SAMUEL WHITBECK

24 April 1892

MY DEAREST BROTHER,—Forgive my delay in writing. I'm sorry I had to leave you so suddenly. As you know, the Duchess of Elsinore asked me to come and stay with her, saying I would bring comfort to her after her husband's untimely death. She has always watched out for me, just as much as you, ever since Mama passed. So, I felt I owed her that.

I know I should have written sooner. To ask if classes are going well. Or whether you've gotten into any mischief without me. But I must admit, I haven't been myself lately. It's like I keep forgetting things I know I've done, almost like someone else is operating my mind.

And to add to it, there's something odd in the air. Why, just the other day, I found out that Anne returned. I thought I'd see her at dinner, but when I asked the duchess, she replied with a faraway look in her eyes that Anne hasn't been herself lately. I can't help but wonder if whatever is ailing Anne has anything to do with my lapses in memory.

I have bags under my eyes—eyes often bloodshot. I feel as if I'm missing sleep. When I wake, my back aches and even more strange are my blackened heels as if I've been moving through the night while asleep—without even my slippers on. And then . . . I am afraid you'll think me mad. But sometimes when I'm alone, I swear I hear someone talking to me . . . I knew I recognized the voice, but I just couldn't place it. Until yesterday. When the new duke, the duchess's new husband, the very brother of her former, joined us at dinner. I must've been daydreaming, for when he called my name, it was the voice from my dreams.

You'll think me silly for even writing this. But if I don't, I worry I'll forget.

Sam, I fear I've been visited by the devil.

Something is rotten here.

28 April 1892

Camilla sneezes, blowing dirt out her nose, then climbs out the grave. "Next time, you're getting buried." She dusts herself off.

"Next time?" I lift an eyebrow. "Isn't the whole idea that this never happens again?"

She shrugs. "Now that I think about it, it wasn't all that bad. In fact, it was kind of fun. What was it you said again?

Never have you loved anyone as deeply as Camilla, that forty thousand brothers could not outdo your love for me?" She doubles over laughing. "I'm never letting you forget that." Out of her pocket, she pulls a potion. *The* potion. With which she faked her death, slowing her heart to a low rate, making it seem like she truly was dead.

I scoff. "You have a strange definition of fun."

"So, what next?" she asks as she comes beside me.

I walk over to a bench just to the left, to the side of the graveyard in which we stand. "I don't know." The part we had planned for, making everyone—especially my uncle—believe that she's dead, is over. "Somehow we have to prove that he's a monster known to others only through penny dreadfuls."

"We're not going to prove he's dead," she says, coming to sit beside me on the bench.

"Well, then, I don't see how else we're going to get rid of him."

"Oh, Anne. Haven't you any imagination?" With a wicked smile, she pulls out the penny dreadful rolled up inside her pocket.

No. 1
No. 2, 3, and 4 are Presented, Gratis with this No.
VINCENT THE VAMPIRE
or the
Knight of Blood
A Romance of Exciting Interest
by the author of
A Maiden's Revenge, Grace Van Helsing
Sold by all Newsagents everywhere
PRICE ONE PENNY.

Camilla flips to a page detailing "Vincent the Vampire" being staked by his lover. She places the open paper in my lap. "We're going to kill him ourselves."

"Kill him?" I stand from the bench, and the pamphlet falls to the ground. "Are you actually crazy? He's my uncle," I whisper as if I'm afraid to speak such truths aloud, as if I can't believe she's suggesting such a terrible thing.

"Well, he killed your father," she says, hands on her hips. "And he put me under his spell, drinking my blood, trying to make me like him. He would've succeeded, too, had we both not figured it out. I'd say it's the lesser evil that he deserves to die."

I shake my head. "We can't go playing God." I take in the graveyard around us where many generations of my family are interred. My gaze lands on a skull, leaning against a tombstone. *Reginald,* the tomb reads, with nothing else but the date of his birth and death.

I walk over to the tomb and kneel in the earth. Then, with my right hand, I pick up the skull. "Alas, poor Reggie," I whisper. "I knew him."

Camilla comes beside me and rolls her eyes. "That is not Reggie's skull, his remains are likely far beneath the earth."

"But it could be his," I say, remembering how he would laugh. Reggie was our jester, but he was more than that to me. Aside from Camilla and my father on his infrequent visits, Reggie was my companion. He'd tell me stories about my ancestors—brave battles fought; noble deeds done. "He always knew how to bring me comfort, and now he's dead. One day, we'll all look like this. No matter how noble, how fair, how great—we're all bones and ashes in the end."

Camilla places a hand on my back. "I know this isn't what

you asked for—I know this shouldn't be your burden to carry. But if he is this beast, this monster we think he is, if we let him go and he kills others, then it will be on us. We made a choice to act, to get this far, we cannot turn back now."

Some choice. "It's not like my father's ghost asked me if I wanted to know the truth. He just told me, taking my free will from me."

"Maybe." She shrugs. "But you chose to believe him, you chose to believe me. We can no sooner turn from our choices than we can the truth."

"What truth?" I ask.

She takes Reggie's skull from me and stares at it. "That your uncle is a monster and monsters must be killed," she says as if it's that simple.

But of course, it isn't. "What if by hunting a monster we become monsters?" I counter.

She places the skull back atop the grave. "Anne—"

A twig snaps. I hold my finger up to my mouth. "Shh," I say as I hear footsteps. Someone is approaching. "Quick. Hide. We can't let whoever it is see you."

Dread fills her eyes. Her thoughts—what if it's my uncle?— are as clear as the twinkling stars above us. "Hide," I say. "Go now."

She darts away, crouching behind a tree. I tense, unsure of what to do. If I run, it makes it look worse, if I stay, what if he kills me? But it's not my uncle at all. Camilla's brother, Sam, rounds the corner of the church, coming into the graveyard. His green eyes are burning bright, and before I can react, he charges at me. I jump to the side, trying to get out of the way. But he's faster and punches me in the jaw.

"That's for my sister," he says.

25 April 1892

LADY ANNE'S JOURNAL

7:59 p.m.

I tried to find Camilla after I saw her the other night, but when I reached the courtyard she wasn't there—just a trail of footprints that eventually disappeared. I decided to go to dinner with my mother, hoping that she'd be there, but all Mother said was that Camilla wasn't well. She barely acknowledged my existence otherwise—so much for her wanting her "dear daughter" to return.

But none of those moments compare to what I saw after dinner. A sight more troublesome than even my father's ghost. I wouldn't dare write it here had I not promised myself I would, that this would be a place where I'd recount all.

I was walking back to my chambers, which are on the other side of the castle from where my mother likes to informally have dinner. My uncle, whom I've only seen once since I arrived, was absent. That time I saw him was bad enough, he and my mother together looked like two people without remorse—even without proof, other than my father's word, I believed he did it. How else would one so casually be with the wife of his own brother or the brother of her own husband— even if my mother and father weren't close?

Anyway, I was walking back to my rooms when I heard a muffled scream. It was coming from a spare bedroom. Through the cracked door, I could see my uncle. Before him was a woman, a maid, by the looks of her uniform. She wore a high collar, which he promptly undid. I steeled myself, certain I was about to witness an affair. Not that it would've mattered what I saw, I told myself, for my mother would never believe me. Of course, given what I saw, she's definitely not going to believe me. With a caress of his hand upon her pale neck, where two other bite marks already were, he bit her, drinking deep.

Then, as if he knew someone was there, he looked up at me. Or rather, he looked in my direction but did or said nothing to acknowledge I was there or that it was me he saw. His eyes, normally bright green, were a deep, dark red—the very color of the blood coating his mouth and running down the woman's neck. As he stared, dread seeped into my heart. A coldness grew there that I have never known.

I tore myself away from his stare and ran all the way to my rooms. When I got here, there was but a simple note:

Dear Stepdaughter,
I would be honored if you'd join me the day after tomorrow. I remember you used to be quite the accomplished equestrian. I hear the trails are glorious this time of year.

Sincerely,
Andrew

He must know I saw him. He has to know that I saw him . . . drinking? From a maid's neck. His sharpened teeth, biting into her and draining her blood. I have to figure out a plan now. All of this must be connected.

Wait, someone's knocking on my door. I must remain calm. I shall return.

10:11 p.m.

It was Camilla. She asked me to save her life.

25 April 1892

MISS CAMILLA'S JOURNAL

10:13 p.m.

I went to Anne and told her that I thought her uncle was a vampire and that he was possessing me. The strangest part is she believed me.

Earlier today, I sent word to the duchess that I was sick—it wasn't that far off from the truth—and went to the old library. The late duke loved that library. The duchess never used it as a result, and the new duke was rarely seen during the day. So, I spent all day there, looking for any clues. Any records, any accounts of what I've been going through. And it's not just me. Something is up with some of the staff, too. They look paler, sickly almost, as if they had lost a lot of blood.

And then I found it, my account, only it wasn't what I expected. It was a penny dreadful, rolled up and shoved between two other books. One of those pamphlets sold on the street, tales written to scare and surprise. The author of this one was a Miss Grace van Helsing. "A romantic suspense author by day and a monster hunter by night," claimed her biography. I might've laughed at that, if, after all this, I could've mustered up a laugh. Instead, I read the stories, all four of them. And then I started finding similarities between the novel's young maiden and myself. The memory lapses, the fatigue, the increased sensitivity to sunlight. She was being enthralled by a vampire, which meant that I was, too.

A grand leap? Maybe. But was it not Sherlock Holmes who said, "When you have eliminated the impossible, whatever remains, however improbable, must be the truth"? I needed another opinion. So, like a detective myself, I headed to Anne's rooms determined to lay out all that I knew.

Maybe she had been avoiding me, maybe she didn't even know I was here. But I was determined to make her listen to me. I needed an ally; I couldn't do this alone.

She opened the door as soon as I knocked, her face the palest yellowish brown, like she'd seen something terrible, like the unfathomable was true. At once, I knew that she knew something too. The dread, the fear in her face all but confirmed it. And when we finished laying out all of the facts, we came to this conclusion:

Her uncle, Duke of Elsinore, was in fact a vampire. And, like any vampire, he must be stopped.

Now, we just have to make everyone think Anne's even crazier so as to not draw attention to our plans, which shouldn't be too hard, given that she told her mother she spoke to her father's ghost. Then there's the matter of faking my death—to get out from the duke's thrall—which will be a challenge. But we have to throw her uncle off somehow. We can't let him know what we know.

Now, we have a plan. Soon we shall have our revenge.

THE DAILY TELEGRAPH.

No. 11,528. London, Thursday, April 28, 1892.
ONE PENNY.

DEATHS.

TAYLOR—On the 27th at Elsinore Hall. Miss Camilla Whitbeck was found drowned, in a brook, of unknown circumstances.

Funeral to be this evening. Of her death, Duchess Penny Taylor said, "One woe doth tread upon another's heel, so fast they follow."

28 April 1892

I stumble back, nearly hitting my head on Reggie's tombstone, as I reel from Sam's punch. "You're not supposed to hit a lady." I spit out blood.

Sam scoffs. "You may be the daughter of a duchess and duke, but you're no lady. Was it not you who, at age eight, convinced me to put crickets into your mother's bed?"

I laugh as the memory returns to me, but Sam does not. "A punch for old times' sake, eh?"

"You shouldn't be here," he says, ignoring me. "You don't deserve to be here."

"Camilla was my friend, I deser—"

"You're the reason she's dead," he yells. "I heard you drove her mad talking about seeing ghosts." He pulls out his sword and points it at my chest. "Tell me why I shouldn't kill you now."

"Sam." I raise my hands. A million thoughts race through my head. Clearly, our plan, spreading rumors about how crazy I am, worked a little too well.

"Don't move." He presses the blade to my cheek. The cold steel drives shivers up my spine.

"I'm not the real enemy here."

"Who is?" He smirks. "God? Are you going to try to tell me that it was just her time to die?" Hand shaking, he brings the blade down to my neck. "Are you seriously going to—"

"Stop!" Camilla races from where she is hidden and stands beside me.

"Camilla?" Sam's voice cracks. He drops his sword. "Is this some kind of cruel trick? What have I done to deserve this?" Tears roll down his cheeks as he looks up to the sky as if sending a silent prayer, as if asking forgiveness for some assumed crime.

"Well, I'd say trying to kill me was pretty bad."

"Anne," Camilla snaps, shooting me a look that says she'll kill me if I continue to make fun of her brother's plight. She takes his hands, now pressed together. "It's really me. I never drowned."

"But I saw you, you were dead." He withdraws his hand and wipes his cheeks. "I saw you," he says again and again.

From her dress pocket, Camilla pulls out a small vial of potion containing a bit of the nightshade we got from an apothecary. "We told them we wanted it for a play, to make the unbelievable real. I suppose it was a play of sorts, one to fool a wicked duke." She grins at me then looks back at Sam. "How did you get here so fast?"

He reaches into his pocket and then pulls out a letter addressed to him from Camilla. "I booked the earliest train as soon as I received this, and when I got here, the duchess told me you'd lost all senses and flung yourself into a brook."

"My letter," says Camilla. "In the midst of everything, I forgot I sent it."

"You said you were haunted by the devil," says Sam. "What's going on here?"

She leans into him, eyes full of sorrow and fear. "Do you trust me?"

Without hesitation, he nods. And then we fill him in.

"You think the duke is a vampire?" Doubt slips into his

voice, but he hasn't left, hasn't run away yet, which means there's a chance he believes us, a chance we can convince him.

"We're certain of it," I say. "But we need proof."

"Which is where this comes in," says Camilla, waving around the penny dreadful. "I found a London address for Grace van Helsing, who's the author." Camilla points at her biography. "What if she really is a monster hunter? I say we find her and ask her all that she knows about vampires. Their strengths and their weaknesses and we use that to really figure out what is going on here."

"And then?" asks Sam.

Camilla looks to me, and I think of all that has transpired. Of my father's death, of how Camilla barely escaped death—or a fate worse than death—of how my uncle is using my mother, of how he'll likely never stop until we're all dead and drained of our blood. And then he'll move on to kill others. Camilla's right. I made a choice. I chose to believe my father, I chose to believe what I saw that night, I chose to believe her. We are all going to die one day. One day we'll be bones and ash. But right now, we are alive. It's up to me, to us, to make sure that my uncle's reign ends here.

"And then," I say, meeting her eyes, "we bring this vampire down."

THE DAILY TELEGRAPH.

No. 11,530. London, Saturday, April 30, 1892.
ONE PENNY.

DEATHS.

TAYLOR—On the morning of the 29th at Elsinore Hall. Lord Andrew Taylor, Duke of Elsinore, was found dead of unknown circumstances. Funeral to be determined. Of his death, his stepdaughter, Lady Anne Taylor, said, "One may smile, and smile, and be a villain."

Does it not, think thee, stand me now upon—
He that hath killed my king, and whored my mother,
Popped in between th' election and my hopes,
Thrown out his angle for my proper life,
(And with such cozenage!)—is 't not perfect conscience
To quit him with this arm? And is 't not to be damned
To let this canker of our nature come
In further evil?

　　　　　　　　　　　—*HAMLET*, ACT 5, SCENE 2

Author's Note

‿ ♛ ‿

When I set out to write this story, I knew two things:

One, that I would retell *Hamlet*.

Two, that there would be a vampire.

I love *Hamlet*. I've studied it. I've performed it. I know so much of it by heart. I also love vampires. They're seductive, and they're terrifying. Though I love vampires in all their forms, I tend to favor vampire media that focuses on charismatic vampires who are tortured souls that hold your sympathy. I have Anne Rice and *Blade* to thank for that. But with this story, I wanted the vampire to be the bad guy, as *Hamlet*'s Claudius is, and so I turned to the original bad guy vampire tale: *Dracula*.

Dracula certainly wasn't the first vampire novel, but it is one of the most well-known. I've read *Dracula* many times, and one of the things I love is that it's an epistolary novel, which means it's entirely told through journal entries, letters, and other forms of correspondence. Because of that, you get these really fascinating plot decisions where someone gets attacked, but then journals about it—otherwise, how else would we know it happened? I also love how much of *Dracula* is inspired by what was going on in the world at the time. I wanted to take part of that, really ground this retelling in a specific time and place, and then have present-tense dialog mixed in with newspaper clippings, letters, etc., so you start the story knowing something is amiss, and bit by bit, you're filled in.

I've always felt that *Hamlet* has a gothic air to it, so I decided to set it in the 1800s, centering around a great English country estate, Elsinore—rather than a kingdom. Many of our great gothic novels were written in the 1800s. I also pulled in details from that time like Somerville College, one of the first two women's colleges in Oxford, dollar princesses—rich, American women who married into the English aristocracy—penny dreadfuls, and so forth.

Also, just a note about those clowns, the ones mentioned in the *Hamlet* excerpt at the beginning: that was a name for peasants, generally speaking, which gravediggers back then would've been. It's also a name for a fool, as in a jester, as the gravediggers' purpose in the play was that of comic relief.

And, finally, Ophelia. I really do adore *Hamlet*, but I have always hated Ophelia's character arc, or lack of well-rounded one. I didn't want to center a romance, I wanted girl power all the way, and so as soon as I knew the setting and the framework, I knew Ophelia would live and that Hamlet would be a girl and that they would be friends.

We Fail

Inspired by Macbeth

Samantha Mabry

> *Unnatural deeds*
> *Do breed unnatural troubles.*
>
> —ACT 5, SCENE 1

I: ICE STORM

The heater was on. The dryness of it was causing the edges of my lips to chap. The car reeked sour, like the beer someone had spilled all over Mateo just before we left the field. I was in the back seat, wedged between Lucy and Laurel, who didn't smell like beer but instead smelled like woodsmoke from standing near the bonfire. Then again, they usually smelled like woodsmoke because of the essential oils they both were in the habit of rolling across their wrists. Duncan was in the passenger seat, up next to Mateo, messing with the old radio. He landed on a station, turned the volume way up, and cried out that this was his and Daniel's favorite, *favorite!* song.

"Hang in there, Drea!" Mateo shouted back in my direction.

I was slumped forward, my arms wrapped around my stomach. Even though it had been over a month since the miscarriage, my body was refusing to accept that there wasn't a baby growing inside of it anymore. I was still struck with sudden nausea and would wake up in the middle of the night with crushing headaches. We'd left the party early partly because of the worsening weather, but mostly because I was afraid of throwing up my drive-through dinner in front of a bunch of my classmates who either pitied me or snickered behind my back. Even now, the nausea still hadn't passed, and the incessant thump of the music, of Duncan and Daniel's *favorite* song, wasn't helping.

Lucy, to my left, reached out with her smoke-scented hand and gave my knee a squeeze.

"Next time," she whispered, "don't let Duncan pressure you into going out if you don't want to."

Laurel, to my right, rubbed the upper curve of my spine in small circles.

"He has no idea," she said. "He doesn't know what you're going through."

"No one does," Lucy added.

I let out a little moan of gratitude so quiet, I'm sure no one could hear it but me.

I'd asked for shotgun so I could take sips of cold air from the open passenger-side window, but Duncan had insisted on taking it for himself. He said he needed the extra space. Typical. Duncan always needed extra space. Physically, he *was* huge, but his bigness manifested in other ways, too: he was loud and always in motion, and when he talked, his skillet-sized hands gestured wildly in the air.

And now, Duncan was dancing in his seat, causing it to jolt back and forth on its squeaky springs and bounce hard against my shoulder. I could smell a fresh hit of stale beer as Mateo reached around with his right arm to try to hold the seat steady, but he didn't turn down the music or ask Duncan to stop.

"I'm okay," I muttered, even though no one had asked, even though it wasn't true.

Duncan was in even rarer form that night: bigger and louder. Earlier that day he'd performed so great at practice— breaking every tackle, so light on his feet, he nearly flew— that the scouts from both North Texas and UT Austin had scheduled interviews with him for the upcoming week. To play football at either place would've been incredible—an honor, really, for any small-town kid—but he was gunning for Austin because his boyfriend Daniel had already been accepted there on early admission to major in architecture.

Mateo, the other starting running back for the team, barely got a second look from the scouts. Maybe he wasn't a powerhouse like Duncan. Maybe he wasn't *quite* as quick. The scouts couldn't see what I knew to be true: Mateo was kind and thoughtful and acted with great care. The opposite of Duncan. In any spare moment, Mateo was studying plays. We'd be watching Netflix together and a three-ring binder would be open on his lap. He was captain of the team, a wonderful leader. He listened and would always pause before he spoke, as if he wanted to get his words just right. He would've been the best father. But Mateo didn't demand as much, so he didn't get as much, and he had a bad habit of deferring to others. He didn't like to "cause problems." So when Duncan insisted on shotgun, Mateo let him have it.

I was clutching my stomach, at the deep void there, while Duncan was bouncing in his seat, singing at the top of his lungs.

And then, there was the wreck.

Lucy gripped my thigh. Laurel screamed. Her scream was swallowed by a monstrous, roaring sound. At first, I thought it was *actually* a monster, but I later learned that the roar was caused by Mateo's old Seville skidding, being thrown onto its side and scraping across black ice. Old cars like his were made entirely of metal, and when metal collides with pavement and ice, the sound is out-of-this-world loud.

I don't remember when the noise stopped, or when the car finally slowed to a halt, or how I got out of the back seat—if I was pulled or if I was thrown.

What I remember next is standing in the field.

Mateo was pacing, taking long strides, trying to get a signal. He punched in some numbers on his phone and then held it to his ear. When that didn't work, he lifted the phone up to the blurry night sky. Lucy and Laurel were standing a ways away, under the protection of the crooked and bare limbs of an oak tree. Their arms were linked.

I could see the road, State Highway 281, but it was farther away than it should've been. That didn't make sense. We were *just* on that road. Mateo's Seville—the car I'd *just* been in, the car that served as the setting to the biggest moments of my life, from losing my virginity to getting pregnant to getting engaged—was on its side, streaked in black, and smoking. A large clump of grass and mud was lodged deep in one of the wheel wells.

I noticed the clump of grass and mud before I noticed Duncan. Most of him was pinned under the car. He was only visible from his rib cage up. For once, he looked small.

"Are any of you getting a signal?" I heard Mateo shout.

He was the only one trying.

Duncan's right arm was under the car, but his left arm was free, curled into a half circle above his head. He wasn't moving it—or he couldn't move it. Misty sleet was falling directly on his face, but he wasn't batting it away. I said his name, but he didn't turn his head in my direction. His eyes were open. Maybe he couldn't hear me.

I walked around to where I was standing in his line of sight and crouched down. Duncan still didn't look at me. He was gazing to the horizon and breathing really weird. There was a spot, dark and spreading across his chest, across the light-gray sweatshirt the scout from UT Austin had given him earlier that day.

"Drea!" Lucy shouted. "Is he okay?"

I glanced over to the girls, who were still under the tree, huddled close, and I swear I could smell woodsmoke from where I was, squatting in the grass, over the stink of exhaust and burnt rubber.

The mixed smells were awful, but I wasn't feeling sick anymore.

"I'm going up closer to the road!" Mateo called out as he broke into a jog. "Drea! Is there something you can do? Hold his hand or something? At least?"

The dark spot on Duncan's sweatshirt was spreading, getting bigger, the blood starting to leach into the orange threads of the embroidery. Duncan was still breathing, but it sounded like water bubbling. His trembling lips were gray with cold.

"Drea," he whispered. "Help."

"Drea!" Laurel's voice boomed.

"What's happening?" Lucy shouted.

"Help," Duncan repeated.

In the distance, at the road, Mateo was shouting. He'd stopped trying to get a signal and was now trying to wave down passing cars, using his phone as a flashlight.

I stood up and started to run.

The soles of my boots crashed down on the crusted grass. A pair of headlights appeared around a bend just as I caught up to Mateo. I grabbed his arm and thrust it down so the light from his phone was hidden against my coat.

"Wait," I demanded, thrilled and breathless. "Just wait a minute."

II: GHOSTS

I spent most of my time in the school's rooftop greenhouse.

There was so much to do. In the days leading up to and immediately following Duncan's death, I was there anytime there was even the smallest sliver of sun. I hammered together boards for some raised beds, revived old soil from the last round of crops, added mulch, and planted hearty vegetables like carrots, kale, and spinach. Early on, some of the plants showed signs of blight, but everything except a couple of the more delicate lettuces survived. Aside from that, my daily routine consisted of checking on the plants in the beds, making sure they were well-watered and bug-free, and then watering, repotting, and rotating the various tiny containers I had set up in rows on folding tables so they'd each get time in the warmest spots. I repaired tears in the hard plastic and rewired the metal structure.

Occasionally, I took breaks to stand out on the roof in the cold sun. Even though it took up most of my time, my work with the plants wasn't for an official class. I did it because I liked it. It was rewarding. It helped me in the process of re-convincing myself that I was capable of creating an environment in which living things could grow and thrive. It wasn't like I was going to graduate at that point anyway. I refused to go to class, and the counselors had urged my teachers and principal to let me take "as long as needed" to heal from my "traumatic incidents," the first of which was losing the baby. The second was the wreck.

The original plan was that Mateo and I were going to get married in late June, a couple of weeks after graduation and three months after the baby came. I'd even picked out the venue online, a little farmhouse just outside of Stephenville that someone had done up all rustic-cute with lights strung from the beams and carpets covering the dirt floor.

Then, in the middle of December, during finals week, I collapsed in the hallway outside the cafeteria. By then, the baby had been dead in my body for days. The Friday after that, during the third quarter of the last football game of the season, Mateo went down hard and a player on the opposing team stepped on his ankle, causing it to twist. I was still in the hospital when it happened, but I'd heard later from Lucy and Laurel about how Mateo had refused to be taken to the locker room. For the rest of the game, he was over on a bench on the sidelines, clapping for his teammates and scowling at the packs of ice that were stacked up on his ankle.

Mateo's doctors said he would heal completely and that he'd be back to normal in two or three months. But he didn't have two or three months to spare. When the college scouts came, he was still a little slow. He couldn't put pressure on his

foot all the way like he used to, so his pivots were less grace-
ful and his timing wasn't as sharp. It wasn't fair that Mateo
couldn't prove to them how bright he could shine.

Through my work in the greenhouse, I've learned that some
plants thrive in even the coldest temperatures. I hadn't known
this before and had assumed all plants require sun and
warmth. My favorite cold-weather plant isn't one of the vegetables. It's the echinocereus, which is also called the hedgehog
cactus. The plant part itself is sort of squatty and small, but
it has really big spines. Sometimes, I prick my fingers on those
spines. I like the tingly feeling that follows, trippy like the tiniest
buzz.

On a Monday morning, a week after the car accident, Mateo
came up to the roof. I was working, crouched down and hack-
ing at some stubborn soil with a trowel, and he waited in the
doorway until I noticed him there.

"I saw Duncan," he said.

This wasn't the first time I'd heard this.

Almost immediately, Mateo had started blaming himself for Duncan's death. On the night of the accident, Mateo
wasn't drunk or speeding, but it was *his* bald front tire on *his*
old car that had hit a patch of black ice and sent us into a spin.

Now, Mateo hardly slept. When he *did* manage to sleep,
he had dreams about Duncan. In those dreams, Duncan was
standing in front of Mateo in an ice-crusted field. There was a
dark circle of blood on his sweatshirt. Jutting out from his torso,
from the jumble of soft organs right under his rib cage, was

a jagged hunk of a passenger-side window, several inches wide and long.

In the hours after the wreck, the doctors at the hospital had told us that *maybe* they could've stopped the bleeding and stitched up Duncan's insides if he'd arrived at the hospital a little bit earlier.

But only *maybe*.

Probably not.

Mateo clung to that *maybe*. It was destroying him, causing him to have bad dreams.

I clung to the *probably not*.

"It was just a dream," I said.

"It wasn't a dream." Mateo leaned hard against the doorframe, causing the whole structure to shake. "It happened just now. In B-Hall. He was wearing that bloody sweatshirt and staring at me. Everyone else was swarming around. They didn't see him. They were just getting their books out of their lockers, running to class."

"Oh," I replied. "I think that maybe you're just stressed out?"

Mateo walked into the greenhouse then collapsed onto a stool in front of a row of small planters stuffed with wispy feather grass. His hands were trembling. I felt bad for him, but it wasn't the best time for me to give him the comfort he clearly needed. I was in the middle of repotting. I was covered in dirt. I waited a moment for Mateo to realize this, but when he didn't, I grabbed an old cloth from my back pocket and slowly started wiping my trowel clean.

"Of course, I'm stressed out," Mateo said. "It doesn't help that Daniel is freezing me out."

"He needs someone to blame, so he blames us," I replied. "That's not so hard to believe."

The night of the accident, seconds after I'd yanked Mateo's arm down and muted the light from his phone, we'd both felt the whoosh of air from a passing car. Mateo had spun toward me, confused.

And then, under that dark sky, I'd said, "You can take his place."

For weeks leading up to that moment, I'd felt this gnawing emptiness. I'd lost the baby, and then, almost immediately, Mateo had lost his chance to land on a good team. Our future was gone, but with Duncan out of the way, we could work to grab it—or, at least, *some* of it—back.

Things weren't really working out that way, though.

"Us?" Mateo looked over his shoulder to confirm we were alone. "Daniel blames *us*? *Me*, Drea. Daniel blames *me*, when really *you* were the one . . ."

"No!" I thrust the tip of the trowel in Mateo's direction. "You wanted it, too. I know it. You let two more cars pass until—"

"Shut up, Drea."

"I was thinking about us!" I shouted.

"Shut up!" Mateo stood up suddenly, swatting my arm away and sending the trowel flying out of my hand and skating across the ground. "You were thinking about *yourself*. You still feel helpless, and I get that, and I think about the baby every *single* day. But it's not fair that you are pulling me into your helplessness. Now, *I'm* the one being blamed. *I'm* the one being haunted. You have no idea what it's like, that feeling— that itchy, awful feeling—of never being left to yourself."

Mateo was waiting for me to reply, but I said nothing. I wanted to pick up the trowel and stab Mateo in the heart with it. And as I stabbed him I'd scream at him about how wrong he was. I knew what it was like to be haunted. My daughter had moved inside me. I'd played her music and felt her flip. Her tiny body was gone, but she was still here somehow. The nausea and the headaches still persisted. She was my ghost, and if I were honest with myself, I never wanted her to leave.

Mateo used to talk to the baby. He would put his hand on my stomach and say, "Sweet Little. Little Sweet." I missed that so much—both of those things: his fingers splayed across my stretched-tight skin, and the sound of the baby's nickname coming from his lips.

"You should go back to class," I told Mateo. "I have a lot of work to do here."

"I'm thinking about telling Daniel," he replied abruptly, like this is what he'd come up to the roof to say to me in the first place—like he'd been scared to say it, up until now. "About what we did that night."

I walked over to a nearby hedgehog cactus and tapped its spine with the tip of my finger.

"And what exactly did we do?" I asked.

Mateo glared at me and then got up and left without answering.

III: ICE STORM

Two days later, Lucy and Laurel came up to the greenhouse. They brought me hot cocoa from McDonald's, which I hadn't asked for and didn't really want. I waited for them to leave, but they didn't. Laurel leaned her hip against a shelf and started tugging lightly at a bright-green bud of barely formed squash on the vine. Its smallness made her fingers look too long, spindly like sticks.

"Mateo looks bad," she said.

"He's not sleeping," I replied.

"He's scared," Lucy offered. "Daniel keeps asking about the night of the wreck, like he thinks Mateo is holding back some important detail. Yesterday, after last period, Daniel full-on shoved Mateo into the lockers, and Coach Jones had to come and break it up."

I sifted my hand through soil, poured fresh into a pot from a just-opened bag. New dirt smelled like air but also sour like decay. It was cat-fur soft and very, very dark in color, like molten chocolate cake. Sometimes, when I was alone, I would pinch some off and hold it to the tip of my tongue.

What Lucy and Laurel were telling me—this wasn't really news. Over the course of just the last two days Mateo was clearly getting worse, wilting and going brittle, barely hanging on. If he were a plant, I could repot him in this new, chocolate-cake soil and water him, and maybe he'd take root and get a second life, but, unfortunately, Mateo was a boy, not a plant.

"Mateo gave us a ride to school this morning in his new car," Laurel said, still fiddling with the squash with her clacking stick fingers. "And he ran over a jackrabbit."

I looked up, startled.

"There was no way he could have braked in time," Lucy clarified.

"Still," Laurel added with a shrug. "It seems like a bad sign."

❦

That afternoon, I prepped the greenhouse for a hard freeze that was supposed to happen overnight. I covered all the beds in burlap and made sure the rough fabric was secured. Then I moved the smaller containers away from the surfaces that would get the coldest, off the ground and away from the plastic tarp walls. By the time I left, all the little plants were huddled together on a couple of tables in the middle of the greenhouse. I covered those tables in burlap as well. If I could've, I would've plugged in a small space heater, but I didn't want to risk the old electrical system of the school. There was no guarantee everything would survive, but it was the best I could do.

The sleet started as the sun went down, just as I was driving home from school, and, that night, I fell asleep to the sound of ice pinging against the windows. The next day was Thursday, and school ended up getting canceled because the roads were too dangerous to drive on. I let my phone run out of batteries and took three baths in a row, draining and then refilling the tub with hot water each time it got lukewarm.

The school reopened on Friday, and I was up at the greenhouse before the sun was fully up. It was clear that something had gone wrong. The door was partially open, but I didn't know how that could've happened. I'd locked the door when I left. Of course I'd locked the door when I left. When I entered, I saw piles of brown on brown—burlap and dirt and dried-up leaves and stems, all mixed up. Everything was shrunken, crisp, the deadest of the dead. One table was shifted into a diagonal, and the other was tipped completely on its side. There were empty planters all over the place. I took a few more steps inside, and that's when I noticed the flash of color on the ground. It was out of place and the brightest blue: bird feathers—no, the *entire* wing of a bird—torn off and spread out. I crouched down, sifting gently through the dirt and lifting the loose pieces of burlap, but I couldn't find the head or the body, just that one wing.

As for what had happened, I could only guess. The bird

had flown in through the door that I'd somehow (how?) left open. A larger animal, like a squirrel or a cat or a raccoon, had rushed in after it. In the great, big battle that ensued, the tables had been bumped, and the plants had fallen. The burlap had come loose. The bird had lost its life and was probably eaten. The plants that hadn't been knocked completely from their soil had been exposed to the cold from the open door. I glanced over and saw that the little squash bud that Laurel had been fiddling with the other day had shriveled on its vine.

I sat on the cold, concrete floor and cried for the plants. Then I cried for myself because just when I'd started to think that maybe I wasn't terrible at keeping things alive, I was proven wrong.

Eventually, I heard movement at the door and looked up to see Lucy and Laurel standing there. Lucy was frowning. Laurel was holding a cup of hot cocoa and taking in the destruction.

"This is, for sure, a bad sign," she said.

IV: ECHINOCEREUS

In all that destruction, there was a miracle: a hedgehog cactus, alive. Somehow, an empty planter had flipped and fallen on top of it, offering a perfect shell of protection.

The hedgehog cactus didn't need sun and fresh air to grow, but I figured neither would hurt. Much of the roof was still covered with ice, but the outside temperature was warmer than it had been the last couple of days. I carefully slow-walked the cactus across the slick roof and placed it on a west-facing ledge. Then I took a step back to gaze at the bluebonnet-blue sky.

"What happened up here?"

I turned to see Mateo. He was wearing a green-and-black flannel, dirty and wrinkled and with a little white stain, maybe a smear of dried toothpaste, across the collar.

"Something got into the greenhouse," I said. "I don't know how. It's a total wreck. That's the only thing that survived."

I pointed at the cactus, smiling, so clearly proud of the little plant that lived.

"I think there's something wrong with you, Drea," Mateo said.

That wasn't what I was expecting him to say, but it also wasn't a lie.

"Well . . ." I snorted. "Well . . . *yeah*."

"You don't regret what we did." Mateo advanced toward me, taking steady steps on the ice. "Even now. All you care about are your plants."

"And what did we do?" I shouted, repeating myself from the other day. "Duncan was already dying."

"Bullshit!"

Mateo rushed forward, and suddenly we were close, less than a foot apart. It was closer than we'd been in a long time, and I could feel the raw emotion cracking brightly between us. We were yelling at each other, yeah, but it was *something*. It felt real.

"You didn't see him like I did," I said. "He was crushed and barely breathing."

Mateo, clearly bothered by the word *crushed*, took a hard swallow and looked down to the space between the toes of our shoes.

"He was my friend," he said.

"I know," I replied.

"We could have helped him."

"No." I put my hand, dirty fingers spread wide, on his chest. "He's gone, and we need to move on."

I said it as much for me as I did for Mateo. We were in this together. *We.*

Mateo wanted to touch me—I could tell by the way his fingers were fluttering at his sides, twitching in and out of loose fists. I was certain we were finally fusing together again after tragedy—*two* tragedies—had threatened to rip us apart. He was weak right now, but I could build him back up. I was ready.

One of my hands was still on Mateo's chest, and the other one went to my stomach. I'd felt the kick there, under the scratchy fibers of my sweater, under skin and muscle.

"He's gone," I repeated. "This is our chance now."

Mateo looked up to meet my gaze. He shifted his weight to the right, onto his bad ankle. The movement was subtle, but I knew what he was doing: testing its strength.

"I don't know," he said.

I moved my hand from Mateo's chest to his cheek, and he leaned into me, nuzzling like a cat.

"I don't know," he repeated.

But then Mateo reached for my hand, the one that was against my stomach, and gripped it.

"Sweet Little," he whispered. "Little Sweet."

After Mateo left, I spent the rest of the day trying to clean up the mess. When I went back to the ledge to check on the hedgehog cactus, school had been out for over an hour, and the sun was already going down. In a far field, people were practicing for track—running sprints and jumping hurdles. They were bundled up in matching sweats, and I could see their breath against the dark. The winter air smelled like smoke from a chimney.

Something off to the side caught my eye—a person. He was standing near the bleachers and was wearing a stained, gray sweatshirt. Once he saw that I was looking at him, he raised his arm. He didn't wave it, though—just held it up in a semicircle over his head. It looked like it had that night in the field, when it was lying limp in the icy grass.

I gasped and took an awkward step to the side. My knee knocked against the planter that held the hedgehog cactus, causing it to teeter and then tip. When I reached out to catch it, my midsection collided with the ledge, and I huffed, extending my arm even farther, spreading my dirty fingers for the air-bound plant. The entire building tilted.

Out ahead of me and down, I could see the tiny cactus, rotating in the cold dark, and as I reached for it again, I felt a sting in the center of my palm from where a spine had lodged itself deep. The plant was soaring. I was soaring with it. My whole world was going end over end.

V: GHOSTS

Lucy and Laurel found me the next morning. They'd gone up to the roof with some hot chocolate, called my name around the greenhouse, and just as they were about to leave, saw an odd pile of loose dirt and some scuff marks near the western edge of the building.

Later that night, people from school gathered in the parking lot, just as they'd gathered for Duncan a few weeks before. They held candles speared through paper cups and said nice things about me.

"Poor Drea," Laurel said.

Lucy nodded. "Yeah. Poor Drea."

Everyone thought I'd fallen on purpose, finally weighed down by grief heaped on grief.

Mateo was there, standing next to the girls, but he wasn't holding a candle. He was in that green flannel shirt from the day before, and when people would come by to offer him their condolences, he wouldn't reply. He was still wilting, and I wondered if he'd ever recover.

I tried to get close and overlap myself with him or fold myself into him. I thought that maybe he could feel me the way I still felt my baby girl. Maybe I could be a flutter in his stomach.

Mateo was wilting, but he was also angry. I could tell. Losing so many things in a row—a baby, a teammate, a scholarship, a fiancée—can fundamentally change a person. It can make them feel like they're hollow and filled to bursting at the same time.

I came even closer, so close, I could hear a series of clicks in Mateo's jaw, like he was grinding his teeth. I tried to tell Mateo that I'd died trying to save a life—that instead of being angry, he should be proud. I don't think he heard me, though. His hard gaze was directed across the lot, to a smirking Daniel. I knew that Mateo was going to act on his new anger, which wouldn't turn out well.

Duncan had been the one who'd thrived on emotion. Mateo had always been the deliberate one. Because of that, I'd had to act for him. I don't like to think about what might happen without me around.

Author's Note

Some interpretations of *Macbeth* (including the most recent film version featuring Michael Fassbender and Marion Cotillard) have claimed that, just prior to the start of the action of the play, the Macbeths lost an infant child. Lines such as Lady Macbeth's in Act I, "I have given suck, and know / How tender 'tis to love the babe that milks me" support these interpretations. It makes some sense then that the trauma of the loss of a child coupled with the pair's overall "vaulting" ambition influences their decisions. I'm a new mother. At the time that I'm writing this, my son is about to turn two. And, of course, having a child changes one's thinking in a lot of ways. This story came about as I shifted to thinking about *Macbeth* as a play about the things people do when they have loved a child and are now torn down by grief.

LATE
ROMANCE

Lost Girl

Inspired by The Winter's Tale

Melissa Bashardoust

A sad tale's best for winter. I have one
Of sprites and goblins.

—Act 2, scene 1

Perdita knew that Zal was different the first time she told him her name. Most people, upon hearing it, immediately mentioned the dog from *101 Dalmatians.* When Zal's eyes lit up at the freshman mixer she had been persuaded by her roommate to attend, she prepared herself for another comparison to a dog in a Disney movie.

Instead, he said, "Perdita, from the Latin *perditus,* meaning lost. With the feminine ending, it would be closer to something like 'lost girl.'"

He was a classics major, Perdita soon discovered, hence the excitement over Latin.

She had asked her Aunt Polina once why she had given her that name. "It came to me in a dream," was all Aunt Polina would tell her. Perdita wasn't surprised by the lack of explanation—she was used to Aunt Polina not telling her things. Years of asking about her parents went nowhere, as did any questions about why Aunt Polina flew downstate so often and how they were paying for Perdita's college expenses on Aunt Polina's modest salary.

Perdita probably could have found out some of those answers, if she'd really wanted to. She could have done some googling, tried to find a trail of bread crumbs that would lead her back home, like Hansel and Gretel. But the thing about Hansel and Gretel is that their parents abandoned them in the woods to starve. Perdita didn't want to know if she'd been left in the woods. It was easier to imagine that she'd just been born there.

Besides, she'd always liked the idea of living in the woods. "You chose which school to go to based on the trees alone," Aunt Polina had said to her, teasing, and Perdita couldn't even deny it. The first time she had stepped on the campus, visiting as a high school junior, she had felt a stronger sense of belonging than she had ever felt in her life. While everyone else on the tour was admiring the stone buildings and the giant library, Perdita's eyes kept drawing back to the dreamy willow outside the science building, or the knobby London plane trees—currently bare, but full of promise—that lined the main plaza, or the eucalyptus grove that served as the western entrance to the campus. She had been thinking of majoring in plant biology but had quickly realized she didn't want to study plants so much as be absorbed into them. She didn't think there was a major for that.

About a month after they'd met at the mixer, when she and Zal were definitely dating but not quite ready to call it that yet, he took her up to the top of the clock tower on campus. She'd never gone inside, thinking it was for tourists, the kind of thing you showed your family when they visited for homecoming weekend. But Zal had gone up before, and he seemed excited about it, so maybe there was something worth seeing up there.

From the platform at the top of the tower, Perdita stared down at the campus's red-tiled roofs and the clusters of trees. She pointed out which building was which in her mind, tracing out her regular routes to class and imagining herself winding through campus like a mouse in a maze. It was interesting but not particularly exciting, and a chilly wind kept whipping strands of her copper hair into her mouth. She started to ask Zal if they could go back down now but then saw the calm contentment on his face. He wasn't looking at campus but rather straight ahead, at the water of the bay and the bridge that connected their side of the bay to the city, where his parents lived. He'd told her a little about his parents, that they owned a highly successful software company and that his dad was not thrilled with his only child's choice of major or lack of interest in taking over that software company one day.

She was still staring at him when his face broke into the most wonderful smile. "I just love seeing the water," he said. "Even if it's not the ocean, it's close enough."

Only now did Perdita actually look at the bay for itself, at the constant motion of the water, never quite still or steady. There was something about its surface that almost looked fake to her, like in kindergarten when the teacher would have everyone shake out a shiny, blue sheet to resemble a river.

"What do you think it'd be like to live underwater?" Zal asked her.

She shrugged. "My pastoral fantasies usually involve burrowing into a hollowed-out tree, personally. I think I'd get tired being a fish—always tossed around, no solid ground."

"You'd get used to it, though," he said at once, like he had already given underwater living serious consideration. "And then if you ever tried to stand on solid land, you'd probably wobble around."

He started to sway back and forth to demonstrate. "Come on, wobble with me."

Well, she couldn't let him wobble alone, could she? She swayed in sync with him, trying not to laugh, and then he took her hands, and they were half swaying, half dancing. "See," he said, "if you were a sea creature, you'd always be moving, just like this, always dancing. That wouldn't be so bad, would it?"

He looked so earnest, dark eyes and long eyelashes magnified in the lenses of his glasses, wanting her to see the same beautiful possibilities that he saw when he looked out on the bay. But all she could think was that she was prone to seasickness and had never really learned how to swim beyond paddling around in the shallow end of a pool, so she would make a pretty pathetic sea creature.

The next time she saw the city across the bay was after winter break. That was how she would measure time from now on, she figured. There was before the winter break of her freshman year of college, and there was after—Perdita B.W.B. and Perdita A.W.B.

"Is everything okay?"

She could have told Zal she was just nervous about today. They were standing on the steps of his Victorian house, where she was about to meet his parents for the first time over lunch. But she knew that wasn't what he meant.

As if the same thought had occurred to him, he added, "I don't just mean about today. Since winter break, you've been . . . weird."

"Weird?"

"Quiet," he quickly corrected. "Distant."

It may have been easier to refute that claim if she were able to look him in the eye as she told him she was fine. But if she made eye contact, he would hang on to that slender thread of connection, and he wouldn't let go until she had told him something honest, something true. The truth—the reason for her distance—was that at any given moment, she was expending a large amount of mental energy trying *not* to think about the events of winter break.

She tried not to think about Aunt Polina's face, pale and pinched, as she asked Perdita if they could talk after dinner.

She tried not to think about Aunt Polina's words, which still threatened to bubble up to the surface of her mind no matter how much she tried to push them down. It was hardest at night, when she'd wake up unexpectedly—that was when all the thoughts attacked, when she was too sleepy and disoriented to put her shields up in time to stop them. Then, she would pluck at the thoughts like flower petals—*she should have told me sooner; she should never have told me at all*—around and around until she fell asleep again or until dawn gave her permission to stop trying.

Shields safely up, she finally turned to Zal and said, "Do you ever think about running away to live in the woods?"

But before Zal could answer or address the randomness of her question, the door opened, and his dad let them both in.

Zal had told her once that his last name meant "born from a fairy" in Persian, a fact he took great delight in. Stepping into the immaculate Parizadeh household, Perdita did indeed feel like a disheveled, hopeless mortal entering a fairyland where she didn't belong. Zal's mom was quick to offer her a tour of the ground floor, pointing out items of interest such as the wall full of Zal's academic awards and the intricate Persian rugs from Isfahan, where her parents had been born. Zal's dad trailed after them, never less than unfailingly polite, and yet Perdita knew with certainty that he didn't want her there—or more accurately, that he had hoped she would be someone else. *Let me tell you what I just found out about myself,* she wanted to say, *I actually am someone else.*

She should have told me sooner.

Zal's mom had to leave before lunch for a business meeting, and Perdita thought longingly of her kind smile when she sat down for lunch across from Zal's stony-faced father. Mr. Parizadeh asked her a few questions, but the ones he really wanted to know—*Who are your parents? What do they do?*—were the ones Perdita didn't want to answer.

She should never have told me.

Perdita excused herself to use the restroom at an opportune moment, and after she had shyly dried her hands on the monogrammed towels, she lingered by a bookcase in the hallway. Angry voices were coming from the dining room.

"We've always taught you how important your education is, and now you're wasting it by learning about statues and fooling around with girls."

"I'm not wasting anything, Dad. You have to give me a chance—and give *her* a chance, too. You barely know her."

"Of course I don't know her—she's hardly told me anything about herself."

"That's not fair," Zal shot back.

"You know I want what's best for you."

"But don't I have any say in what's best for myself?"

"You're still so young. You think you know what's best for *now*, but not in the long run. I don't want you to make mistakes that you'll regret later."

"You can't stop me from ever making mistakes, Dad."

There was a tense silence, and then Mr. Parizadeh said, "That's true. But I'm your father and I care about you, so I can't support them. I'll give you a choice—you can have *one* mistake. You can have your statues or your girlfriend. If you don't pick one, you'll have to pay your own tuition."

Another silence followed, this one even heavier than the last, before Zal said, "Mom would never agree to that."

"We'll see."

Knots were forming in Perdita's stomach. They were fighting. They were fighting because of *her*. She had made Zal fight with his father, and his parents were probably going to fight with each other, too. What if his parents split up over this? What if his dad really did stop paying his tuition? What if Zal chose her but then had to lose that light in his eyes whenever he talked about the accusative case in Latin? *What if he* doesn't *choose me?*

She closed her eyes, trying to ignore the tightness in her chest. When she opened them again, she was looking at a photo on the shelf in front of her. Or no, not a photo—a framed cover from a tech magazine. Zal's parents—several years younger—were standing with another man whose face she couldn't place, all of them joining hands and smiling at the camera. And then she read the caption, which mentioned the unknown man by name, and she flinched.

The rest of the lunch passed, set to the soundtrack of forks scraping on plates. On the metro back to campus, Zal was still quiet, his hands clenching and unclenching in his lap.

Perdita had never seen him this upset, this unsettled, and she hated that it was her fault.

"So," she said, "do you ever think about running away to live in the woods?"

She was rewarded with Zal's surprised laugh, breaking through some of the tension. "You overheard us, I'm guessing?"

She nodded then thought for a second and said, "You should choose your major."

"I'm not going to choose."

She looked at him in surprise. "What do you mean? He'll stop paying your tuition."

Zal shook his head. "It was an empty threat. He's just trying to use you to scare me out of my major. And . . . even if he does mean it, I'd be fine. Lots of people aren't lucky enough to study what they love. I can still take classes that interest me even if I don't major in classics. It's not even that big of a deal." But he sounded like he was trying to reassure himself as much as her. "My mom would never agree to it, anyway," he added weakly.

"They'll fight over it, then," Perdita said. "It's not worth it."

"What's not worth it?"

She gestured to the space between them. "This."

He frowned. "You don't think this is worth it?"

"No, I mean—it's not worth *that*. Not worth being in trouble with your dad or causing family turmoil."

"It's fine. It was just an argument. We have them all the time."

"That doesn't matter. Just because it's been okay before doesn't mean it'll always be okay."

"*If* my dad doesn't back down, I'll figure something out."

"That's not a solution."

"Then what *is* a solution?"

Breaking up, she wanted to say. But she kept thinking about that magazine cover, about dads arguing with moms, about the ways kids sometimes had to step up and be the adults their parents refused to be even though it wasn't fair. *She should never have told me. She should have told me sooner.*

She told me now. I might as well use it.

"I can ask my dad to talk to him," Perdita said.

He looked at her with such genuine confusion that it was almost comic. "I thought you didn't . . ."

He trailed off, both of them hearing the rest of the sentence. *I thought you didn't have one.* "It turns out I do," Perdita said. "He's retired, but years ago, he and a couple of his college friends founded a software company together. It was hugely successful, but he asked them to buy him out so he could retire early." She looked at him, seeing the rest of the story come together in his perplexed face.

"My parents' business partner . . . the guy on the magazine cover . . ."

Only Perdita A.W.B. could finish his thought by saying, "That's my dad."

※

From so many miles up, the ocean looked deceptively flat and still. Perdita had wanted the window seat, but she was beginning to regret it, feeling boxed in and short of breath. Maybe when the seat belt sign was off, she could move over to the aisle. The flight wasn't full, so there were only the two of them in their row of three seats, with Zal taking the middle seat as if it weren't the most loathed position in the history of commercial flying. He didn't think about things like that, though. He just saw a seat next to Perdita and took it.

"Thanks for coming with me," Perdita said for probably the fortieth time.

"Of course," Zal said. "I'd much rather spend spring break with you. I could use some space from my dad."

"I wouldn't know the feeling," Perdita muttered.

The mortification on Zal's face was immediate. "Oh, hey—I'm so sorry."

"No, it's fine. I was just . . . I was trying to be funny. I didn't mean to make things weird." She laughed, then, because things were already extremely weird.

"I haven't wanted to pry, but . . . you know you can always talk to me about it?"

"You won't believe it. It sounds like a story I just made up."

"That might actually help," Zal said. "Tell it to me like a story—like a myth or a fairy tale. Reframe it all in your own words."

"I don't see how that helps. It doesn't change anything."

"You've heard of catharsis, right?"

She smiled. "I've heard of it, but what I really want to know is what it means in the original Greek."

She turned to look at him, because nothing was more beautiful than the way Zal's eyes shone at the mention of a word with Greek or Latin roots. *If this doesn't work, I can't let him choose me.*

"It means something like purification or cleansing. It's why stories can make us feel better about our emotions. They give us the opportunity to clean out our mental chaos and feel the emotion from a safe distance. You don't have to tell me anything, of course, but just for yourself, it might help to do some journaling, or—"

"I'll think about it." The words came out more sharply than she intended, so she added, "Thank you."

He took her hand, brushed his lips against her knuckles.

She closed her eyes and tried to take a short nap to make the flight go faster, but her shields had been obliterated permanently, so Aunt Polina's voice kept jolting her awake every time she started to nod off. Words and phrases from that winter conversation swam in her head.

Difficult birth—fell into a coma soon after.

Your brother, you never knew him.

Unmarried, so no right to custody.

I think you're both ready now.

Finally, she gave up and her eyes snapped open. "Okay, let's try it."

"What?" Zal said, half-asleep himself.

"The cleansing. Catharsis. I'll tell you a story."

He resettled himself in the chair so he was turned to his right, facing her, giving his full attention. *I think I love him*, she suddenly realized, but that was not helpful right now. *I can't let him choose me.*

She thought it out first, planning her story in her head, measuring it against what Aunt Polina had told her. It wasn't an exact parallel, but it was close enough.

"Once upon a time, there was a princess who was lost."

She stopped. "No, that's not right. I'm going to start over.

"Once upon a time, there was a queen who was accused—no, that's still wrong.

"Once upon a time, there was a king—a father—who thought he was right . . ."

The king and queen lived happily together with their son in a beautiful castle on the boundary of the human world and Fairyland. But

because the boundary was so close, a lot of sprites and fairies often came through to the human world to wreak havoc. One day, a mischievous sprite jumped up to sit on the king's shoulders and started whispering lies in his ear. The sprite was invisible, so the king couldn't tell the difference between the sprite's whispers and his own thoughts. When the sprite kept telling him his queen had been untrue to him, the king began to think it himself, and then he began to believe it.

The king and queen started to fight, and the king threatened to banish the queen from his kingdom, even though she was carrying their second child. The first child—the prince—was distressed about his parents' feud but too young to do anything about it.

🌹

"Rhiannon," Zal murmured.

"Like the song?"

"Kind of. She was a mythical Welsh queen who was framed and falsely accused of murdering her children."

"Does it have a happy ending?"

"I think so—but I'm not as familiar with Celtic myth. Anyway, keep going."

🌹

The queen's one powerful ally was her younger sister, a witch. The witch tried to appeal to the king, but he wouldn't listen to her, even though she warned him he would regret his decision. The queen had her child—a daughter this time—but the king was convinced she was a changeling, fairy-born, neither his nor human. He ordered the child to be left out in the woods, for the fairies to claim if they wished, and he banished his wife.

The queen asked her sister to watch over her daughter in her absence, and the witch promised her that she would make things right. She put a spell on the queen, turning her into a tree, and hid her away in the woods, where she visited her every month to make sure that she was safe from harm.

❀

"Daphne," Zal said at once.

"I think I know that one. The laurel tree."

He nodded. "She escaped from Apollo by turning into a laurel tree."

"I wish I could turn into a laurel tree," Perdita said, leaning her head on Zal's shoulder.

He kissed the top of her head. "Please don't. I would miss you too much."

She sighed dramatically. "Fine. I promise I won't turn into a laurel tree."

"Thank you. What happened to the prince? The son?"

Aunt Polina's voice answered in her mind: *Heart condition, exacerbated by stress.*

Perdita took her head off of Zal's shoulder and leaned back toward the window. "He died of a broken heart," she said stiffly.

After a cautious silence, Zal said, "And the girl?"

She looked at the college hoodie he was wearing, at the mascot emblazoned across it. "Eaten by a bear."

He gave her a look halfway between amusement and suspicion. "Hmm, I don't think that part's true. I think she survived."

Perdita took a breath.

❀

When the king found out that his son had perished from despair, his grief was so strong that the sprite couldn't stomach it any longer and flew away. The king began to realize that he had been wrong, and that he had destroyed everyone he had ever loved. He sent the witch to bring back the princess, but it was too late. The witch, having promised her sister she would protect the child, had taken the princess to a fairy ring, giving her to an enchanted bear that promised to keep her safe in Fairyland. When the witch returned to the king, she told him that she would only reunite the king with his daughter when he had proven that he was pure of heart. The king, ashamed of his actions, agreed.

The witch wasn't sure if she had made the right choice, but she was young, and alone, and missed her sister, and didn't know what the right choice was. Maybe . . . maybe there was no right choice. Maybe the only thing left for the witch to do was try to lessen the damage already done.

Perdita paused, and she didn't realize how long she had paused until Zal said, "Hey . . . you doing okay?"

She nodded, cleared her throat, and continued.

The king sold half of his kingdom so he could shut himself away in his castle with only his grief. Meanwhile, the girl grew up in Fairyland, not knowing anything about her origins, and she fell in love with the Fairy Prince . . . even though his father, the Fairy King, wasn't happy that his son had fallen in love with a human girl.

"I bet he wasn't," Zal muttered. "Tell the Fairy King it's none of his business."

The girl kept trying to remind the Fairy Prince that he shouldn't jeopardize his relationship with his family just for her.

"Tell the girl that the Fairy Prince cares about her too much to let her go without a fight."

Perdita felt an involuntary thrill at those words, though she didn't know if she was flattered or scared for him, for what he was willing to give up. She pushed the thought aside.

The Fairy Prince fought with his father because of his love for the girl, and the Fairy King threatened to banish his son if he ever saw her again. But the Fairy Prince was loyal and loving and true, so he and the girl decided to leave Fairyland behind and return to the human realm, to beg the human king's intercession.

Zal nodded. "I like that Fairy Prince. She should keep him around."

Perdita tried to smile. "Maybe she will."

"How does it end?"

Perdita shrugged. "They all get eaten by bears."

He laughed. "They go see the king, though, right? What happens when they see him? Does he recognize the girl as his daughter? Does she know what happened to her mother?"

Perdita fidgeted in her seat. *I really should have picked the aisle.* "I don't know," she said. "I don't care. None of this actually matters. It's just a story."

Zal winced, and she didn't understand why until he said, "I know. I know these things don't seem that important—myths, stories . . . statues." At that last word, Perdita's heart gave a lurch of regret. She hadn't meant to, but she had dismissed everything he loved and cared about as thoughtlessly as his father had. "But the stories we tell ourselves help us make sense of the world. It's something humans have been doing for thousands and thousands of years—so if it's not important, then why do we keep doing it?"

She let his words linger in the air between them, thinking about the time Aunt Polina had taken her to see the redwoods. Perdita remembered standing in front of one of them, her head tilted up to see it towering over her, silent with the awe of knowing that this tree had been around for centuries. She was so tiny beside it, but when she placed a hand on the trunk, she had felt connected to something infinite, something sacred. She wasn't sure if she could find that same feeling by telling this story, but she could try.

She nodded. "I get it."

He smiled. "How does the story end?"

🌹

The lost princess returned home with her Fairy Prince. The king received them both, but . . . but years of grief and solitude had hardened him. The girl and the Fairy Prince reminded him too much of the children he had lost, and so he sent them away, not wanting to be reminded of what he had done.

🌹

She paused, looking at Zal as if to ask if that was a suitable ending, but he still wore the expectant stare of a child waiting for a satisfying end to a bedtime story, so she continued.

🌹

But then the king noticed something—a charm around the girl's neck, that had once belonged to his lost queen. He recognized it instantly, and he knew that the girl must be his daughter, the one he had condemned to the wilderness so long ago. He told her the truth then, told her what had happened, what he had done to destroy their family, how he had forsaken her when she was born. He told her everything, and the girl . . . the girl decided that there was only one way to make sure he would never hurt her, or anyone else, again. She took the dagger she had brought with her from Fairyland and plunged it into the king's heart, taking her revenge.

"And then I guess she would be arrested for committing regicide and executed, right? The end."

Zal sighed. "I have to say, I'm not a fan of that ending."

Perdita shrugged, wedged so far into the corner of her seat that her shoulders barely lifted. "What do you want me to do about it? It's a tragedy, isn't it? Like all those Greek plays you tell me about. Fate decides that your life is messed up and there's no way it can end except for bloody revenge."

"But why does it have to be a tragedy, just because of what our parents decided to do?" he asked. He was shifting in his seat, clearly agitated. "Don't we have any say in how things work out? Isn't it our turn to make our own choices?"

"It's not always that easy," Perdita said. She crossed her arms over her chest. "Sometimes . . . sometimes other people make bad choices but you're the one who has to suffer for them. Sometimes things are broken and you can't fix them."

"I disagree."

"Well, too bad," she said sharply. "That's how it is."

He opened his mouth to respond but then shut it again, leaning his head back against the headrest. "Is that how you want it to be?" he said, more softly.

"It's not up to me."

"Maybe not always in life. But in the story . . . the story can end however you want it to end. Even if it doesn't make sense. Even if it doesn't seem likely. The Greeks loved a deus ex machina."

"What do you want me to say, then?"

When the king found his lost daughter, he immediately went to his knees in tears. He apologized to her for all the harm he had done her, told her he would never be able to atone for it, but that he hoped to try, to be the father she had always imagined having. The girl looked at this stranger who was her father and didn't know what to do or how to feel. She had never seen the worst of him, only heard about it years after the fact, and so she didn't know whether to believe that he was capable of doing good, or if he would hurt her again, or if they would just disappoint each other. She didn't know if he deserved her forgiveness or if she was capable of giving it.

Just then, the witch appeared and told them that she had been waiting for this day. She brought them to the woods, to the tree that she had been watching over. And then she said to the tree, "It's time. Awaken," and the tree became flesh again. The queen was miraculously alive, and she embraced her daughter for the first time after so many years apart. The royals wept together, their broken family made whole—or as whole as it could ever be. The Fairy King saw this reunion through the fairy ring, and moved by it, he regretted his own hasty dismissal of his son. He crossed into the human world to give his son his blessing in whatever he chose to do.

And even though the princess still didn't know if she could forgive, or could ever fill up the void her parents' absence had left in her, or could become someone other than the lost girl she had always been, at least . . . at least this time, it was her choice to make. The end.

Perdita's cheeks were warm, her throat tight from holding back tears, and she felt a little queasy. But most of all, she wanted to hide under her seat along with the flotation device she prayed she would never need. *Childish,* she thought. *Pathetic.* She wished she had stopped at the murder ending.

Zal just looked at her. "Ah," he said at last. "Demeter."

She let out a relieved laugh, some of the tears shaking loose. "I hate you."

"Nah, I'm pretty sure you love me."

She nodded. "Yeah, I do. Which one was she?"

"Goddess of the harvest. When her daughter was abducted to the underworld, Demeter grieved so much that she let the world fall into endless winter. Only when her daughter comes back to her for part of the year does spring return again. It's about the seasons, the cycle of death and renewal—loss and return."

She turned away from him, looking out the window, at the hint of the coastline below the clouds, and imagined the ebb and flow of the waves. Loss and return. *What do you think it'd be like to live underwater?* Zal had asked her, and she'd thought she didn't know the answer, but maybe she did. All this time, she had believed she belonged among the trees, wishing to be rooted to the solid earth, but maybe she was wrong. Maybe she was actually a sea creature, subject to forces beyond her control and yet always finding her footing again and again and again.

"Perdita?"

She turned to him.

"I just want to tell you how much I appreciate that you're doing this for me—for us. I know it must be hard. Or maybe I don't *know* but—"

"Zal," she said, interrupting him. *Wobble with me,* she

wanted to say. But instead she said, "Whatever happens . . . fight for me, okay?"

He smiled at her, eyes shining like she was Latin roots and Greek conjugations and Sophocles plays all in one. "That was always the plan."

She settled her head comfortably against his shoulder and said, "Which ending do you think will happen?"

"The one where we all get eaten by bears, probably."

Perdita laughed, and at the same time, the seat belt sign turned off with a little ding. "Finally," she said. She stood and shuffled to Zal's other side, settling back down in the aisle seat, finally able to breathe.

> *What you do*
> *Still betters what is done. When you speak, sweet,*
> *I'd have you do it ever. When you sing,*
> *I'd have you buy and sell so, so give alms,*
> *Pray so; and, for the ordering your affairs,*
> *To sing them too. When you do dance, I wish you*
> *A wave o' the sea, that you might ever do*
> *Nothing but that; move still, still so,*
> *And own no other function. Each your doing,*
> *So singular in each particular,*
> *Crowns what you are doing in the present deeds,*
> *That all your acts are queens.*

—FLORIZEL, ACT 4, SCENE 4

ABOUT WILLIAM SHAKESPEARE

William Shakespeare was born in April 1564 in Stratford-upon-Avon, England, to John Shakespeare and Mary Arden. (His exact date of birth is unknown, though he was baptized on April 26.) At the age of eighteen, he married Anne Hathaway, with whom he had three children: Susanna and twins Judith and Hamnet, the latter of whom died in childhood.

After 1585, there is nothing known of Shakespeare's life until 1592, when he was already in London and known as both an actor and a playwright. The following year, the plague broke out in the city, closing theatres for the rest of the year and turning Shakespeare to poetry. In 1593, he published *Venus and Adonis,* and the following year, he published *The Rape of Lucrece* and joined the prestigious acting company Lord Chamberlain's Men, which later became known as The King's Men.

Together with a few other members of the company, Shakespeare became a part owner of London's famed Globe Theatre in 1599. Many of Shakespeare's most famous works were performed there, including *Julius Caesar, Hamlet, As You Like It, Othello, Macbeth,* and *King Lear.*

Shakespeare published a book of 154 sonnets in 1609 (though they were written considerably earlier), and retired to Stratford a few years later. He died there on April 23, 1616, and was buried two days later at Holy Trinity Church.

Acknowledgments

It takes the work of so many people to make such a beautiful volume happen, and I feel impossibly lucky that I've had the good fortune to have the excellent team at Flatiron behind me for not one but two of these amazing collections. Thank you once again to my wonderful, insightful dream of an editor, Sarah Barley; her fabulous assistant, Sydney Jeon; my amazing publicist, Cat Kenney, and publicity manager Chris Smith; the killer marketing team of Nancy Trypuc, Jordan Forney, and Katherine Turro, and copyediting/production team of Manu Velasco, Lauren Hougen, and Eva Diaz; audiobook producer extraordinaire Matie Argiropoulos; magnificent cover designer Jon Contino and art director Keith Hayes, who knocked it all the way out of the park once again; Devan Norman, who designed these absolutely beautiful pages; managing editor Emily Walters; and, of course, agent Victoria Marini and her assistant, Lee O'Brien, for getting it into their capable hands.

To the contributors who poured their Shakespearean hearts and souls into this work—Kayla, Lily, Melissa, Patrice, A. R., Bri, A-M, Joy, Samantha, Kiersten, Emily, Austin, Lindsay, Tochi, Cory, and Mark—you have made the most incredible collection and I hope you love it and take as much pride in it as I do. Thank you for opening Shakespeare up to a wider audience in the very best, most brilliant, and most creative ways, and for trusting me with your work.

So much love and thanks to the friends (and agent Patricia Nelson) who keep me calm and guided through this and every process: Katherine Locke, Marieke Nijkamp, Maggie Hall, Emery Lord, Becky Albertalli, Tess Sharpe, Jess Cappelle, Sharon Morse, Candice Montgomery, Jessica Spotswood, Maxine Kaplan, Lev Rosen, Becca Podos, Sona Charaipotra, and too many more to name. Sasha, Barrie, and Liz—our monthly dinners turned weekly Zoom chats mean the world to me, and I am so lucky to have you in my life these past [More Decades Than I Care to Mention].

This book was largely written and edited during a global pandemic that changed the world as we know it in a million ways. It feels trite to thank all the medical professionals and essential personnel who kept everything going while I locked myself in my house for months, but I'm going to do it anyway: thank you. And thank you (as promised!) to *checks current name of WhatsApp group* Kind of a Big Deal [eggplant emoji] for kinship and sanity.

A huge debt of gratitude to all the bloggers, bookstagrammers, booktubers, booksellers, librarians, and teachers who helped both *His Hideous Heart* and this book find its readers, including but absolutely not limited to Rachel Strolle, Cody Roecker, the whole gang at Books of Wonder and East City Bookshop, Kimberly Gabriel, Eric Smith, Bethany Robison, Adriana M. Martínez, Amal El-Mohtar, Kate Welsh, Beautifully Bookish Bethany, and Bookish Valhalla.

Finally, to my family—you are all my adventures and happy endings. Thank you for everything.

About the Authors

⁓ ♛ ⁓

DAHLIA ADLER is an editor of mathematics by day, a book blogger by night, and an author of young adult and romance novels at every spare moment in between. Her latest novels are *Home Field Advantage* and *Cool for the Summer*. Dahlia lives in New York with her family and an obscene number of books. You can find her at dahliaadler.com, or on Twitter and Instagram @MissDahleLama.

K. ANCRUM is the author of the award-winning thriller *The Wicker King*, the interstellar lesbian romance *The Weight of the Stars*, and the Peter Pan thriller *Darling*. K. is a Chicago native passionate about diversity and representation in young adult fiction. She currently writes most of her work in the lush gardens of the Chicago Art Institute.

LILY ANDERSON fell in love with the Bard when she was ten and never looked back. In the twenty years since, she has performed, adapted, and directed Shakespeare plays, as well as retelling *Much Ado About Nothing* as her debut novel, *The Only Thing Worse Than Me Is You*. Her other works include *Not Now, Not Ever* and *Undead Girl Gang*. You can find her at mslilyanderson.com.

MELISSA BASHARDOUST received her degree in English from the University of California, Berkeley, where she rediscovered her love for creative writing, children's literature, and fairy tales and their retellings. She currently lives in Southern California with a cat named Alice and more copies of *Jane Eyre* than she probably needs. Melissa is the author of *Girls Made of Snow and Glass* and *Girl, Serpent, Thorn*.

PATRICE CALDWELL is a graduate of Wellesley College and the founder of People of Color in Publishing—a grassroots organization dedicated to supporting, empowering, and uplifting racially and ethnically marginalized members of the book publishing industry. Born and raised in Texas, Patrice was a children's book editor before shifting to become a literary agent. She's been named a *Publishers Weekly* Star Watch honoree and featured on *Bustle*'s inaugural "Lit List" as one of ten women changing the book world. Patrice's debut fantasy novel is out September 2022 from Wednesday Books/Macmillan. She is also the editor of *A Phoenix First Must Burn: 16 Stories of Black Girl Magic, Resistance, and Hope* as well as a YA paranormal romance anthology out in fall 2022. Visit her online at patricecaldwell.com, Twitter @whimsicallyours, and Instagram @whimsicalaquarian.

A. R. CAPETTA and CORY MCCARTHY coauthored the bestselling Once & Future series. They are also the acclaimed authors of over a dozen solo titles, including Cory's feminist romcom *Now a Major Motion Picture* and near-futuristic thriller *Breaking Sky*, and A. R.'s witchy head rush known as *The Lost Coast* and the romantic, Italian-inspired fantasy *The Brilliant Death*. After meeting at Vermont College of Fine Arts, they began flirtsparring much like Benedick and Beatrice. A. R. and Cory now raise a young maverick in the snow-swept mountains of

Vermont . . . and continue to banter as if it were an Olympic sport.

BRITTANY CAVALLARO is the *New York Times* bestselling author of the Charlotte Holmes novels, including *A Study in Charlotte*, and with Emily Henry, the author of *Hello Girls*. Her most recent novel, *Muse*, was released in early 2021. Her poetry collections *Girl-King* and *Unhistorical* were both published by the University of Akron Press. Cavallaro lives with her family in Michigan, where she teaches creative writing at the Interlochen Arts Academy.

SAMANTHA MABRY lives and writes in Texas. Her books include *A Fierce and Subtle Poison*, *All the Wind in the World*—which was longlisted for a National Book Award in 2017—and, most recently, *Tigers, Not Daughters*.

JOY MCCULLOUGH is the author of the YA historical novel *Blood Water Paint*, which was longlisted for the National Book Award, finalist for the William C. Morris Award, finalist for the Amelia Walden Award, and winner of the Pacific Northwest Book Award and the Washington State Book Award, and the middle grade novel *A Field Guide to Getting Lost*, a Junior Library Guild selection. She is also a playwright with a degree in theatre from Northwestern University and has Shakespeare's words etched into her skin. She lives in the Seattle area.

ANNA-MARIE MCLEMORE is a nonbinary fairy prince whose family taught them to hear la llorona in the Santa Ana winds. They are the National Book Award–longlisted, Stonewall Honor author of *The Weight of Feathers*, *When the Moon Was*

Ours, Wild Beauty, Blanca & Roja, Dark and Deepest Red, and *The Mirror Season.*

TOCHI ONYEBUCHI is the author of the young adult novel *Beasts Made of Night,* which won the Ilube Nommo Award for Best Speculative Fiction Novel by an African, its sequel—*Crown of Thunder*—and *War Girls,* a Nommo and Locus Award finalist. His adult debut was *Riot Baby.* He holds degrees from Yale, the Tisch School of the Arts, Sciences Po, and Columbia Law School. His fiction has appeared in *Asimov's Science Fiction, Omenana Magazine, Uncanny,* and *Lightspeed.* His nonfiction has appeared in *Tor.com, Nowhere Magazine,* and the *Harvard Journal of African American Public Policy,* among other places.

MARK OSHIRO is the young adult author of *Anger Is a Gift,* winner of the 2019 Schneider Family Book Award and nominated for a 2019 Lammy Award, as well as *Each of Us a Desert,* and their middle grade debut, *The Insiders.* When they are not writing, crying on camera about fictional characters for their online Mark Does Stuff universe, or traveling, Mark is busy trying to fulfill their lifelong goal: to pet every dog in the world.

AUSTIN SIEGEMUND-BROKA and **EMILY WIBBERLEY** are the authors of *Always Never Yours, If I'm Being Honest, Time of Our Lives,* and *What's Not to Love.* They met in high school, where they fell in love over a shared passion for Shakespeare. Austin went on to study English at Harvard so he could continue to impress Emily with his literary analysis, while Emily studied adolescent psychology at Princeton. They live in Los Angeles, where they've combined their interests and decided to write stories of high school, literature, and first love.

LINDSAY SMITH is the author of *Sekret* and other novels for young adults. She writes for Serial Box's *Marvel's Black Widow: Bad Blood, Orphan Black: The Next Chapter,* and *The Witch Who Came in from the Cold.* She has also written for comics, RPGs, and more. She lives in Washington, DC, where she works in international cybersecurity.

KIERSTEN WHITE is the *New York Times* bestselling and Bram Stoker Award–winning author of more than a dozen young adult novels, including the And I Darken trilogy, *The Dark Descent of Elizabeth Frankenstein,* the Camelot Rising trilogy, and the Slayer series. She lives in Southern California with her spouse and three children, none of whom are allowed to read her books.

DON'T MISS...

"A superb collection
of young adult
short stories inspired
by Edgar Allan
Poe's work."

—*The New York Times Book Review*

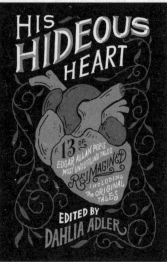

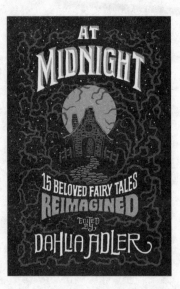

A new collection of retold fairy tales
from fifteen award-winning and
bestselling writers, including Melissa
Albert, Darcie Little Badger,
and Malinda Lo

FLATIRON
BOOKS